The Lost Mother's Christmas Miracle

IRIS COLE

VIDORRA HOUSE

©Copyright 2024 Iris Cole

All Rights Reserved

License Notes

This Book is licensed for personal enjoyment only. It may not be resold. No part of this work may be reproduced in any form or by any electronic or mechanical means including information storage and retrieval systems, without written permission from the author.

DISCLAIMER

This story is a work of fiction, any resemblance to people is purely coincidence. All places, names, events, businesses, etc. are used in a fictional manner. All characters are from the imagination of the author.

Would you like a free book?

[CLAIM THE FOUNDLING BABY HERE](#)

Table of Contents

Disclaimer..iii

Part One..1

   Chapter One 3

   Chapter Two..27

   Chapter Three..39

Part Two 50

   Chapter Four...51

   Chapter Five 61

   Chapter Six 71

Part Three 91

   Chapter Seven 93

   Chapter Eight..107

   Chapter Nine 117

Part Four 129

   Chapter Ten 131

   Chapter Eleven 145

   Chapter Twelve..157

   Chapter Thirteen..165

Part Five 177

   Chapter Fourteen..179

Chapter Fifteen 191

Chapter Sixteen 203

Chapter Seventeen 215

Part Six *227*

Chapter Eighteen 229

Chapter Nineteen 239

Chapter Twenty 249

Chapter Twenty-One 259

Part Seven *268*

Chapter Twenty-Two 269

Chapter Twenty Three 283

Part One

THE LOST MOTHER'S CHRISTMAS MIRACLE

Chapter One

Helen Nicols' heart fluttered between her ribs like a trapped bird seeking freedom. The wild thunder of its wings pounded in her ears, and she tried to take deep breaths, steam curling from her nose and mouth with each one. She could only hope the little child by her side couldn't hear her racing heart. It seemed impossible; its thudding filled her whole world.

Small fingers tightened on hers. "Mama?" a small voice whispered.

Helen ignored the tiny voice. She feared that, if she looked down, she would start to cry—or, worse, back out of her decision. She'd agonized about her choice enough. She knew what she had to do — what was best for everyone, and if she looked down now, she'd never be able to do it.

Instead, Helen kept her eyes up and focused on the milling crowd that filled the market square. Once, this had been a place of joy for her. A place where she'd buy eggs and flour and fish for dinner, anticipating an evening of warmth, love, and laughter. But that felt like a different lifetime now, though it had only been two years. It felt like all that happiness had happened to someone else.

Now, the marketplace held only horror. All those smells she'd loved—fresh bread, raw dough, smoked fish, salt, and crisp sugar—were mere reminders of what she couldn't have. Her shrinking stomach no longer panged with hunger; it seemed to have given up. Instead, the smells only seemed to fuel the weakness that seeped through her muscles and suffused her limbs.

No one in the crowd spared her a second glance. One was enough for them to judge her unworthy of their presence. The neighbours who'd once come over to borrow sugar now dodged around her, failing to recognize her bony visage. They sneered and crossed to another stall as Helen shuffled past. They wore wonderful wool jackets and knitted scarves that kept out the biting wind. Helen did not. That wind cut through her to the very bones.

It was difficult not to look at the candles in the windows or the wreaths on every doorway. Difficult not to look at them and remember how Christmas had been only a few years ago.

The small hand on hers shivered. "Mama," came the little voice again.

No, Helen, she coached herself. *No looking down. You must do what you planned. You must.*

The heartless crowd hastened past her, not reading or not caring about the agony in her eyes. The sky pressed down like a lid, crushing and grey. There would be snow again tonight. Helen would wake up sodden and shivering.

The little one by her side would not.

That thought drove her to keep looking. She turned left and right, scanning the muffled crowd. The scarves and hats, the warm mittens and the cosy coats, all only made her feel colder and made her struggle more to identify the one she'd come for.

"Mama," the small voice whispered.

Helen spotted him at last. He leaned against a wall across the marketplace, picking his teeth with his fingernails, his fingers greasy from whatever he'd just eaten. Maybe he'd give the little one something, too. Surely he'd see how hungry she was. It had been so terribly long since they had had anything to eat.

Food, shelter, warmth. These were all the things that were on the line. Things that Helen could no longer provide. Let alone all the festive joys that should belong to this child at this time of year. The warm home, the laughter, the Christmas tree... Perhaps that was too much to hope for, yet Helen had nothing left except for hope.

She could either do this, or watch her precious daughter starve.

"Mama!" the little one insisted.

Helen inhaled deeply and stepped toward the man. He spotted her and turned, grinning, to wave at her. His manner suggested that this was an ordinary business deal to him, not the heart-wrenching affair that it was to her, and as he wiped his greasy hands on his shirt, a sudden burst of revulsion filled Helen. She couldn't imagine passing the tiny hand in her own to the dirty paw of this stranger. Nausea bucked in her chest, and she had to pause and inhale deeply several times to tame it.

Her eyes lit on the plane tree struggling for life on a corner of the marketplace. How many times she had paused to chat with friends beneath the welcoming shadow of its branches! How she longed, now, for those days! But they were long gone. This despair had become her reality. She could do nothing but face it.

"Come on," she croaked. The words fell between her lips, desiccated and worthless.

She had to pull to make the child walk with her.

Little feet stumbled on the paving stones, and a tiny whimper of protest rose, a sound of complete exhaustion birthed from hopeless hunger. *Not anymore*, Helen told herself. *Not after I do this, no matter how painful.*

They reached the plane tree, and Helen tugged the child forward so that she stood with her back to the bark.

"Mama, please," said the little voice. "Please, I'm so hungry. That man has bread. May I have some bread?"

May I, not *can I*. She had taught her daughter well before everything fell apart. Tears burned Helen's eyes, but she fiercely blinked them back. Steel resolve hardened within her, the same determination that had kept her alive in this brutal world, only to lose what mattered most to its cruelty.

She took a deep breath and steadied herself. Then, slowly, Helen knelt down and summoned the courage to look her daughter in the eye.

The sight of her child's face never failed to hurt her, as though some invisible hand had thrust a hot poker into her soul. She had her father's eyes: bright, piercing blue, like jewels captured in flesh. The mass of red hair around her face came from Helen, though hers was richly scarlet where Helen's held tones of auburn.

She gazed at the child for a few moments, drinking her in. She wanted to remember her, all of her. If she had known her last moments with Adrian, she would have held him a little longer, would have memorized the contours of his body and the brightness of his smile so that she could carry them with her forever.

"Mama," the girl prompted.

"My sweet darling." Helen gently brushed a strand of red hair behind the child's ear. "Don't worry. There'll be bread for you very, very soon."

More than bread. There would be oranges, maybe, and sweets. There would be Christmas; something very different to last year's. Last Christmas had been simply another day huddled in a freezing alley.

The girl's eyes lit up. "There will?"

"Yes. There will." Helen hoped it was true. "But first you must wait a little while, sweetheart. Can you wait a little while?"

The girl slowly nodded. "Here?"

"Right here," said Helen. "I'm going to look for bread." The lie landed on her heart like a cannonball. "I'll be back." Another lie, this one far heavier, so crushing that she almost gasped at its weight as it encased her chest like her ribs had become lead.

The little one nodded. "All right, Mama. I'll wait here."

"I know you will, darling." Helen's hands trembled as she cupped the girl's face in them and planted a gentle kiss on the top of her head.

"Mama, why are you shaking?" the child asked.

"It's a little cold, darling, that's all." Helen straightened and stepped back. Leaving her felt like the world was ripping. It felt like clawing out her own heart or her own eyes and casting them to the wind, but she would have done so to save her child. Helen would have done anything in the world to save her child... even this.

The little girl looked up at her, tiny and vulnerable, four years old and the most beautiful thing on which Helen had ever laid eyes.

The words spilled out before she could stop them. "Merry Christmas, my darling."

The child blinked. "It's Christmas?"

When she was only two years old, this little girl had spent weeks bouncing up and down in excitement for Christmas Day.

Something shattered inside Helen to realize that Christmas barely mattered to this four-year-old, an age where this blessed season should be filled with perfect wonder.

"Almost," Helen croaked.

"Oh." The child shifted her weight. "Mama… you said there'd be bread."

"There will." Helen fought back her tears. She traced her fingertips down Beryl's cheek, feeling the soft, warm skin. "I love you, darling," she whispered. "I love you, Beryl."

Beryl gazed at her, mute and surprised. Helen knew that if she did not walk away at that moment, she never would. She turned on her heel and strode off, though it felt like her very skin tore at the parting, especially when the little voice floated through the crowd in pursuit and struck her heart like an arrow: "Love you, Mama."

Tears streamed down her cheeks. Helen kept her head low and did not wipe them until she had rounded one of the stalls and knew she was out of sight. She brushed her eyes on her sleeve and kept walking, head down, shoulders trembling with sobs, until she reached the man where he leaned on the wall.

Simeon Cragg belched and looked at her without interest as she reached him, trembling and crying.

"Well?" he demanded.

"She's—she's over there." Helen pointed at the plane tree; only the branches were visible over the stalls now. "She's waiting for you. If you tell her I said to go with you, she will. She'll make no fuss. She's a good girl." Her voice cracked. "The best."

"You could've brought me the child like we arranged," Simeon grumbled.

Arranged. It was a far kinder word than what had truly taken place.

Helen stared at him mutely, remembering his many approaches each time she passed him, his many offers to "take the girl off her hands." Never in a thousand years had Helen thought she would be forced to say yes to Simeon Cragg.

"You said—" Helen's sorrow strangled her. She had to clear her throat to be able to breathe, then speak on. "You said that there was decent work for her."

"Oh, yes. Don't you worry your head about that, Mrs. Nicols." Simeon chuckled. "It's a perfectly good job. Sweeping chimneys. Old Smudge wants her because she's little and skinny, you see. Fit well in the narrower chimneys, she will."

Helen swallowed. Her Beryl, sweeping chimneys! Adrian would be heartbroken. He always used to give sweep children pennies when they passed them on the street, soot-blackened and sorrowful, looking—

She pushed the thought away. Adrian was long gone.

"She'll be warm?" Helen asked. "And fed? You're sure?"

"Yes, yes." Simeon waved a hand. "Of course. They live in a tenement right next to Smudge's. Three meals a day, a roof over their heads, nice and warm. Work inside, too, not in the rain and cold."

Thunder rolled through the grey sky. Helen swallowed hard, imagining her Beryl with a full belly and warm clothes. The thought made everything possible. She would do whatever was required to ensure that for her daughter. *Even this*.

"Maybe," she whispered, "maybe she'll even have Christmas, don't you think?" She searched Simeon's eyes with naked desperation. "Maybe she'll get to hear some carols and—and have a sweet, or—or something."

"Christmas? For chimney sweeps?" Simeon laughed.

Helen's heart plummeted. "Please. They all deserve to feel happy at this time of year."

Simeon's eyes narrowed, and his laughter vanished. "Yes, sure," he said. "Sure. Smudge'll have Christmas for them. He'll give them toys and light a tree."

Helen closed her eyes. She couldn't hear the sarcasm in his voice; she had to cling to the image of Beryl beneath a bright tree, laughing.

"It's better than you can do for her, Mrs. Nicols. Now, are you going to let me take the child or not?" Simeon demanded.

Helen met his eyes, her heart galloping in her chest, wild and terrified. "Yes," she whispered. "It is better than I can do for her." Her own mother couldn't feed her, couldn't find somewhere warm for her to sleep. Clinging to her would be pure selfishness. Helen fought the tears as they filled her eyes. "Please, take her."

"All right, then." Simeon dug in his pocket and produced half-a-crown. "Here." He slapped it into Helen's palm.

Helen's heart bounded. Half-a-crown! A pang of wild relief ran through her at the thought of all the food she could buy with this, food she didn't have to share. Instantly, revulsion filled her. Was she this pleased she'd sold her daughter? What monster had she become? It was all she could do not to retch where she stood.

"Pleasure doing business with you, Mrs. Nicols." Simeon leered, then strode away.

Helen's knees had turned to water. She sank to the grimy pavement and sat with her back to the wall, tears rolling over her cheeks. They made her vision filmy and blurred, but she could still peer beneath the stalls to see Beryl's skinny legs and hole-ridden shoes where she stood beside the tree. She watched Simeon plod over to her in hobnailed boots. Beryl hesitated, but then slowly shuffled forward.

The tiny shoes with their many holes fell into step beside the hobnailed boots, and Beryl walked out of Helen's life as she watched with tears streaming down her cheeks.

The sea was the colour of slate. It rippled beneath the grey sky as snow trickled down in fat, white flakes, each as cold as the kiss of death when it landed on Helen's skin. She sat on the cold stone bench, not caring that it froze her, and gazed at the featureless horizon where grey sea met greyer sky.

A distant sound echoed from the street behind her. The carollers were too far away for Helen to hear the words, but she recognized the melody, and her memories supplied the lyrics.

I saw three ships come sailing in
on Christmas Day, on Christmas Day,
I saw three ships come sailing in
on Christmas Day in the morning!

"Oh, Adrian," Helen whispered. "Oh, if only your ship would come sailing in!"

Her tears spilled over. She covered her face with her hands, fighting to hold them back, longing for her husband with everything in her. Even after all this time, the memories flooded her so easily, so brilliantly. Adrian, after all, was impossible to forget.

They had first met at this time of the year. Helen would always remember that beautiful, special Christmas six years ago.

The bag of laundry was heavier than usual. Helen tried to think of the extra pennies it would bring her and not of the interminable weight as she plodded down the street, the bag's strings digging into her shoulder with sharp pain.

Curse those rich folks, *she thought.* Curse them and their foolish Christmas parties, where they dined on stuffed peacock and candied orange peel while the poor of London starved in the streets and the workhouses!

She gritted her teeth against the pain and tried to walk a little faster. Darkness came so quickly at this time of year. Already the lamplighter made his rounds, bringing tiny golden flames to the wrought-iron streetlamps on every corner. The little pools of yellow light seemed inadequate faced with the real darkness of an English winter.

Why anyone would celebrate in the dead of winter, Helen didn't know. It made no sense to her. This time of year held nothing but cold and suffering.

She paused and gazed through the window of a nice home, one with a garden and multiple stories. Through the drawing-room window, she could see the shape of a bright green tree set up in the corner, its colour brilliant against the grey wallpaper. Candles flickered amid its branches; oranges and gingerbread men hung among the dark sprigs. Parcels wrapped in brown paper lay at its feet.

Parcels! Toys! Trinkets! And still the poor starved! Bitterness rose in Helen like a flood, and she turned her back on it and kept walking.

Reminders of Christmas faded as she strode nearer to her cottage by the docks. Only a few cottages here had the pennies to spare for wreaths on their doors, the hollyberries bright as blood against the snow that caked the roofs and doorsteps. The wreaths grew less and less common as she neared her home.

She was only a block away from the tumbledown cottage where she lived and worked—washing endless mounds of laundry for the better-off—when the rattle of carriage wheels cut through the sound of blowing wind. Helen jumped aside almost too late as a donkey cart careened down the street. The little beast was white-eyed and wild with fright; the cart skidded across the iced paving stones. Its wheel barely missed her. Instead, it collided with her laundry bag, and the strings sailed from her grasp.

"No!" Helen cried in despair.

The bag landed heavily on the pavement and split open. Clothes spilled into the gutter, mingling with the yellow-grey slush within.

"No!" Helen gasped again. She ran to the clothes that lay everywhere, cursing as pedestrians trampled over them. At best, they tripled her workload. At worst, she would have to pay for these garments, and she could barely afford the rent as it was—

A pair of heavy boots crunched across the pavement toward a little girl's best Christmas dress.

"Please, no!" Helen cried.

The boots stopped several inches short of the dress, then furrowed as their owner knelt.

"That was awful." The voice that spoke was rich and warm, with a husky edge, like the sound of the sea beating against the docks in a wild storm. It held both gentleness and wilderness, like a mother wolf cleaning her cubs with the same teeth that could pull down a deer. "I'm so sorry. He nearly ran you over, you poor thing."

Sympathy was seldom part of Helen's daily life. It never had been. She doubted she had ever heard someone speak to her in such tones, and now she looked up slowly and incredulously, doubting that she'd heard right at all.

The man who crouched on the pavement opposite her had eyes so blue that they made her gasp. They were the blue of the sky on a clear winter's day, or the blue of the sea right after sunrise, bright as jewels. The deep tan of the skin surrounding them only made them seem all the brighter. The skin wrinkled at the corners of them when the man smiled, and he had a thick black beard that curled profusely around his strong jaw, almost as abundant as the black hair that fell over his forehead in rich ringlets.

"Are you all right?" he asked in that wonderful, husky voice.

Helen opened and shut her mouth several times before any sound would come out. Her tongue felt suddenly as dry as sandpaper.

"Yes," she croaked.

"Good. No thanks to that fool," said the man scornfully. "Here." He held out the girl's dress; its fabric looked impossibly delicate against his big, callused hands.

She snatched it up and stuffed it into the bag, then grabbed a shirt and did the same. What if his kindness was a mere act? Having grown up in the workhouse until the washerwoman hired her when she was fifteen, in Helen's experience, kindness was never genuine. He was trying to take the garments. He wanted to steal from her!

"Easy, there!" The man laughed, a good-natured rumble that made it difficult to stay on her guard. "I mean you no harm." He said it almost playfully, as though the alternative was too absurd to consider. Before Helen could grab them, he snatched a dress and a pair of trousers from the paved street and tucked them into the bag.

The bag! He wanted to take it from her! Helen's grip tightened on it, but the man barely noticed. He tucked another shirt into it.

"I'm Adrian," he said. "Adrian Nicols. What's your name?"

Helen swallowed. "Helen." She held back her last name as though it was a weapon he might use against her.

"A beautiful name. It suits you." Adrian straightened and smiled again, displaying white teeth. The wind combed through the thick hair of his chest, made visible by the open buttons on his white shirt beneath a leather jerkin. The fabric rippled around his shoulders and arms, revealing the tight curves of strong muscle. "This is terribly heavy. May I carry it for you?"

"No." Helen seized the bag and pulled it close to her chest.

Adrian did not resist. "All right, then. Do you pass by here often?"

Helen planned her escape route and began to edge along the sidewalk past him.

"I'll look out for you, then." Adrian smiled and spread his hands. "I'm a sailor at home for the winter. I have nothing to do with my time. If I see you pass again, I'll be here to help you."

Help her! A likely story. Helen skirted past him and jogged away, clutching her precious laundry, her heart sinking in anticipation of a long night's washing.

"Oh, Adrian," Helen whispered, gazing at the rippling sea. "How kind you were, even then." The memory of his smile and husky voice made her eyes sting.

What would he say about what she'd done with his child?

The thought shattered her. Helen lay down, pillowing her head on the cold bench, and wrapped her arms around herself. Exhausted sleep fell upon her like a coma, and with it came the memories, a tide she couldn't hold back.

The Christmas tree towered over a corner of their living room, aglow with candlelight, tinsel, and paper chains. Helen peered around the living room door, biting her lip as she tried to hold back her giggles.

Adrian crouched beneath the Christmas tree, carefully adjusting one of the brown paper-wrapped parcels that lay at its feet. She'd tied the parcels with bright ribbon, and Adrian admired the candlelight's reflection in the satiny surfaces now as he carefully lifted one parcel and gave it an experimental shake, as though trying to work out what lay within.

The sleepy bundle in Helen's arms gave a tiny sigh. She cuddled the baby closer, stifling her laughter, and quickly stepped through the door.

"What are you doing?" she asked, her tone playfully accusing. "You can't open those yet. You have to wait for Christmas Day!"

Adrian jumped up, big muscles flexing beneath his white shirt, and spun around. The guilt in his eyes made Helen want to laugh aloud.

"I was only looking," he mumbled, shuffling his feet like a boy caught in mischief.

Helen laughed. How could she ever have hated Christmas? How could she misunderstand its magic and wonder so? Perhaps it was because her life had held neither of those things—until Adrian came into it, and changed everything.

"Wait." Adrian's eyes widened. "What did you do to Beryl?"

Helen giggled as she held up the baby. "Look at her!"

Adrian gasped and clasped his hands to his cheeks, his eyes wide with joy.

He was unlike so many men in that way; he never feared the expression of his emotions, and now, he glowed with wonder.

"Oh, Berry!" he cooed, extending a big hand toward the baby. "Look at you!"

Beryl opened her eyes and giggled. Though her hair was only a few inches long, it was already copper-red, a brighter shade than Helen's. The colour complemented the bright green ribbon which Helen had used to tie a sprig of the baby's hair on top of her head.

"She's big enough for ribbons!" Adrian cried. "Oh, Berry, you're growing up too fast." He held out his hands and gave Helen a pleading look. "May I?"

Helen knew that it was unusual—perhaps even improper—for a man to hold a baby. But who was here to judge? It was just the three of them, her perfect little family. She smiled and handed tiny Beryl to her father.

The child seemed puny in Adrian's callused hands, but she giggled in delight at the sight of her father's face. Her tiny hands tangled with his rich beard as he chuckled at her, eyes alight.

"Merry Christmas, my little darling," Adrian whispered. He leaned closer so that his big, sun-beaten nose touched her tiny, soft one. "Merry Christmas."

Helen watched the scene and wondered how she could ever have hated Christmas, the most wonderful time of the year, a time when her family was together, warm, and safe. It turned out that all she'd needed to love Christmas was this... Adrian and Beryl, here by her side.

Helen's eyes snapped open.

The dream had never turned into a nightmare. Instead, the memory still played behind her eyes, smelling of orange peel and pine leaves, Adrian's rich laughter rolling through her mind as it combined with the high-pitched coos and giggles of Beryl.

Perhaps it would have been better if the dream had dissolved into something horrific. But as it was, the only nightmare was the one that Helen woke up to.

Tears made her face feel stiff and half-frozen. Her body ached from sleeping on the stone bench, and the wind blowing in off the sea brought fistfuls of sleet with it, driving needles of cold into Helen's bare face with every gust. It teased her auburn hair and pulled it over her face, making sleet gather on her eyelashes. Hunger made her belly feel like a cruel hand had reached in and brutally ripped her stomach from her abdomen.

But none of those harsh realities could compare with the fact that Helen was completely alone. Beryl was gone. She'd given her away.

"Oh, Beryl!" Helen cried.

She sat up, arms wrapped around her chest, her pounding heart stinging with every beat. The image of Adrian holding that baby, love and joy shining in his eyes, burned through her mind. She'd sold that baby. She'd given her to a stranger for half-a-crown.

Suddenly, the nice fantasy she'd made up for herself about giving Beryl a Christmas filled with food, love, and presents vanished like mist before the sun. She knew it wasn't true. Beryl would be forced to sweep chimneys, to climb into their sooty interiors and breathe their filth. Hadn't a little boy recently died in a chimney? Adrian had said something about it when he saw it in the news...

"Oh, Beryl," Helen croaked. "Oh, Adrian. What have I done? *What have I done?*"

The half-crown burned in her pocket like a coal. She hadn't been able to bring herself to buy bread with it yesterday. Now, it seemed like a miraculous foresight. It was her only means of getting Beryl back.

She scrambled to her feet, blood pounding in her temples. Urgency overwhelmed the hunger that weakened her muscles. Her half-frozen feet pounded on the stone paving—somewhat numb, somewhat burning—as she ran back to the marketplace.

How long had she slept? It was daylight now, bright, like morning. Did it matter? Helen had wandered the streets for two days without Beryl before collapsing on the bench by the sea. Though she knew her little girl had long since left the marketplace, she searched the area, desperate to spot bright red hair, freckled cheeks, and eyes as pale blue as jewels.

"Out the way!" a gentleman grunted, furious.

Helen stumbled back, narrowly avoiding the fat, well-dressed man. He scoffed, shocked that he'd had to speak to her to make her move out of his way. She didn't care that she'd offended him. All she cared about was getting Beryl back.

Beryl wouldn't be here, she realized as reason slowly overtook her panic. But Simeon Cragg would be. He'd be able to tell her if he'd already given Beryl to that chimney sweep. He'd know where Helen could find her baby girl and get her back.

She stopped in the middle of the marketplace and turned left and right. Three men on stepladders surrounded a pine tree set up at its centre; they lifted ropes of tinsel from boxes and wrapped it around the tree. The smell of gingerbread wafted across the square. A handful of children in pale robes wandered around its edges, singing "Angels We Have Heard on High."

But she didn't see Beryl—or Simeon Cragg.

"Hey, you. Miss. Miss!"

Helen blinked, suddenly realizing that the man at the fish stand nearest her was talking to her.

"I beg your pardon," she croaked.

"Well, you won't get any pardon from me," said the man rudely. "You're in the way of my customers. Go and beg somewhere else."

Helen felt no pain or irritation at his words; this was simply how men addressed her. Besides, she felt nothing at that moment except a desperate need to find Beryl.

"Sir," she said, "do you know Simeon Cragg?"

"If I tell you, will you go away?" the man demanded.

Helen vigorously nodded.

"Yes, I do know him. I watched the bobbies carry him off for stealing half an hour ago. Now go away," said the man.

Helen's heart skipped. "The police arrested him?"

"That's what I said, isn't it?" the man snapped. "Leave!" He reached for the knife he used to clean fish; scales and guts clung to its surface.

Helen ignored it. "Was a child with him—a little girl?"

"No," said the man.

"Sir, do you know a chimney sweep called Smudge Blackwood?" Helen asked.

The man brandished the knife. "I told you to leave!"

Helen backed away. She nearly collided with a little flower-seller, who clutched a basket of oranges and cried out when her fruit nearly spilled on the ground.

"You!" Helen barked.

The little girl cowered, expecting to be struck. "I'm sorry, ma'am. I didn't see—"

"Do you know Smudge Blackwood?" Helen demanded.

The girl shook her head, wide-eyed and mute.

The streets had not been kind to her little face; it was creased and scarred, permanently bruised, her eyes unnaturally large against her pinched and fragile cheeks. The world had been brutal to this child, who was only a few years older than Beryl.

Would Helen's precious little one end up the same way?

No! Helen thought.

"Smudge Blackwood?" someone asked. "The chimney sweep?"

Helen turned around. A crossing-sweeper leaned on his broom nearby, his shabby clothes hanging from his bony frame.

"Yes," she cried desperately. "I need to find him."

"He lives nearby," said the sweeper. "Take that street until you reach a cotton mill, then turn left. You'll see many old brick tenement buildings. It's the third street on your right, second house on your left."

Helen memorized the directions with the heart-pounding urgency of terror. "Thank you," she cried, then turned and ran.

Neither her shoes nor her body were in any condition for running, but Helen couldn't bear to walk, to be separated from Beryl for a moment longer than necessary. Her arms cried out to be wrapped around her little girl's body. Her breath rasped in her throat as she jogged past the rumbling, clattering cotton mill with its noxious dust pouring from its windows, and she turned sharply, passing between the buildings that crowded close around the narrow street.

Each several stories high, they were built of single rows of plain brick. None of the windows had glass in them anymore, and soot streaked the walls both inside and out. Not a scrap of rubbish marred the pavement; it was picked clean and bare, everything scraped up and taken away to be sold, down to dog faeces and dead rats.

A few rotting pallets lay against one wall. Beside them, a homeless man crouched on a slightly better pallet, his eyes reptilian and wild. He hissed as Helen passed, and she quickly crossed the street.

She didn't blame him. A good pallet could be the difference between life and death.

She counted the buildings and finally came upon the tenement building the crossing-sweeper had indicated. It crouched miserably among its fellows, as run-down and bare as the others. The door's paint was so flaked that its original colour was invisible. Specks came off on Helen's knuckles as she knocked.

She strained her ears and heard little voices, and her heart turned cartwheels. One of the children inside had to be Beryl.

She knocked again, her heart clenched, and finally the door swung open. A sneering man with dark hair and angry eyes glared down at her.

"Please, sir," said Helen, "I'm looking for Smudge Blackwood."

The sweep's eyes narrowed, and he stepped back. "Knew I shouldn't have given my real name," he muttered to himself.

"So you are Smudge Blackwood," said Helen.

The sweep stepped back, as if to slam the door, but Helen stepped into the gap and pulled out the half-crown. She dangled it in front of his eyes and saw them widen with greed.

"You bought a little girl from a man named Simeon Cragg," she said. "I want her back."

Smudge's eyes narrowed again. He looked from the half-crown to Helen's face.

"Beryl is my child," said Helen. "Please. Take the money. Just give me my daughter."

Smudge scoffed. "Firstly, I paid three shillings for her, and I spent money feeding her last night, too. Your pathetic half-crown won't begin to cover what you owe."

"I'll get more money." Helen thrust the half-crown at him. "Please, take it. I'll get more money. I promise you, I'll—"

"It doesn't matter," Smudge barked. "I'm not letting you take the child."

Helen's heart stuttered to a halt in her chest. This possibility had never risen in her mind.

"B-but why not?" she croaked.

"What do you think would happen if these wretches discovered that Beryl's mother bought her back? They'd think all their mothers would do the same." Smudge sneered. "They'd start looking for ways back to their families. They'd be even more trouble than they already are."

Helen's breath caught. "Please, sir. Please. I won't tell anyone. Please just give me—"

"I won't give you anything," Smudge hissed. "Leave. Now."

A small voice sobbed in a nearby tenement, too far away for Helen to hear clearly, but what if it was her Beryl? What if her little girl was crying in her room at that moment, terrified and alone?'

"No!" Helen shrieked.

Smudge cried out as she thrust the money into her pocket and tried to push past him to get to her little girl.

"Give her to me!" Helen yelled.

Pushing against Smudge was like trying to push a wall to the ground. He seized her shoulder and shoved her back so that she staggered out of the building.

"*Beryl*!" Helen shrieked.

"Shut up!" Smudge roared.

"Beryl! My baby!" Helen screamed.

Smudge's face twisted in fury. He sprang outside, slamming the door behind him, and lunged at Helen. She screamed and tried to escape, but he was too quick. His hand closed over her arm like an iron shackle and he yanked her closer to him, then struck. The back of his free hand rang across her face, knuckles meeting her lips, crushing them against her teeth. Blood filled her mouth, and she fell silent.

Smudge seized the front of her dress in both hands, painfully pinching, and pulled her close to his face. His breath smelled of rotten teeth and cheap tobacco.

"Go," he hissed, glaring into her eyes. "If you come back here, I'll kill you."

Helen's breath froze. Looking into his wild eyes, she knew that he meant every word.

Smudge drew back a fist. Helen ducked, trying to avoid the blow, but there was no way to escape it. It smashed into her cheekbone, drawing a gush of hot blood, and she cried out as pain blossomed over her face.

Smudge released her dress. Helen staggered away, a hand cupped over her cheekbone, tears stinging in the wound below her eye.

"I'll kill you," he repeated.

Helen looked at the madness in his eyes and felt her heart turn to a block of ice within her. Face throbbing, she spun around and ran into the streets as fast as her frightened legs would carry her.

She only slowed when she reached the docks and knew that no one was chasing her. Sobbing and shaking, she sagged to her knees at the edge of an abandoned pier, ignored by the bustle of sailors around her.

"I'm so sorry, Adrian," she gasped. "I can't get her back. I'm so sorry. I'm so sorry."

Dry blood made her fingers stick together. She leaned over the murky water and stared at her reflection, at the blood on her cheek, the swelling around her eye. With trembling hands, she reached into the cold, stinking water and rinsed her fingers, then splashed it over her face.

The cold snatched her breath and made her wound burn, but it couldn't match the agony that she felt in her chest, as though her heart had been ripped out and a raw wound left behind.

She had given up her only child, the one in whose veins Adrian's blood ran. She had to face the reality that she had sold Beryl because she feared that they would both starve if they did not. Why had she not tried harder? Why would she do anything but cling to her child? Now Beryl was with that horrible man, the man who had beaten Helen, living in that awful tenement, sweeping chimneys.

The thought made Helen retch. She reached into her pocket and drew forth the coin that Simeon Cragg had given her for her daughter. Though Helen knew only the few scraps of arithmetic she had learned in the workhouse as a small child, in between starving and being bullied, poverty had sharpened her calculating skills. Half-a-crown was two shillings and sixpence, which made thirty pennies. That was a loaf of bread every day for a month. It was a full belly for four entire weeks.

It could keep her alive until well after Christmas. It was her reward for giving away her daughter—no, not only her daughter... Adrian's daughter.

I sold his child for a month's worth of bread.

Horror stung Helen's chest. Without thinking twice, she opened her fingers and allowed the half-crown to fall. It plopped into the water and sank away into the same sea that had taken Adrian from her.

Chapter Two

Though she had known the interior of this workhouse for decades, its exterior felt strangely alien.

Helen stood beside the front gate in the tall brick walls that surrounded this place, trapping its inmates within. Loops of wire guarded wall, preventing escapees from slipping into the streets when their matrons or overseers were not looking.

In Helen's experience, however, someone was *always* looking inside the workhouse.

She wrapped her arms around her body, partly against the chill from the cruel wind that howled between the warehouses surrounding her, partly against the icy pang that came from within. The workhouse itself was a bare, cold, brick building, its windows tiny slits like narrowed eyes looking upon the streets. Stone-paved courtyards surrounded the building. Their wrought-iron fences allowed Helen a glimpse within at the men, women, and children—also separated by gender—who worked within. The children were meant to play, but instead huddled together, arms around each other against the cold.

The men and women worked. The clink of breaking rocks filled the air as the men made gravel. The women hunched over lengths of heavy rope, picking oakum with hammers and nails.

Technically, one was allowed to leave the workhouse whenever one liked. It was no official prison. But with the spectre of death stalking the streets with its cruel weapons of starvation, frostbite, and disease, the workhouse kept many trapped within. Here, at least, there were warm beds and three meals a day—though those meals might consist of a bowl of cold gruel over which one had to fight other women, and those beds might be hard, louse-ridden pallets shared with two or three others who thought nothing of using their knees and elbows to defend their space.

It was better than dying on the streets. Working would be better than sitting on a corner, begging, having nothing to distract her from the evil that hung on her shoulders. Her own evil. Her sale of her very own child.

Helen stepped forward, and a harsh voice cut through the still air.

"What do you call this? Do you presume that I am stupid enough to believe you spent all day doing *this*?"

The voice was coarse and feminine, with a familiarity that cut through to the base of Helen's spine and froze her where she stood. Her head swivelled toward the yard where the women in their ugly striped dresses picked oakum.

A harsh matron, dressed in black and rake-thin, towered over a girl no more than fourteen or fifteen years old. The girl sobbed, hands tucked to her chest. A length of rope lay at her feet with only a few inches' tar chipped from it and lying in black flakes on the stone.

"Look at this!" the matron shrieked. "You've not finished one length, and there are a dozen more waiting for you. What good would these few scraps be?" She kicked at the tar, which floated away from the girl. Several other women pounced on it and grabbed the scraps to add to their own.

The matron didn't care; the girl didn't notice.

"I'm sorry," the girl whimpered. "So sorry."

"I'll leave you out here all night," the matron snapped. "Or would you prefer a stay in the refractory ward?"

The refractory ward! The very words struck terror deep into Helen's heart. She, too, had been locked in that hateful place—that solitary confinement—for the smallest of infractions. Alone and in utter darkness, Helen had feared that she would go completely mad. She had feared that the world had ended and left her behind.

It reminded her why she had left the workhouse in the first place. Better to take her chances on the streets, to fight that cruel spectre of doom, than to face one more day in the refractory ward.

Slowly, body aching, belly empty, Helen turned from the workhouse and wandered away.

"Hello, there!"

Helen started, hands tightening on the bag of clean laundry she carried. It had taken her all night to wash the Morrisons' stupid party clothes for their stupid Christmas party, celebrating nothing but the ability to be rich and eat roast goose. She dared not cause a single wrinkle in the fabric. If she did, they would be sure to reduce their payments for her services—or, worse, employ one of the hundreds of other washerwomen who filled London.

She forced herself to relax and loosen her grip. The voice was familiar, and she knew by now that it meant her no harm.

"Hello! Hi!"

Helen turned as the shaggy-bearded man with the piercing eyes, the one who had introduced himself as Adrian, stepped from a nearby cottage—as he always did when he saw her go past. He was smiling easily, his thumbs hooked in his pockets. The wind caught his white shirt and flattened it against the powerful curves of his chest and arms.

"May I help?" he asked, extending his hands.

Helen backed away. "No, thank you."

"All right," said Adrian easily. "I'll walk with you, then."

Helen didn't protest. She took a shortcut through a chaotic part of the docks on her way to the Morrisons, and she'd noticed that when Adrian walked with her, the men no longer called out horrible things or attempted to take the washing away from her. A lost bag of party clothes would permanently ruin her.

"How are you?" Adrian asked, falling into step beside her.

"Well enough," said Helen.

"Your hands look sore," Adrian noted.

Helen glanced at them. Painful welts on her dry knuckles throbbed in the cold air. "Part of washing, that's all."

"Not a nice part, though, is it?" Adrian shook his head. "At least it's nearly Christmas."

"Yes," Helen muttered. "There'll be a few quiet days. This is the last Christmas party before it's all over and I have to start washing things for New Year's Day parties."

Adrian laughed. "And it's almost Christmas!*"*

Helen glanced at him. "What on earth do you mean? What does Christmas mean to a woman like me?" Bitterness born of exhaustion filled her tone. "I have no tree, no gifts, no decorations. I barely have a piece of smoked fish, let alone roast goose." She stopped suddenly, wondering why she'd poured out this speech to Adrian.

"A great pity," said Adrian softly. "A great pity. I pray that that will change for you someday."

The way his eyes rested on her made sudden warmth blossom through her belly. She looked away, afraid she might blush.

"Still," said Adrian softly, "Christmas is for all of us, and costs nothing. That's the point of it, isn't it? Someone else paid for us all and made His gift free for us all."

"What gift might that be?" Helen grumbled.

"Forgiveness," said Adrian. "Freedom." His eyes shone. "Peace and joy."

Helen said nothing for several more minutes. Her arms ached; Adrian paced beside her, whistling a Christmas carol without a care in the world. She glanced at his much-patched shirt and scarred hands and wondered if he had any more than a piece of fish for his Christmas dinner, either. Yet he seemed so rich in all the things he'd mentioned. His joy seemed boundless, his peace eternal.

"I think," said Helen quietly, "it might be very nice if you would carry the washing, please."

Adrian's eyes lit up as though she'd given him a great prize. He took the bag from her and carried it with tremendous care as they continued side by side through the streets of London.

Helen woke with a gasp, raising her head as cold sprayed against her cheek. She blinked, snow covering her eyelashes, and confusion filled her. How long had she slept? Had the snow grown so deep as to bury her?

"You!" a voice barked. "Move out of the way!"

Another spray of snow fell on her face. Helen wiped it away as she scrambled to her feet. The shopkeeper sweeping the pavement before his store brandished his broom, threatening to cover her in snow again.

"Get away from my shop!" he ordered.

Helen cleared her throat. "Yes, sir. Sorry, sir." She backed away. "Do... do you have a piece of stale bread—"

"Leave!" The man waved the broom again.

Helen scrambled away, her joints stiff and sore from sleeping sitting up with her back against the bakery. The delicious scents had lured her there in the early morning, but now the baker was open for business, and she knew that everyone in the marketplace would chase her off lest she scare away their customers. It was a slightly nicer square than the one where she'd sold her only child. She couldn't bear to go back there.

She shuffled to the pump at the centre of the square and bent over it, hoping for a trickle of clean water instead of drinking only melted snow. But it was thoroughly frozen when she tried the handle.

A sigh escaped her on a cloud of steam. Her shrinking belly felt as though it had shrivelled up and vanished. How long had it been since she'd eaten? Three days? Four?

Impact thudded into Helen's shoulder. She stumbled back and spun around, ready to defend herself, but saw no attacker; only a young woman with an armful of clothes in a terrible hurry. The clothes she carried look new—the cloth still thick and dark—but her own dress was ragged, with a tattered hem, an unmended hole in the skirt, and several hasty patches on the bodice.

Had she stolen them? Helen hardly cared, but perhaps she was about to sell them and get money, which she might give

Helen if she begged. It was a vague hope, but that was the only kind of hope that Helen was ever afforded these days. She turned and shuffled after the hurried girl, head hanging, exhausted feet aching with every step.

The girl did not go far. She darted down a narrow alley beside a slop-shop. Helen had spent many moments gazing through the glass at the warm clothes within, thinking of how much a good coat or a scarf could benefit her as winter crept toward its shortest days and longest, darkest nights. She had once pitied the poor wretches who bought clothing from slop-shops instead of buying fabric and making their own; she had learned to sew in the workhouse, and made all the clothes she, Beryl, and Adrian needed herself... in those days. Those far better days.

Now Helen could afford neither fabric nor second-rate slop-shop clothes.

She forced the thoughts and memories away as she moved quickly past the store. The narrow, bare alley offered a brief respite from the wind. Helen glimpsed a tattered skirt disappearing around the store's corner and followed it.

A knock made her jump before she reached the corner. She pressed herself to the wall, the brick rough against her, and made no sound as she crept to the corner and peered around it.

The girl with the tattered dress knocked again at a narrow back door. It swung open, revealing a stumpy man with flecks of red hair on his head and jaw. His eyes were yellow and rheumy.

"Finally!" he barked. "What took so long?"

The girl trembled as she held out the pile of clothes. "Four dresses, sir. As you ordered."

"Pah. I ordered them for this morning. It's already ten o'clock!" the man scolded.

"I'm sorry, Mr. Gifford, sir." The girl hung her head.

"It'll have to do. I was hoping you would make five," the man growled.

"I'm sorry, Mr. Gifford," said the girl.

"Well, don't stand there being sorry. Go and make more!" the man snapped.

"Yes, sir." The girl backed away, then hesitated.

"I suppose you want to be paid for this pathetic attempt." The man sighed. "Very well." He dug in his pocket and produced three pennies. "Now go."

"Thank you, sir!" the girl gasped, accepting the pennies. Their copper flashed brightly in the dull light, and Helen's gut tightened at everything they could represent: loaves of bread, old newspapers to use as a bed, or perhaps even a few hours at an inn, sleeping out of the cold.

The girl trotted off, not sparing Helen a second glance, and the man began to close the door.

"Sir, wait!" Helen cried, springing forward.

The man sneered, but Helen spoke quickly. The words spilled from her in a torrent as she jogged towards him.

"I can sew," she said. "I hear you need more dresses, and I can sew them very fast. I've made all kinds of things. I was a washerwoman and a mender once, too. My sewing is good and fast."

She stopped, breathless, before the door. The man looked her up and down, his yellowed gaze unmerciful upon her bony hips and protruding shoulders.

"Do you work for me, girl?" he demanded.

She was a woman and mother, not a girl, but she did not attempt to correct him. "Not yet, sir."

"Not yet, huh?" The man chuckled. "You're in luck. Christmas parties are around the corner. People come in at all hours of the day, looking for new things to wear to their parties."

More rich frippery, Helen thought, leading to this man's abuse of that poor, frightened girl. Where was Adrian's Christmas, the one that was filled with peace, love, and joy? The one that was about goodwill to all men?

"I need more workers," the man added. "But let me tell you, it's no joke, working for Barnabas Gifford. I expect you to do as you're told. If I say I need five dresses, you should make five—or you won't be paid at all."

Helen vigorously nodded. "Yes, sir. I'll do anything, sir. Anything." She gulped.

Barnabas Gifford sneered. "Yes, I can see that." He scoffed. "I need two dresses by tomorrow morning."

Two dresses in a day! Helen strangled her protests.

"A penny per dress," Gifford added.

Two pennies... They represented food, real food, something hot and hearty. If she could make two pennies every day, she could eat again.

"Yes, sir. Thank you, sir," she croaked.

"I won't have you sitting on the street, getting my fabric all dirty, either," Barnabas snapped. "There's a tenement down the block—second building on your right toward the river. You'll stay in room number four." He reached into shadowy shelves beside the door and held out two bolts of cheap fabric. "Here."

Helen took the fabric. "Yes, sir."

"Go on. Make the dresses." Barnabas shooed her away.

"Sir, I... I need a needle and thread," Helen croaked.

"I've given you fabric and a tenement to stay in," Barnabas snapped. "What more do you want from me? Now go away and do as you're told!"

Helen cringed, not daring to contradict him. "Yes, sir." She turned away.

"One more thing, woman," Barnabas growled. "What's your name?"

She looked up. "Helen, sir. Helen Nicols."

"Don't think about stealing my fabric, Helen Nicols," Barnabas hissed. "I'll know, and I'll make sure you hang for it."

Helen's toes curled. "Yes, sir."

She shuffled off, hugging the fabric, her heart pounding. Desperate to place the fabric somewhere it would not be damaged, she headed in the direction Barnabas had indicated, and a few minutes later stood before a tenement building not unlike the one in which poor Beryl now lived. The only real difference was that a little stream splashed along across the street from the tenement, a humpbacked bridge offering a passage to the marketplace whence Helen had come.

The agony of missing her child dulled any worries that may otherwise have risen when she gazed at the tenement, at its thin walls and the gaps where bricks had gone missing, at the windows where many panes had been replaced with wood or cardboard. She shuffled to the building, pushed open a door that creaked and swung on a loose hinge, and gazed dimly at the room numbers painted on the pitiful doors, which had never been painted and looked as though they were cobbled together with planks from old pallets.

The one with the number 4 painted upon it had a draught whistling beneath the door that stung Helen's ankles when she pushed it open. Peering into the room, she was at once transported in her mind to the workhouse, to those last few horrible moments before one was forced into the refractory ward. The tenement reminded her all too painfully of that awful place. It had four walls, yes, but was no wider than its door.

Chinks of candlelight from the tenement above her trickled through the gaps in the ceiling. The draught came from a missing brick in the back wall.

That was all. There was no stove, no fireplace, and no bed; only the cold wooden floor.

It was better than an alleyway. Helen told herself this as she crouched and carefully placed the fabric on a clean patch of floor, then retreated and shut the door behind her. Anything would be better than an alleyway. She repeated it to herself over and over again as she strode down the hall and into the city to beg for a single penny, enough to buy a needle and thread and a stub of candle, to illuminate her work in that dark and cold place.

Helen's eyes burned in the sunlight to which they had become unaccustomed in the past several days. She squinted against the light, which poured with unusual richness upon the marketplace, lighting up the snow-laden roofs and the banks of sparkling snow that lay where they had been shovelled in the streets. Bright bunting brought colour to a scene of black, white, and grey, matching the rosy and wind-nipped cheeks of passers-by.

"Merry Christmas!" one called to the other as he hastened past, his scarf's tails streaming in the wind.

"Merry Christmas!" the other responded.

Helen shook her head as she stumbled across the marketplace, eyes stinging with sunlight and exhaustion.

Christmas was yet days away. Besides, why would anyone think it merry? So many suffered at this time of year. There were so many like her.

She carried two bolts of fabric under her arm—enough for three dresses, which Barnabas expected her to finish by this time the following morning. It was impossible, but Helen knew she would have to do it anyway, no matter how late she would be forced to stay up that night.

She stopped and gazed at the marketplace with feverish eyes. The bakery and the candle maker stood side by side. Fresh bread glowed golden in the window: a penny per loaf.

Her stomach growled. She'd had nothing but a piece of fish and an apple the day before. A whole loaf of bread would be glorious... but first, she turned to the candle maker's window. Most of the display was occupied with beautiful Christmas candles in lovely shapes and colours, but she spotted a few stubby, ordinary ones near the bottom. The cheerful sign beside them was decorated with sprigs of holly and held their price: a penny each.

Helen's toes curled. How long would she work tonight? She could, perhaps, do a few hours' work by daylight, but the tenement admitted so little that it strained her eyes to do and swiftly became impossible when afternoon came. She would need as many as ten hours' candlelight to finish her work if she moved quickly.

Those little candles barely lasted six hours each.

Tears of hunger and frustration stung her eyes. Helen's shoulders sagged; she had no choice. She turned away from the golden loaves and staggered into the candle shop instead.

Chapter Three

The stream was filthy, yet when Helen closed her eyes, the sound of the running water sounded clean enough. She could almost imagine that it was the little stream by the meadow outside London where Adrian used to take her and Beryl for picnics sometimes in better days. Beryl was little then, just learning to walk, and they were talking about having another child someday. Helen was excited for the idea.

They would sit on Helen's favourite chequered blanket, eating bread and ham and cheese and fresh green apples from the basket she had packed, enjoying the surface of springy grass and heather. It was only a short stagecoach ride outside London, a simple extravagance that Adrian's new position as first mate could easily afford him on those rare and precious summer weeks when he was not at sea.

The splashing of the stream awoke more memories in Helen: the smell of crushed grass, the crunch of apple between her teeth, and Beryl's laughter as she chased butterflies on her wobbly feet. She could almost feel Adrian's strong fingers wrapping around hers.

But it was all a dream, a memory, something that would never come back to her. When she opened her eyes, they were all gone: Adrian claimed by the sea, Beryl, by Helen's own selfishness. There was no meadow; only the bustling streets. Factory workers in busy clothes hurried to and fro. An old man shouted at a stray dog, then aimed a kick. The little animal dodged and ran away.

Helen saw these things instead of the mistletoe hanging from the eaves of the buildings or the holly sprigs pinned to the lapels of passers-by. She saw none of the smiles, nor did she hear the jovial cries of "Merry Christmas!" even among these destitute folk as they hastened along the street. Her agony had rendered her deaf and blind to the good and beautiful. Instead, she saw only the bleakness of her own heart reflected in the world, making it all seem so dull and grey when her memories were filled with breath-taking colour.

She gazed into the rushing stream, its waters greyish and soiled as they parted around heaps of rubbish and the occasional ice-edged rock. The steam was narrow, it was true, but very deep here where it rushed beneath the bridge and swollen with precipitation from the endless snow. The pool that swirled beneath Helen must have been ten or twelve feet deep.

More than deep enough to drown in.

The thought chilled her, yet at the same time, Helen couldn't bring herself to raise her head and look away from those dingy waters.

"Hello!"

She watched as a scrap of something—perhaps a leaf, perhaps paper—scudded by on the sluggish current. How small and pitiful her life felt, like that sad floating object, tiny and fragile, effortlessly crushed. It zipped through an eddy around a nearby rock, then sank when the water pulled it under. Helen felt her own chest close in empathy.

"Hello there! Miss? Miss?"

The voice came nearer. Helen finally raised her head, reluctant to face whatever fresh cruelty the world brought upon her today.

A little old lady stood a few feet from her at the edge of the bridge. Despite the poverty written in the lines of her face and the hard calluses on her chapped and gnarled hands, the old lady seemed lit up with an internal glow that had nothing to do with her hollow cheeks and pale skin. She had bright green eyes that danced with internal merriment, as though laughing at some glorious secret hidden within. Her pure white hair formed a cloud around her head, only partly tamed by the wool hat perching thereon.

"Hello, dear," said the old lady. "You live in number four, don't you?"

Helen dumbly nodded, though she would hardly call it living. She worked, she slept, she sometimes ate. Her existence had been whittled down to nothing else.

"It's lovely to meet you," said the old lady. "I'm Sally Adams. I live in number five, right across the hall."

Helen returned her gaze to the water.

The old lady moved a little closer. "You can call me Sally. You work for the slop-shop, too, is that right? I've seen you there when I go to bring my dresses and things to Mr. Gifford."

Helen said nothing.

"There's plenty of work with Christmas coming up." Sally chuckled. "Why, I hardly knew my old hands could still make two dresses in a day. At least it gives us a little more in our pockets, doesn't it, dear? I've bought some tea and I thought I'd make a lovely, hot pot. Why don't you join me?"

Helen blinked at her. The words barely seemed to penetrate her mind, but she thought vaguely of how nice it would be to have something hot in her stomach.

"How much?" she croaked.

Sally frowned. "I'm sorry, dear?"

"How much for the tea?" Helen croaked. "I don't have anything."

"Oh, dear, you don't have to pay me a penny. I'm being neighbourly, that's all." Sally laughed, as though the thought of paying for everything was ludicrous. "Come on inside and warm your cold bones with a nice cuppa, how does that sound?"

Helen gave the stream one last glance, then shuffled toward Sally, still carrying her fabric bolts under her arm with the brown paper bag containing her candles. Sally tucked Helen's limp hand over her arm as though they were old friends and strode toward the building with a surprising spring in her step for a lady of her age.

"Have to make clothes," Helen mumbled.

"Me too, dear, me too. I'll get started as soon as I've put the kettle on. I have three shirts to make today, how about you?" said Sally.

"Two dresses."

"Isn't that nice? You'll get tuppence for that, and somebody will have a lovely time at a Christmas party, dancing and enjoying your dress." Sally laughed. "Pity the light's so low at Christmas, isn't it? I couldn't find any candles in the marketplace today. They were all out of the ones we can afford, but that's no matter. Maybe the moon will come out tonight and give us a little light to work by. What do you think?"

Helen nodded dumbly.

Sally strode to number five and pushed the door open. "Welcome, dear. Have a seat!"

At first glance, the tenement was the twin of Helen's, except for a few more luxuries, if they could be called that. There was a pallet covered with newspapers and a threadbare blanket in one corner. Three wooden crates stood in the other; two were smaller, arranged like seats around the larger one. Sally went over to the smouldering coals in the tiny fireplace across the room and hung a tin kettle over them.

"Nice hot tea," she said, placing a paper bag on the crate she used as a table. "Do sit, dear."

Helen sank onto one of the smaller boxes, but did not relinquish her hold on the precious fabric and bag of candles she carried. Sally sprinkled tea into the kettle, then sat on the box beside Helen.

"Did you find any food today?" she asked.

Helen shook her head.

"That's all right. I've plenty," said Sally, producing from the same bag a half loaf of bread. It was hardly anyone's definition of "plenty," even for a single person, but Sally cheerfully tore it in half and offered some to Helen.

Helen stared at the bread, then at Sally, then back again.

"Do go on, dear," said Sally.

Helen reached out with a trembling hand and took the bread. It lasted only seconds as she scarfed it down too fast; the dry bread stung her stomach, and she had to fight the urge to retch as it curled in her too-empty belly. But then Sally placed a mug of hot tea at her elbow, and Helen sipped. She couldn't remember the last time she'd had something hot to drink.

"Oohhh, thank you," she whispered as the weak but warm tea slid deliciously down.

"Of course, dear." Sally smiled as she arranged a needle, thread, scissors, and fabric on the table. "Do you feel better?"

Helen thought shamefully of the bridge and nodded. "Yes, thank you."

"Good." Sally chuckled. "What's your name?"

"Helen," she said.

"A beautiful name, Helen. I saw that you don't have a table or anything in your tenement," said Sally. "You can sit with me, if you like. It'd be lovely to have the company."

Helen stared at the old lady as she squinted at the fabric, then painstaking began to cut out the same pattern she'd doubtlessly made a thousand times. She didn't know how to thank this sweet old woman for extending a hand of friendship at the moment when she most needed it. Sally felt like the only glimmer of sunlight on a cloudy day, but Helen couldn't articulate that.

Instead, she said quietly, "I have candles. We can share."

Sally smiled, and a tiny pocket of warmth gathered in Helen's heart for the first time since she'd given Beryl away.

"Sally!" Helen called, stepping into the tenement building. "I'm here!"

A merry greeting rose down the hallway, and Helen smiled as she stepped inside, her arms laden with fabric and a few small parcels wrapped in brown paper. A band of scruffy street children shuffled past, lifting up their reedy voices to sing "O Christmas Tree."

O Christmas tree, O Christmas tree,
How lovely are thy branches!

Helen shook snow from her hair and shut out the billowing wind, which left several snowflakes on the hallway floor.

She strode down to tenement number five and popped her head around the door. Sally sat at the table, working on a piece of sewing by the light of the last candle.

"You'll never believe it," said Helen. "The baker had too much gingerbread. He was selling it at half price to keep it from going stale." She placed the parcel triumphantly on the crate. "It's a little dry, but it was only a penny for this piece."

"Lovely!" cried Sally. "Did you get candles, too?"

"I did, and more fabric from Mr. Gifford. He was less difficult about accepting both your work and mine from me today," said Helen.

"You're such a dear. My poor old knee hated walking all that way. You're saving me such pain by walking to the slop-shop for me every day."

"You're saving me effort," said Helen, "by carrying on with the sewing while I'm gone. Mr. Gifford tried not to show it, but he was pleased that we've made so many things this past week."

"That's wonderful. I'm pleased, too." Sally set the sewing aside and smiled. "Merry Christmas, my dear Helen. I praise the Good Lord for bringing you into my life."

Helen sank onto a makeshift chair and found herself smiling. She couldn't quite say the words back, but she felt them differently now that she was friends with Sally.

"Come on," she said eagerly, unwrapping the gingerbread. "I'm so hungry! This will be delicious."

"It surely will, especially because I have a little surprise of my own for you," said Sally.

Helen laughed. "What?"

"Well, I put half a penny aside for something nice at Christmas weeks ago," said Sally. She reached below the crate and pulled out a tiny brown paper packet, which she placed on the table. "Here it is. Just enough for one night, but it'll be special in any case."

Helen gasped. "Is—is that sugar?"

"That's right, dear," said Sally. "A little sugar for our tea tonight." She sprinkled it into their tin cups.

"Oh, Sally, that's lovely." Helen sipped. "Ahhh! I can't remember the last time I tasted sugar."

"I remember when we used to have sugar sometimes in the workhouse when I was a wee lamb." Sally smiled. "Did you, too?"

"I did," said Helen softly, "but there was a time when I had sugar anytime I liked."

Sally tilted an eyebrow, an invitation to say more, but didn't pressure Helen to speak. Instead, she broke off a piece of gingerbread and ate it with every sign of relish.

"I wasn't always poor," said Helen. "I've told you how I worked for a washerwoman after running away from the workhouse, but then... then... one day, a sailor came by, a handsome, wild man named Adrian, and he carried my washing for me."

Sally grinned. "Did you like it?"

"Not at first," said Helen. "I refused to let him, at first, but then I saw that he really was good and kind, not cruel like everyone else I'd ever known. So I let him. And then... well, I married him."

"Was he a good man?" Sally asked.

Helen hung her head. "The best," she whispered. "The very best. The kindest... the gentlest. Christmas was very different with him around."

"I remember my first Christmas as a married woman. It was beautiful," said Sally, with a wistful sigh.

Helen remembered, too. But her first Christmas as Adrian's wife was very different. "Adrian was a sailor, like I said," she said softly, "and he was out at sea for our first Christmas as husband and wife. They wintered in Newfoundland. We had a tiny cottage, and he'd left me enough money to get by, but it was terribly quiet and lonely in that little house without him."

"Ah, I'm sorry, dear." Sally touched her hand. "I remember the quiet the first Christmas after the war took my John."

"Yes... well." Helen hung her head. "Adrian came back... that time."

Sally tilted her head.

"Then he took an expedition to South America with an explorer," Helen whispered. "He was a wonderful navigator by then, the best... we had everything we could have wanted. Adrian said that he would never have to go to sea again if he went to South America on this expedition, even though he knew he'd be gone for months, maybe a year. I waited in hope for the first year." Her voice cracked. "I waited in despair for the second. Beryl was only three when I finally accepted that he was dead."

"Oh, my poor dear," Sally murmured, resting a hand on her knee. "You had a little girl?"

"A perfect little girl." Pressure constricted Helen's chest. "She was just like her father. I... I tried, but we owed money on the house, and... and with Adrian gone..." Tears filled her eyes.

"You poor thing," said Sally. "I'm sure you did your best."

"I did, but it wasn't enough. We lost the house... we lost everything. I couldn't feed her anymore, Sally." The raw pain tore from Helen. "I sold her to a chimney sweep. I couldn't feed her. I didn't know what to do."

She saw Sally's eyes widen faintly with shock, and she had never hated herself more than she did in that moment. She lunged to her feet, almost about to flee, but Sally grabbed her arm and then pulled her down into a gentle embrace.

"It's all right, dear," Sally murmured. "It's all right."

"It's not all right," Helen sobbed into Sally's chest. "I betrayed her, Sally. I couldn't get her back."

"Perhaps the Good Lord will lead you back to her someday," said Sally. "His mercies are great, my darling. Look here. Look at our little Christmas."

Sniffling, Helen gazed at the few small items on their crate; the bits of gingerbread, the packet of sugar, and the bright candle.

"Christmas isn't just about rich folks and roast geese," said Sally softly. "It's a time for believing in miracles, no matter how small, or big. Christmas is a time for hope. Sometimes, when things feel the hardest, that's when a little bit of Christmas magic can surprise you. Maybe, just maybe, something good is still waiting for you, even now."

Helen leaned her head on Sally's shoulder for a few long moments.

"Now, let's eat this gingerbread!" said Sally, laughing.

Helen bit into the gingerbread, and though cold and a little dry, it was surprisingly good. Yet she ate slowly, with less appetite than she'd had a moment before, Beryl weighing heavily on her heart.

That night, she lay alone in her tiny, bare tenement, lying on a pile of old newspapers with a flour sack for a pillow and a tatty old blanket. She thought of her little girl's bright blue eyes. Longing threatened to crush her.

Christmas is a time for hope, Sally had said. Helen felt only a tiny flicker of that hope in her chest, but she clung to it. It was enough for her to close her eyes tightly and make a quiet vow.

I'll come back for you, Beryl, she whispered in her heart. *Every day of my life, I will fight for the means to be able to care for you. And when I have them, I will seek you again, no matter how long it takes. No matter what, I'll find you again, my love.*

She sent the promise winging away into the night, interweaving with the falling snow and rising carols, and then wept herself to sleep on that cold and lonely Christmas Eve.

Part Two

Chapter Four

Two Years Later

*I saw three ships come sailing in
On Christmas Day, on Christmas Day,
I saw three ships come sailing in
On Christmas Day in the morning!*

Helen shivered, crossing the street to avoid the band of carollers that wandered past, their piping young voices filling the street despite the frigid wind that nipped at Helen's exposed wrists and fingertips. The younger carollers skipped along, shouting their lines with enthusiasm. Several looked to be about six—the same age that Beryl would be now. One little girl had bright red hair, but her eyes were dark.

Helen paused to watch her skip by, belting out her lines, and her heart sagged within her. *Oh, how different things would be if only my ship had ever come sailing in.*

She tugged her bonnet closer around her ears and hurried onward, ignoring the mistletoe and holly wreaths already going up on the shops around her.

It was still a month before Christmas. How could these fools have the time and money to spare to start preparing for that silly holiday so early?

The only thing that wasn't unseasonable on this frigid December day was the weather. There was no snow yet; the pavement was cold and dry, slippery with ice. But the lowering sky promised that either rain or snow would fall soon. Helen hoped it was snow. She was exhausted from being soaked to the bone with rain most mornings when she hurried to the slop-shop, and often Barnabas would dock her pay for bringing damp clothes to him.

She prayed he wouldn't do so today. It had been two days since she and Sally had last eaten, and the flesh had melted from the old lady's bones that winter.

Helen reached the alley at last and knocked. Barnabas flung the door open with a sneer.

"Where's that Mrs. Adams?" he demanded. "I haven't seen her in months."

"Her knee troubles her in the cold, sir," said Helen for what felt like the hundredth time.

Barnabas scoffed. "Did you bring my shirts?"

"Yes, sir. Six shirts," said Helen.

She extended the pile of clothing to him, and Barnabas roughly counted the shirts, then tucked them under his arm. "Very well." He held out a coin.

Helen took it, then froze. "T-tuppence, sir?"

"Same as always," Barnabas snapped. "A penny for three shirts. Is there something wrong with that, Mrs. Nicols?" His eyes narrowed.

Helen cringed. "N-no, sir, it's just... It's just..." She gripped the tuppence with trembling fingers.

"Spit it out, woman," Barnabas barked. "If you're unhappy with your work here, I'd like to know about it. I'm sure there are dozens of women in this city who'd love to have it."

"No, sir. Please, sir, that's not what I mean," Helen croaked. "It's just—well, bread is two pennies and a half for two loaves these days."

"You have enough money for bread, then. I don't see your difficulty." Barnabas sneered.

"Yes, sir, but c-candles are getting… are getting more expensive too," Helen croaked.

Barnabas waved a hand. "I tire of your stories, woman," he snapped. "Work for me, or don't. I don't care."

"Please, sir, I want to work for you," Helen gabbled. "Please, don't send me away. Please—"

Barnabas dropped three bolts of cloth in Helen's arms. "Four dresses by morning. Don't be late," he barked. "Christmas parties are starting."

"Yes, sir," said Helen. Oh, those accursed Christmas parties! It was only another reason to hate this season.

She turned and stumbled into the street, hugging the fabric to her chest. As she limped toward the bakery, praying that the stubs of candles they still had would hold for the night, the first fat snowflakes began to fall. Helen stumbled to a halt and stared up at the sky, watching the white flakes tumble down, glittering. They settled on everything: the pavement, the rooftops, the dark hats of the men and women passing by, like tiny stars against the cotton and velvet.

Tears burned in Helen's eyes. The first snow always reminded her of the same thing: kneeling by the plane tree, looking into Beryl's beautiful little face for the last time.

Love you, Mama. Her tiny voice still echoed in Helen's mind, choking her with its piercing clarity in her memories.

Helen hung her head and kept moving. With every step, her tears fell as swiftly as the snow.

The soft voice rang around the hallway as Helen finally ducked into the tenement building, clutching the dense, heavy loaf under her arm. Sally's voice was old and reedy now, but it held a quavering beauty as it rose against the low ceiling.

O holy night, the stars are brightly shining
It is the night of our dear Saviour's birth!

Helen couldn't help smiling as she strode to number five and pushed the door open. Sally sat at the table, bent over her sewing, her trembling hands working the needle through the fabric, her eyes creased as she squinted in the low light of a stubby candle.

"Ah, Helen, dear." She looked up, her smile unabated despite the milkiness that had grown in her eyes over the past two years. "You're back."

"I have bread, Sally," said Helen, "and I was terribly lucky. A rag-and-bone man was selling a candle stub for ha'penny." She placed it on the table.

"Ahhh, wonderful. Providence has helped us again, my dear," said Sally. "Let's open up this nice bread and have ourselves breakfast." She said it casually, as though it hadn't been days since their last meal.

Helen tore chunks from the loaf and they ate it with their hands in silence. Despite its density, the dry bread tasted wonderful after such hunger, and Helen washed it down with greedy gulps of cold water from the pump outside.

She wondered how long it would be before the pump froze and thought longingly of the taps she used to have in her home with Adrian, which she could simply turn for an abundant supply of hot or cold water as she pleased. Things were so different here.

Sally suddenly laughed.

Helen jumped. "What?"

"Oh, sorry, dear." Sally lowered her tin mug. "I was just getting a little sad, you know, and tired, so I thought of a time when my John made me laugh." Her eyes danced. "He was such a silly man. A true gentleman, but he could be a fool at times. Once, he was digging in the garden when I came up behind him suddenly and patted his back and said, 'Boo!' Well, dear, my John was the bravest man I'd ever met. He'd have fought a wolf with his bare hands to save his family. But he jumped clean over the garden fence that day." Sally threw her head back and emitted a delightful peal of laughter. "I'd never seen anything so funny in all my life!"

Helen smiled. "Adrian liked a practical joke, too."

"There you are, darling. Isn't it nice to think of happy moments?" Sally smiled. "Tell me a happy time from your life. I would love to hear it."

Helen's mind flitted through that short, yet blissful period of her life that included Adrian. She smiled suddenly, remembering.

"Have I ever told you about Adrian's proposal?" she asked.

Sally smiled. "No, but please do."

Helen closed her eyes. The memory was so clear that she could almost smell the sea.

Helen was walking down the street when she saw it.

The laundry bag was heavy in her arms. For the first few weeks since Adrian left to go out to sea, it had felt so much lighter thanks to all of his promises. He'd told her that he loved her and was going to marry her—as soon as he came back from this voyage to India. But that had been three months ago, and now autumn lay chilly on London's streets, and still there was no sign of Adrian's ship.

She plodded toward the basement she rented, the laundry heavier than ever, starting to believe that he'd never come back. Then something told her to lift her eyes beyond the cottage roofs to the sea, and she saw the flag flying from the proud mast of the merchant vessel she'd know anywhere. The vessel where Adrian worked as a sailor.

Helen's heart turned over in her chest, a wild cartwheel of joy. Her hands turned numb. The laundry tumbled from her grip and landed in the street. She tripped over it as she scrambled down the street, laughing and crying, then sprinted toward the docks as quickly as her legs could carry her, her skirt swishing between her flying limbs.

She reached the docks, breathless and wild with excitement, as the great ship steered into the harbour. Her eyes searched the gunwale as she stood on the docks, hands clasped over her chest, heart fluttering wildly beneath them. Sailors' heads and warms bristled over the gunwale as they waved to the crowd of people waiting at the dock. She searched, trembling, until she spotted it: a head of fine, dark hair.

Her heart leaped. "Adrian!" she cried. "Oh, Adrian!"

A gruff laugh echoed across the harbour, carrying effortlessly toward her. A white-shirted figure sprang from the ship and cut a swift figure into the still water in a burst of spray.

Helen laughed and sobbed as she ran to the pier, reaching it as Adrian swam strongly to its edge.

"Oh, Adrian, you fool!" Helen laughed through tears as she reached down to help him onto the docks. "What are you doing?"

"I've been away from you for weeks, my love." Adrian scrambled onto the damp wood, his eyes alight. "I couldn't wait a single moment longer."

"Oh, my love!" Helen cried, flinging her arms around his sodden body.

Adrian returned her embrace and swung her around, his skin warm despite his soaked clothes, his big heart thumping against hers. She laughed and landed on her tiptoes, and he cupped his wet, rough hands around her cheeks, bent down and kissed her with fierce joy.

She clung to him. "You came back."

Adrian drew back, eyes shining as they met hers. "You were here, waiting."

"Of course." Helen reached up to touch his face with shaking fingertips. "Where else would I be? You're the world."

"Oh, my darling." Adrian kissed her forehead. "I have waited so long. I can't wait any longer."

He sank suddenly, and Helen's heart stopped as he landed on one knee and reached into his pocket. The tiny box he withdrew was soaked, but when he opened it, tiny droplets sparkled on the face of the ring. She clasped her hands to her mouth. The world seemed to spin around her.

"You deserve gold and diamonds, my love," said Adrian. "This is just silver and jasper, but all the same... will you marry me?"

Helen raised her eyes to his. "If you proposed with a wooden ring, or none at all, there could still be no other answers, my love." She choked out the word. "Yes. Yes!"

He slipped the pretty ring onto her finger, but its sparkle was dull compared to the shine in his eyes. Then he wrapped his sturdy arms around her and kissed her with such love and passion that Helen thought he would never stop, and in the same breath, did not want him to.

"Oh, how lovely." Sally clasped her hands beneath her chin. "That must have been wonderful, dear."

Helen blinked. She'd lost herself so deeply in the memory that she'd almost forgotten that Adrian was long gone, and Beryl with him. She wiped tears from her eyes as she turned to the fabric bolts and unrolled them.

"Come on, Sally," she said softly. "Let's just make these things."

Sally gave her a questioning glance, but said nothing. They began to work in crushing silence.

Yesterday's snow had become today's slush. Helen tried to stay out of the worst puddles of it as she hurried along the pavement, but her shoes and socks were already soaked. Her toes had gone through the fierce pain of freezing and now turned numb.

The church bell was just striking eight when she jogged into the alley and hammered on the door. The last peal died away as Barnabas opened it.

"You're late," he growled.

Helen swallowed the lump in her throat. "Please, sir, four dresses. As you ordered." She held them out.

Barnabas sneered, then grabbed the top one and unfolded it, swinging it left and right as he carelessly inspected its seams. "Very well," he grunted. "I'll accept this, I suppose." He took the other. "Here."

It was tuppence again. Only a penny, for all the day's work. Helen could only hope that the rag-and-bone man might have candles again, but to be fair, she had eaten the day before. Eating two days in a row was too much to hope for these days.

Barnabas handed the dresses to a hapless young assistant, who scuttled off to the shopfront while Barnabas yelled at her. He turned back to Helen and grabbed four large bolts of cloth from the shelves near him.

"Here," he barked, shoving them into her hands. "We're closed for the weekend, as usual. On Monday morning, I expect eight dresses."

Helen's heart flipped. "E-eight?"

"You have three days to do it," Barnabas snapped. "I don't see the problem."

"But sir, we usually make one dress per day each," Helen cried, "and that's hard enough. We stay up late into the night to finish, sir. Please—"

Barnabas raised a hand sharply. Helen cowered, expecting a blow, but instead the man merely sneered.

"Listen to me, you filthy wretch," Barnabas hissed. "I don't have time to argue with you every day. In fact, I'd have thrown you from my tenement months ago, if I had the women to spare. But my dresses sell as quickly as they come into the store. People want dresses for their Christmas parties, and they'll get them here. Do you understand?"

Helen gulped. "Sir, I don't know if we—"

"Finish the eight dresses by Monday morning," Barnabas snapped, "or you're finished, you and that old wretch Mrs. Adams. Do you understand me, Mrs. Nicols? This is your final chance."

Helen's heart thumped, and her mind raced back to the promise she'd made herself on that cold, lonely Christmas. *I will find you again, Beryl.* Without the slop-shop, she had no way of doing that.

"Yes, sir," she croaked. "Very well, sir. We'll do that, sir."

"Good," Barnabas grunted. "And don't go expecting anything more from me, either. You'll get a penny per dress as usual."

"Yes, sir," Helen whispered.

Barnabas waved an impatient hand. "Now go. And don't come back unless you've made eight dresses."

Chapter Five

"Eight dresses?" said Sally, faintly. "Are you sure he said *eight*?"

Helen nodded dumbly. They sat facing each other over the table, the bolts of fabric stacked high between them. A brown paper package of candles sat on the table beside the fabric.

"I don't know what to do," Helen croaked. "We work twenty hours a day as it is and barely manage to finish one dress each. Now we have to finish four dresses each in three days, or we'll lose our jobs."

Sally rubbed her face with raw, red hands. "You didn't happen to find us any food, did you, dear?"

Helen shook her head. "I'm sorry, Sally. I... I bought all the candles I could."

Sally glanced longingly at the bean tin resting on the mantelpiece above her tiny fireplace. The charred, blackened tin contained all their savings in the world: sixpence. They'd saved it painstakingly, ha'penny for ha'penny, over the past year.

"I could take the savings," said Helen.

"No." Sally shook her head. "No, we'll be all right without food for a few more days, dear. It's far more important for us to save that money for when we truly need it. If we grow faint with hunger by tomorrow or Sunday, you could take it then, dear."

"I agree." Helen nodded. "We'll have extra money next week, in any case. Mr. Gifford will give us eight pence for those dresses."

"That's not bad, dear. But that's if we manage to make them all," said Sally.

"We have to," Helen protested. "If we don't, we'll lose our job!"

"I understand that, dear." Sally pulled the fabric nearer and picked up her scissors. "But we can only do so much. We'll simply have to do our best and trust the Lord for the rest, won't we?"

Helen hung her head, watching for a few moments as Sally began to cut. Then she gritted her teeth. "No."

Sally looked up. "What did you say, dear?"

"I said, no. We're not going to leave this up to anyone but ourselves," said Helen firmly. "We can't afford to lose our jobs, Sally. We'll be out on the streets in the middle of winter, and then what?"

Sally blinked. "But what more can we do than we already do, dear?"

"We can work through the night," said Helen.

Sally's jaw dropped. "Love, surely you're not expecting—"

"Sally, we have to," said Helen. "It's only three nights. We can stay awake for that long." She grabbed her fabric and got to work. "We can make it."

"Three nights? Nobody can do that, dear," Sally protested.

"We can," said Helen. "Sally, we have to. What will we do if we don't have our jobs anymore?"

Sally looked into Helen's desperate eyes. Something softened in her expression. Her eyes gentled toward acceptance.

"All right, dear," she said softly. "If you believe we must, then we shall."

Three days and three nights dragged past in painful, candlelit monotony. They bent over the crate and worked in silence, cutting and measuring, stitching and folding, labouring over every crease and ruffle as the dresses slowly took shape.

Helen's eyes burned. Several times, she shook Sally awake when the old woman nodded off over her sewing. She made Sally promise to do the same for her. It grew harder and harder to blink instead of simply falling asleep, and they took to drinking freshly melted snow, the water so cold that it stung their teeth. The brief bursts of pain helped them to stay awake.

Apart from the quick excursions outside to gather more snow for melting or to visit the lavvy, Helen and Sally remained rooted to their chairs throughout that long, dark weekend. All that changed to mark the passage of night and day was when Helen could blow out the candle for a few brief hours during each morning; then the light faded, and she would light it once more.

Their hunger grew. On Sunday, Helen considered using their precious savings for food, but there was no time. They still had more than one dress each to finish in the next twenty-four hours.

Their chatter faded into silence. No more laughter remained in the tenement, only the two women bent over their work in the flickering candlelight, eyes burning and strained, fingers numb and aching. Sewing, sewing, sewing.

The church bell had struck two in the morning on Monday when Helen finally raised the finished dress. "Four dresses," she croaked. "I've finished four dresses."

Sally placed two last stitches, then tied off the thread and set the needle aside. "Me too, dear," she said, gently stroking the front of the dress after laying it on the table. "We're all done."

"Oh, Sally, we did it." Tears stung Helen's eyes. "See? I told you we could."

Sally faintly smiled. Her cheeks were the colour of old, dry ashes, and her hands shook where she sat.

A pang of worry ran through Helen. "Are you all right, Sally?"

"I'm just fine, dear," said the old woman softly. "Tired, that's all. Very, very tired."

Helen grabbed Sally's arm. Despite the fierce aches soaking through her own body, she guided the old woman to her pallet and gently lowered her to the straw mattress.

"I'll bring food in the morning," she promised, "all the food you can eat."

"That's nice, dear," Sally whispered, her eyes closing.

Helen tucked the blanket around her. "Thank you, Sally."

The old woman gripped her hand and squeezed it with unexpected strength. Her eyes fluttered open.

"It's going to be all right, dear," she whispered. "Trust in Providence, and all will be well."

Helen squeezed her hand. "We don't need Providence. We have each other."

Sally's face twitched into a faint smile. Her eyes fluttered closed, and she dropped into sleep. Helen gave her hand another gentle squeeze, then turned and staggered to her own bed.

Despite her exhaustion, Helen woke at the crack of dawn out of sheer habit. She sat up with a gasp although her limbs ached fiercely and her head throbbed for want of sleep.

Eight pennies, she thought. *Eight pennies!*

She sprang to her feet, filled with sudden excitement. They had done it. They had finished their work, and today, they would eat their fill. She washed her face quickly in a basin of cold water, pressed her hair down beneath her grimy bonnet as well as she could, and then tiptoed into Sally's tenement. The old woman lay peacefully, her face a grey mask, exactly as Helen had left her the night before. Her pallor sent a jolt through Helen. Perhaps she had asked too much of dear Sally. But it would be worth it; she would soon be able to eat a good meal for the first time in months. She would soon feel better.

Loathe to wake her friend, Helen quickly gathered the dresses and left.

The eight garments were heavy in her arms and slowed her as she staggered to the marketplace. Her heart pounded as though she was sprinting even though she merely walked, but she smelled freshly baked bread as she crossed the marketplace, and it sent a jolt of hope and energy through her. Soon, she would be bringing that fresh bread back to Sally, and seeing the colour return to her friend's cheeks would make everything worth it.

The church bell began to strike eight when she knocked on the door. Barnabas swung it open, then blinked in surprise.

"Mrs. Nicolls," he spluttered.

"Eight dresses." Helen thrust them into his arms. "As you ordered, sir."

"Well—well, I should hope so." Barnabas quickly hid his surprise. "You and Mrs. Adams will make two more for tomorrow." He struggled to drape the dresses over a nearby rack before retrieving more fabric.

Helen's heart sank. *More clothes?* She wasn't sure what else she'd expected, but her surprise fled in the face of sheer delight as Barnabas held out two precious coins and dropped them into her palm. A sixpence and a tuppence. They represented more money than Helen had had at the same time in years.

"Go on, then," Barnabas grumbled. "Get your work done!"

Relief flooded Helen's blood. She turned and ran toward the marketplace like a little girl, making a beeline for the fragrant bakery.

"Sally!" Helen cried, bounding through the tenement door. "Sally, I'm here, and you'll never guess what I have!"

The brown paper bags in her hand crinkled promisingly with two loaves of fresh bread, as well as fish, turnips, radishes, potatoes, and carrots. She could make a good, hearty broth with this—the kind of hot and wholesome food she and Sally seldom tasted.

Her excitement rushed through her as she darted into number five. "Sally, wake up!" she said, laughing. "Look what I've brought for us!"

The old woman slumbered on, eyes closed, hands tucked beneath the blanket.

Helen put the kettle on. "I'll make tea now—with sugar *and* milk, if you can believe it. He gave me eight pennies, Sally. Eight!" She turned to the pallet and laughed.

"Wake up, you poor sleepyhead. I know you're tired, but a cup of tea will do you the world of—" She stopped.

Sally didn't stir. Nor did her chest rise and fall beneath the blanket. She lay utterly still, her face grey and motionless, still with the stillness of death.

Helen's breath left her in a tiny gasp. "Sally?"

She staggered to the pallet and fell to her knees beside it, grasping the old woman's shoulder. "Sally!"

When her fingers touched the frigid flesh, Helen knew instantly that Sally was gone. But her heart could not accept what her eyes saw and mind processed. She flung the blankets back, saw the dark stains of blood pooled beneath the skin of Sally's arms and neck, and still refused to believe.

"Sally, wake up!" Helen yelled, gently slapping her cheeks. "Wake up!"

The sensation on her palms appalled her. It was like slapping old leather, and Sally's neck didn't move. She was stiff.

A cry of panic, disgust, and horror poured from Helen. She stumbled to her feet, screaming and sobbing, hands clasped over her mouth.

"Sally!" she moaned. "No, no. Sally! Sally! Please! Oh, no! Sally, wake up! Wake up! *Wake up!*"

Her screams died away with no response. Helen sank to the floor, hands over her face, and wept until she could weep no longer.

No one else came to the funeral, if one could call it by so grand a name.

The old priest stood over the little grave in a cemetery that was far too crowded and had far too many mounds of fresh earth, several of them painfully small. He droned to his audience of one as the gravediggers shovelled dirt over Sally's cheap coffin. It had cost three of the precious few pennies Helen had had left. The plot of land had been the most expensive. After the priest's paltry fee, the grave itself had robbed her of everything she had, even the candles she'd sold to street urchins to make up a last desperate penny.

She stood over the grave, watching as shovelful after shovelful of dark earth landed on the unstained wood. It sounded dull and hollow, as though the coffin contained nothing, a mere husk. And Sally had seemed like a husk when the undertaker's men came to load her onto a cart and carry her away. It was not as though the woman who'd been a mother to Helen had died. It was as though she had gone somewhere else, somewhere far away that Helen could not follow.

She felt her face trembling with her effort to keep her tears at bay, but still could not stop them. One rolled down her cheek, blazing hot in the frigid air, as the gravediggers patted the last soil onto the neat little mound that marked the place where Sally lay. The old priest had gone. She vaguely remembered that he'd patted her shoulder, but couldn't remember him leaving.

Then she was alone, standing over Sally's grave. A plain wooden cross stood at her head. It looked like any one of a hundred other graves like this in the cemetery, but at least Sally lay in peaceful repose in her coffin, not rotting in a heap of bodies like most paupers.

A terrible smell drifted across the cemetery toward Helen from the grave on the other side, the one where the men burned straw to hide the stench of unburied corpses, whose limbs lay tangled in a rat-nibbled heap.

"You have your dignity, Sally," Helen whispered. "I made sure they kept your dignity. I—" She stopped. "I tried. Oh, Sally, I tried."

The strength left her in a rush that stole her breath. She fell to her knees on the cold earth, sobs ripping from her. Her fingers clawed against the frozen ground and tore her nails.

"I'm so sorry, Sally," she cried. "I'm so sorry. I thought we could do it. I thought you'd be all right. I didn't know!" The words tore from her in a ragged scream. "I didn't know that you would die. I didn't know I was killing you."

She covered her face with her dirty hands and wept, but there was no one to comfort her. Adrian had left to make her life better, and lost his life instead. She had sold Beryl to feed herself. She had killed Sally to keep her job.

Everyone she touched, she drove away. She would always be alone.

Chapter Six

Helen knelt on the cold ground for a long time until the grief turned to numbness, and the numbness, to exhaustion. Her feet somehow carried her back to Sally's tenement, where she stood and stared at the untouched fabric lying on the larger crate. She reached for it and brushed her fingers across the rough surface. Hatred bubbled deep within her.

Helen slept then, and woke the next morning with a deep, burning fire in her chest. The hatred had kindled to breath-taking rage. Hunger made her stomach burn as she rose and stared at the fabric once more. Those dresses were well overdue at the slop-shop today, but when she stared at Sally's bed, at the indentation her body had made in the mattress when she closed her eyes for the last time, she couldn't care about the money. She could care only about her grief.

Her arms trembled as she seized the fabric, shoved it under her arm, and stormed from the tenement.

Despite her hunger and exhaustion, anger provided her aching limbs with tireless fuel. She stormed through the streets, steam curling around her face.

Her fury was so bright that she almost thought she would melt the snowflakes as they fell around her. They landed on her cheeks like icy kisses.

A little girl sang on a street corner in front of Helen as she strode toward the slop-shop. The child had wind-nipped cheeks and wide eyes, and held a bony hand in front of her as she sang, waiting for alms.

"Gloria in excelsis Deo," the child sang, stumbling over the difficult words. "Gloria!"

Helen shoved her aside, and the child gave a cry of surprise. Helen had no time for God's glory. To her mind, He had let her down. Sally had trusted Him, and look where it got her!

She barely noticed the miserable huddle of seamstresses shuffling into the alley toward the slop-shop's back door. Several scurried out of her way as Helen shoved past them, seething. Her body trembled as she reached the door first and knocked thunderously.

"Mr. Gifford!" Helen roared, pounding on the door again. The other seamstresses drew back with twitters of worry. Several looked ready to bolt, but stayed nearby, clutching the garments they'd made and desperate for those pitiful few pennies Mr. Gifford gave them in exchange for their lives.

"*Mr. Gifford*!" Helen cried, hammering again. She knew she was being reckless and did not care.

The door swung open, and Barnabas glared at her, his lower lip dangling in an ugly sneer.

"You wretched woman!" he barked. "What do you think you're—"

Helen threw the fabric in his face, feeling a moment's satisfaction as he gasped and scrambled to catch it.

"You killed her," she hissed.

Sudden silence fell on the seamstresses behind her. Barnabas scoffed as he unfolded the fabric. "What is the meaning of this, woman?" he roared. "Where are the dresses I ordered you to make?"

"Curse the dresses!" Helen bellowed. "*You killed her*! Did you hear me?"

Barnabas scoffed. "What are you talking about?"

"Sally, sir. Sally Adams," one of the seamstresses piped up. "She's dead."

"Well, then all of you will have to work twice as hard to make up for it," Barnabas snapped. "This is no time of year for people to go around dying. We have Christmas parties, and—"

"Curse the Christmas parties!" Helen yelled, to gasps of horror from the other seamstresses. "Curse it all! And curse you, too, Mr. Gifford. Curse you!"

Barnabas' eyes flashed. "Watch what you say, woman!"

"I am tired of watching what I say," Helen yelled. "I told you, you killed Sally Adams! You and the terrible pressure you put on us all. How are we meant to do so much work in so little time? How can we both eat and work when you give us so little money? You're killing us, Mr. Gifford, just as you killed my Sally!" Her voice cracked, tears streaming over her cheeks.

"Get out of my sight," Barnabas hissed. "You've gone mad." He raised his voice. "She's gone mad!"

"No, she's not." Another seamstress stepped forward. "I worked right through the weekend. Hardly slept a wink. I felt all shaky Monday morning, like I was half dead."

"Yes, so did I!" another seamstress agreed.

"Me too," said another. "I thought the work would kill me."

Barnabas' eyes widened.

"It *did* kill Sally Adams," said Helen. "You did it. You killed her!"

She pointed imperiously, so outraged that she was nearly surprised that fire or lightning did not spray from her fingertip as she aimed it at his face.

"Take your fabric, Mr. Gifford," Helen snapped. "I won't work for a murderer!"

The other seamstresses suddenly fell silent. Barnabas' face twisted in fury.

"Go," he growled. "Leave."

"With pleasure!" Helen snapped.

She turned on her heel, both terrified an exhilarated, and Barnabas shouted the next words out of her. "If you set foot in my tenement again, you'll be trespassing, do you hear?"

Dismay sank in her belly like a cold stone. Why had she not thought of that? Why had she failed to consider that she would be homeless?

"And one more thing!" Barnabas yelled.

Helen stopped and stared at him, panic writhing in her. How quickly would he be able to send someone to stop her from returning to the tenement? She still had a tin mug and a blanket there as well as her needle and a half spool of thread. She would need them to find work with another slop-shop.

"You'll never work as a seamstress in this city again," Barnabas snarled. "Never. Shop owners know each other, you miserable wretch. I'll make sure everyone knows what kind of a woman you age. No one will employ you again!"

Helen whirled around. "You're a murderer. None of us should work for you again!" she cried.

Barnabas snatched a cane from behind the door and lunged with a roar of anger. Heart pounding, Helen spun and bolted into the cold, weary streets that were now her home once again.

How was it that she always found her way back to the sea?

Helen's legs dangled over the edge of the pier. It was at the very edge of the shipyards, with the grey Thames extending toward the ocean before her, the ships looming to her right, and London swarming the river's muddy banks on her left. She sat on the borders between worlds: not quite in the joyous chaos of the shipyards with the sailors calling out in their terms that sounded like another language as they moved back and forth on the decks or unloaded barrels and crates from the bellies of the great ships, nor in the bustling crowd of the streets where urchins begged money and stallholders cried their wares as cabbies shouted instructions while their horses muscled through the traffic.

Helen was apart from it all. The pier creaked softly beneath her, and her feet dangled over the cold river. Only a few feet of water lay below her hole-ridden shoes this close to the bare banks. The tide was moving out. The water was murky brown, with bits of nameless debris floating on its reeking surface.

She sat with her hands folded in her lap, watching the tide slowly leach away. Her strength was leaving her as surely as that tide. How long would it take to die of hunger? Five days? Six?

Barnabas had not joked about his friendship with other slop-shop owners. They had all chased her away the moment she knocked on their doors, as though Barnabas had given them all a description of her. She had tried to beg. She had searched for work.

She had found none.

Movement caught her eye. A small figure slithered down the muddy bank; a child, no older than eleven or twelve, Helen guessed. He clutched a mud-encrusted canvas sack in one hand and waved it with determination as he scuddled down to the river.

The mud at the bottom of the bank was knee-deep and sucked at the boy's feet. He landed in it with a splash, and Helen expected him to draw back. Instead, he crouched down without hesitation, placed the sack on a nearby rock, and then pressed both hands into the mud.

Helen gave a tiny gasp of horror. The mud stank like the rest of the Thames, reeking of all London's filth, which poured from the homes, streets, and factories into the river. Everything from toxic sulphur to human waste piled into that river and lay mixed with the mud, leaving a shimmering, oily layer on its surface. But the boy seemed not to care. He rummaged through the mud, running his fingers through the chunks of debris and human excrement, heedless as it splattered on his face and clothes.

Helen couldn't watch. She looked away, then blinked in surprise as she spotted dozens of others—mostly children—doing the same thing along the shore. Several carried sacks; others had buckets. The smaller ones congregated farther away, where the bank was steeper. Older ones frequently yelled at them, causing the littler children to retreat several feet. All dug through the mud as though expecting treasure.

A glad cry caught Helen's attention. It was the first boy she'd noticed. He straightened, cupping something in his palms. Smaller children edged nearer; he snarled at them like a savage beast, driving them back. Then he wiped the object in his hands with his muddy fingers and held it up in triumph.

It was a glass bottle, Helen realized, of the sturdy, red-tinted type that apothecaries used. She had seen them for sale at pawn shops for as much as a whole penny each.

The boy tucked the bottle into his sack and crouched into the mud once more. Helen couldn't stop staring at the now-heavy sack as it bumped against his hip. A whole penny—for that, the boy could buy a little bread. He would not sleep empty-bellied tonight.

Unlike her.

Helen moved slowly, her limbs jerky with desperation. The urge to move came not from her heart but from something more primal—the simple, animal instinct to survive. Without thinking, without feeling, she rose from the pier and stumbled toward the muddy bank. Streaks showed on its surface where the children had scrambled down it earlier. It squelched beneath her foot, filthier and more disgusting by far than the slush of the streets, and she tried not to touch the mud as she slithered down to the bottom.

The boy bared his teeth at her like a rabid dog. "This is my spot!" he barked. "Find another."

Helen didn't have the energy to argue with the child. She merely stood there, staring at him, and something in her hollow eyes made him look frightened. He shuffled aside, keeping only a wary eye on her as she edged toward the mud.

It sucked into her shoes and stockings as soon as she stepped in it. Each time she lifted her foot, a fresh gust of the horrific smell assailed her nostrils. Nausea rose in her throat, and she retched harmlessly; there was nothing left inside her to bring up.

She slowly extended her trembling hands to the mud. Sharp pains from the cold ran through her feet and ankles, echoed by her fingers when she pressed them into the half-frozen filth.

It was sloppy and grainy on her skin, accompanied by noisome lumps that broke apart and stank worse when she touched them.

Horror shuddered down her spine, but this was the only fate she had left. Head down, arms aching with cold, Helen joined the mudlarks in their quiet struggle to survive.

Helen's stockings were still damp even though it had been hours since she left the river. Over the past week, she had learned to go mud-larking in the morning whenever the tide allowed, meaning that she rinsed herself at the pump during the warmest part of the day. The water was still brutally cold, stinging her skin when she hastily brushed the clumps of mud from her arms and legs, and there was no time to dry off thoroughly before she thrust her trembling and goose-pimpled legs into her stockings and pulled on her shoes once more. One reason was because the cold was enough to make her toes blue in mere minutes. Another was that the locals did not take kindly to the filthy mudlarks washing themselves beneath the public pump—even less so to the woman exposing herself all the way to the ankles to do so—and so the bobby would often drive them off.

Now, the hem of Helen's dress, still soaked, dragged more dampness across her legs as she walked. Her dress was stiff and hard from mud, which remained caked beneath her fingernails. She bent and picked up a handful of snow, then rubbed it over her fingertips until it melted into frigid water and washed away a little of the filth.

She had to clean her hands as well as she could, or the stallholders might sneer at her few pennies when she approached them for food.

She gazed dully at the small collection of stalls at the edge of the shipyard. They were tumbledown and faded: one sold bits and bobs scrounged from the street, an old lady in the corner sold gruel to anyone who could bring their own bowl, and the one in the middle sold scraps of fried fish—one for a ha'penny. Helen had earned tuppence for the few tiny treasures she'd discovered in the mud that morning: a lamb bone, a monogrammed handkerchief caked with filth, and a copper nail.

Her stomach rumbled. She staggered to the stalls, produced a cracked wooden bowl from her apron pocket, and purchased a bit of gruel and a piece of fish. After tearing into the fish with her teeth, she sat down on a roll of discarded rope at the shipyards' edge and ate the hot gruel quickly with her fingers. It burned, but its warm goodness flooded her belly, easing the steady pain in every cell of her body.

"Hey, miss," someone grunted. "Ain't you want a spoon?"

Helen looked up, instinctively clutching her bowl to keep it from being taken; it had cost her a precious half-penny from the stand that sold miscellaneous scrap from the streets.

A man leaned on a lamp-post a few feet away, hands in his pockets. His clothes were frayed and sun-bleached, but he wore a good, warm oilskin coat and hat. His cheeks had the pink look of the newly clean-shaven, but his hair still hung in his eyes in a shaggy brown tangle.

Helen knew a sailor when she saw one, and she edged away slightly.

"Here." The man dug around in his pocket and produced a tin spoon so thin that it nearly bent between his thick fingers.

"Got it with a bowl of stew at the pub. I've got plenty at home. You can have this one."

Helen's eyes narrowed. "I have no money," she rasped.

The man's eyes travelled up and down the length of her body. "I'm not asking for money, sweetheart."

There was no aggression in his eyes, but the bare-faced lust of his expression crawled over Helen's skin like cockroaches. All the same, her fingers *did* burn.

"Go on." The man gestured. "Take it. It's yours."

Helen snatched the spoon from his hand like a hungry animal. She backed out of reach quickly, but the man merely smiled.

"The name's Jerry," he said. "You come here often?"

"Sometimes," Helen growled.

"You have a name?" Jerry asked.

She glanced at the spoon, then at the man. He'd given her something for free, she realized, asking nothing. The last person who'd ever done that for her was Sally.

"Helen," she whispered.

Jerry smiled. "Nice to meet you, Helen. Maybe I could buy you a drink sometime."

Helen blinked. "I don't drink."

Jerry shrugged. "A bowl of real food, then."

She stared at him, knowing exactly what he wanted in exchange, but that bowl of real food—maybe rabbit stew or chicken soup—sounded like heaven to her. Perhaps it wouldn't be so bad…

The thought of being with another man smote her like a hot coal to her heart, and suddenly the intervening years fell away and she was standing in that church again, gazing into the eyes of the only man she'd ever loved.

"Do you, Adrian Bartholomew Nicols, take this woman to be your lawfully wedded wife?"

The vicar's question resounded through the little church by the sea. Its open windows admitted the salt-scented breeze, mingling with the smells of the white peonies and dahlias that filled the church. Only a few people sat in the pews, but it didn't matter. The only thing that mattered to Helen was Adrian's bright blue eyes as they pierced her soul.

"I do," Adrian murmured, his hands tightening on hers.

"And do you, Helen Saunders, take this man to be your lawfully wedded husband?"

"I do," said Helen.

The vicar smiled. "Then it is my honour to present you as husband and wife. You may kiss the bride."

Adrian wrapped his arms around Helen and drew her closer as the old woman at the keyboard coaxed a joyful chorus from the church organ. His arms were warm and brawny as they encircled her torso, but his kiss was fresh and light, pure and gentle, filled with love. Real love. She had scoffed at it once, had failed to believe in it, but in that moment Helen melted into all of its joy and all of its glory. Adrian had come back for her. He was here for her. He'd filled her life with joy.

She kissed him back with all her heart, revelling in the glorious vow she had taken: that she would love him, and only him, for all time.

"Miss?"

Helen gasped, touching her lips as though she could still feel Adrian's wedding day kiss resting there. She flew to her feet.

Jerry tilted his head. "I don't mean no harm, miss. You don't have to be afraid of me."

Helen believed him, but she backed away anyway, clutching the bowl and spoon. Revulsion boiled in her at the thought of what she had nearly done for a square meal. She turned on her heel and fled back toward the Thames.

Helen trembled as she tugged her shoes over her damp stockings. Grains of mud still chafed between her toes as she tied the frayed laces, but she couldn't stand another moment of rinsing the mud from her hands and feet in the grimy Thames. High tide caused the greyish water to slop against the pier, but it still seemed to be hardly anything other than mud, grubby and smelly when she dipped her feet into it.

She laced up her second shoe and sat cross-legged, not caring how vulgar it was, for the little warmth she could gain by tucking her feet under her legs. Shivers rolled up and down her spine, grasping every muscle along the way with cruel hands, forcing her exhausted body to jerk and twitch in a bid for warmth. Her hunger had become a constant gnawing feeling at the core of her being. It forced her to her feet despite her exhaustion.

A wisp of music drifted across the shipyards as she shuffled to the pier's end. The snow fell swiftly, thick and white, dusting everything in a layer that sparkled as pure white as icing sugar.

The music came from a group of carollers wandering window to window in their robes, candles in hand.

"I saw three ships come sailing in

"On Christmas Day, on Christmas Day,

"I saw three ships come sailing in

"On Christmas Day in the morning!"

Helen hung her head, deafening herself to their singing. Candles glowed gold in the windows of the nearby shops; even the fire that the old woman with the gruel used seem brighter against the pure white snow. Scraps of bunting draped the stalls, with bits of holly and mistletoe clinging to their ragged roofs. Helen found it stupid. Why spend any money on decorations when one could buy food instead?

She staggered past the stalls, heading toward the rag-and-bone man whose cart always stood down the block, when Jerry stepped from the door of a modest tenement building nearby.

"Merry Christmas, Helen!" he called.

Christmas already? She'd been mud larking for days, then... always with Jerry intercepting her on her way into and out of town. She couldn't bring herself to say it back.

Jerry stepped forward, blocking her path. "I have something for you," he said.

Helen blinked at him. He held out something wrapped in brown paper.

"Take it," he said. "It's all right. I won't bite."

It smelled good. Helen took it and unwrapped a bunch of sugarplums, the dark, plum-shaped balls of dried fruit and nuts dusted with a generous layer of sugar. She gasped despite herself. Her hunger overruled her common sense, as it always did with Jerry's little gifts, and she seized one and thrust it into her mouth.

"Good, aren't they?" said Jerry. "I'm sure you know how to make them."

Helen had made them for Beryl, in another life. She ate another one in hungry gulps, breathing heavily.

Jerry grinned. "I love them. There's plenty more at home." He paused, retreating a step. "If you'd like."

Helen didn't speak until she'd eaten all six sugar plums. The sugar made her blood buzz with sudden energy, and she wiped her mouth with the back of her hand, then carefully sucked the last traces of sugar from her skin.

"You must be so cold and hungry," said Jerry gently. "I do wish you'd come home with me."

Helen smoothed the paper and folded it to sell. "I... I can't, Jerry."

He sighed. "Maybe you will, someday."

Helen met his eyes and didn't say what she was thinking: *Maybe*. The plums were so good after years of gruel, bread, and plain beets and carrots. Her conscience itched, but lacked the hot-coal agony of previous days.

How bad would it really be to go with Jerry, and have a roof over her head and food on her table again?

"I have to go," she said quickly. "Sorry." She pushed past him and hurried down the street on her sore, cold feed.

"I'll be here tomorrow," Jerry called. "It's Christmas, after all. You shouldn't spend it alone on the streets, Helen!"

He shouted the last words after her as hot tears burned her eyes.

Adrian's fingers interlaced with hers. They were large and warm against hers, and he wrapped his free hand around hers. "Oh, your poor hand is freezing!"

"It's all right," said Helen.

"We can go inside, if you like," said Adrian. "I don't want you to be cold."

Helen tilted her head back and smiled at him with adoring eyes. Adrian's breath steamed around his face, blowing between the thick jungle of his black beard. The candles around them reflected in his eyes as they stood on the front step of their house.

"Let's stay a few minutes longer," Helen murmured.

Adrian smiled. "All right, then."

Warmly swaddled in her thick blankets, baby Beryl slumbered in the crook of Helen's arm, her cheeks rosy and her eyes closed. She had no idea that it was cold outside despite the sparkling white snowflakes that drifted slowly down all around, sizzling when they met the bright flames of the carollers' candles. They came from their local church and wore white robes, which were bathed golden by their candles as they sang.

Helen closed her eyes and leaned her head on Adrian's shoulders as the carol wrapped around her like an embrace. She had everything she needed in that moment, on that blessed Christmas Eve: a belly full of roast goose and black pudding, her baby in her arms, and the warm, solid presence of her husband by her side.

"I saw three ships come sailing in

On Christmas Day, on Christmas day!"

The sigh of deep contentment huffed between Helen's lips and woke her. Her eyes snapped open, and she sat up with a gasp, disoriented in the semi-darkness. Where was Adrian? Where was Beryl? Why was it so dark, and why did her body ache so fiercely? She flailed for her bedside lamp, but her hand rattled on rubbish instead—broken glass and splintered wood. She gasped and jerked her hand back to her chest.

The cold and dark pierced her to the core, making her hunger seem even worse. In one moment, all the tragedies of the past few years crashed down upon Helen's head as her dream faded and reality returned.

Beryl was gone, and Adrian was dead.

Piercing agony shattered her chest. Helen covered her face with her hands and wept, heedless of who might hear her keening sobs as she poured her grief into her palms. She cried until she had no strength left, and then she sat in the alleyway for a long time, staring through the gap in the end at the filthy Thames as the tide receded.

She could weep all she liked. It would not reawaken Adrian. The image of Sally lying in her coffin filled Helen's mind. She saw the still pallor of Sally's face, felt the waxiness of her limbs as she'd tried to wake her.

That was how Adrian was. Gone.

Her options seemed stark in her mind then. She could cling to the memory of a dead man and return to the mud, grubbing in the filth on a day so cold that ice crackled in the mud as she sought the scraps that gave her survival. Or she could go to Jerry Tiller—who might not speak of marriage, might not even love her, but had never seemed harsh or cruel. She could sleep in a warm bed and eat hot meals.

He could not be Adrian, but no one ever would be again. Adrian was dead.

She rose mechanically, like a puppet tugged by strings, and shuffled from the alley.

Jerry's tenement building was not large, but it had received a fresh lick of paint before the winter. The door was bright red, making the deep green of the holly wreath seem richer than ever. It shuddered as Helen knocked. Candles shone in the windows, and a string of colourful bunting hung beneath the eaves, dusted with snowflakes.

The door opened, allowing a gust of fragrant air to fill Helen's senses. The air was warm and smelled of roasting meat and buttery vegetables, and her shrivelled stomach screamed in desperation.

Jerry's eyes widened. "Helen!" he said.

"Hello." Helen cleared her throat. The last scraps of guilt fell away from her at her second breath of the delicious smell. "May... may I come in?"

A grin lit Jerry's eyes. They were murky brown, and held no cruelty. "Yes, of course, of course, come in." He pulled the door wide and stepped aside.

Helen moved into a far more comfortable tenement than she'd expected. Jerry was an uncouth fellow, a common sailor, but he had to make decent money on the ships judging by the wool rug in front of the hearty hearth, where a fire crackled and filled the room with more warmth than Helen had felt in months. A round table stood in the centre of a small but well-appointed kitchen.

"Mrs. Knox down the road makes meals for the sailors to buy," Jerry explained. "Her Christmas lunch is always good. Would you like some?"

Helen's eyes flashed past the sturdy furniture and locked on the simple dishes resting on the round table. There was half a roast chicken, its skin crispy gold, and baked potatoes swimming in the chicken's savoury juices. Roast vegetables—carrots and turnips—lined the chicken. She would have thought nothing of making this for dinner for Adrian years ago.

No, she told herself firmly. *Adrian is dead. I will no longer think of him.*

There was no point in dreaming of Adrian anymore. There was no longer any Adrian; there was only what she had to do to survive in that moment.

"Yes," she croaked, hunger and despair making the sound more like an animal cry of pain and terror than any human word. "Yes, please, I'd love some."

"Sit down, then!" Jerry smiled and pulled out a chair, then seized a plate from a nearby cabinet. "Sit and eat."

Helen had not eaten a free meal since Adrian's money ran out. *No! No thinking of Adrian.* She had not eaten a free meal in years, then, and this one was hale, warm, and abundant. Though Jerry tore the chicken apart with his hands and ate like a sailor, ripping flesh from the bone with his teeth, Helen had seldom tasted meat so delicious. She ate in great starving gulps at first, not caring what he thought (perhaps hoping to repulse him), but as she approached her fill, she savoured every bite. The greasy fat covered her chin. The buttery potatoes melted in her mouth.

When she had eaten enough that her belly felt painfully distended, Helen realized that there was still food left over when Jerry produced a generous helping of plum pudding. He divided it between them, and Helen relished every mouthful of the sweet, fruity confection.

She was almost breathless when she finally laid down her fork. "Thank you so much, Jerry," she said. "That was absolutely wonderful." She meant every word; she hadn't eaten her fill in years.

Jerry beamed. "Good! Now, come and sit by the fire. I'll make us a pot of chocolate."

"You have chocolate?" Helen cried.

"I do. We brought it by the barrel from South America," said Jerry, "and everyone on the crew was given some as part of our wages."

Adrian had— *No.* Helen jerked her thoughts away from the treats her late husband often brought home from his voyages. She focused instead on how glorious it felt to sink into one of the rattan chairs by the fire and slip off her shoes to warm her cold toes at the leaping flames.

Jerry placed a mug of crudely made chocolate in her hands. It had been so long since she last tasted it that she hardly cared how badly made it was. She sipped slowly, toasting her sore feet, as carollers passed by outside.

A flash of brightness caught her eye. For the first time, she noticed the little Christmas tree he had set up in a corner. It was little more than a pine branch, but it dripped with tinsel, ribbons, and paper chains.

Quickly, Helen looked away. She focused on the flames instead, half-closing her eyes as she sipped the warm chocolate. When last had her body felt such genuine rest and contentment?

When she opened her eyes, Jerry was watching her. His expression shone with excitement.

"Tomorrow we'll take you to the milliner," he said, "and we'll buy all the dresses you like." He extended it like a gift, like bribery, but Helen looked down at the holes in her stockings and thought of thick wool ones that would keep her legs warm. Her big toe had gone a worrying shade of blue. She had seen mudlarks missing toes before, and knew that would soon be her fate, if she had stayed out there.

"Is that all right, Helen?" Jerry prompted.

Helen lifted her head. She had made up her mind; she knew what she had to do to stay alive, and she would do it.

"That would be perfect," she said. "Thank you very much, my dear."

Jerry's eyes lit up at the term of endearment. When she finished her cup of chocolate and set it aside, he extended a hand to her. Part of her crawled, but she ignored it. She placed her fingers in his, and took solace in the thought that at least he was very gentle when he helped her to her feet and led her up the stairs to his bedroom.

Part Three

Chapter Seven

One Year Later

They were setting up the Christmas tree in the market square when Helen came by. Three sturdy young men hoisted it upright and packed its trunk firmly into place, pine needles fluttering onto the cobbles as they worked. The needles smelled wonderfully fresh and fragrant.

Helen paused, smiling up at the tree as her shopping basket nestled on her arm. The streets glistened, still damp from last night's rain, but for now the sunshine glimmered between the branches. Soon they would be all draped in ribbons.

"Look, look! The Christmas tree! The Christmas tree!"

Excited little voices came from all around as children scampered across the square, getting under the men's feet and eliciting oaths and barks of annoyance from them. The children hardly cared. Their bright eyes saw only the tree.

A deep ache cut through Helen's chest, and she swiftly turned away, but it did nothing to allay the fierce burning in her heart. Her mind constantly sought to drag her back to Christmas Eve nearly three years ago, the night she had promised herself that when she had the means, she would look for Beryl. Her sweet child would be eight years old now.

Suddenly, Helen's thick stockings and comfortable new shoes felt like a rebuke.

She pushed the thought away. Jerry would never accommodate the idea of a child, and it was his money that jingled in her pocket as she strolled toward the bakery.

Halfway across the market square, the cobblestones seemed to swim in her vision. Helen staggered and squeezed her eyes shut as the uncomfortable dizzy spell swamped her. The square was empty, and no one noticed as she bowed her head and fought the dizziness away.

The spell left her clammy and shaking. She wiped her gloves over her sweaty cheeks. That was the second time it had happened that morning. Perhaps she was coming down with a cold.

She kept her head down, her bonnet mostly covering her face, as she pushed the door open and stepped into the fragrant, cosy space.

"Be with you in a minute, ma'am," the baker called. He stood on a low stool at the back of the bakery, hanging a paper chain across the room.

"Thank you," Helen murmured.

The baker dismounted his stool and turned to the counter, smiling. "Now, what can I get— Oh." He stopped. "It's you."

Helen's hand tightened on her shopping basket. "I'd like three loaves of bread and two of those sweet cakes, please, Mr. Bishop."

"You keep your name out of my mouth, you young hussy," the baker snapped. "I'm amazed you dare show your face in public, living in sin with that sailor as you do!"

Helen's toes curled. It had not taken long for the truth to circulate among the local community, and she ducked her head, shame washing through her in a warm tide. *You don't understand*, she wanted to tell the baker. *It was Jerry or death.* Yet even she had begun to doubt that.

"My money's as good as anyone's, sir," she said, slapping the coins on the counter.

The baker glanced around furtively. His shop was empty. Helen made sure never to go into a shop if other customers were present; she had no chance of being served then.

"Very well," said the baker, "but serving you is against my better judgment!" He crammed the bread and cakes into paper bags, heedlessly crushing the crusts, and thrust them over the counter. "And for Pete's sake, leave by the back door before anyone sees you."

"Yes, sir," said Helen quietly. "Thank you."

She scooped up the paper bags and ducked out of the back door; she believed she knew the back way of every shop in this part of London by now. Hugging her parcels to her chest, she turned toward Jerry's cosy tenement. She would spend the day curled up by the fire, reading and mending his clothes.

Alone.

She darted down the alleyway and stepped into the street, and sudden nausea seized her throat. Helen stumbled and leaned against the bakery wall as her head spun. This time, the spell was far more intense.

Familiar panic rose in her chest. What if she was ill? What would she do?

Calm down, she told herself. *If you're ill, Jerry will pay for the doctor*. The thought made breathing feel much easier. She tucked her hair beneath her bonnet strings and smiled. The security of not fearing for her life each day was worth the shame.

Helen adjusted her parcels and set off briskly toward another shop across the square. This one had pill bottles and packets of powders and glass jars filled with writhing leeches on display in the window, and she looked both ways to make sure no one was watching before she stepped inside.

The interior was murky and ominous with the presence of darkly coloured glass bottles on the tightly packed shelves. Labels in flowing handwriting proclaimed words and names that Helen couldn't begin to read despite her education in the workhouse. She edged up to the tall counter, behind which the apothecary loomed, an imposing figure with heavy jowls and long white whiskers.

Helen had seldom been to the apothecary and couldn't remember if he knew she was the neighbourhood hussy or not.

"Excuse me, sir," she began politely. "I... I've been feeling unwell, and—"

"I'm an apothecary, not a doctor," said the man sharply. "There's little I can do for you."

Helen retreated a step. The doctor was also a deacon in the church and made sure that everyone knew it; she would have no luck with him.

"Yes, sir," she said. "I was thinking that you might be able to tell me what I could use for—"

"I don't have time for this," said the apothecary. "Please leave."

He did know, then, and Helen was as much a pariah here as she was anywhere else. She turned and shuffled toward the door, but before she could reach it, a slender figure stepped from behind the shelves.

"Excuse me." It was a young woman in a black dress; her face was haggard, but her eyes were kind. "May I help you?"

Helen glanced at the counter.

"Don't mind my father." The girl smiled. "He's gone to the laboratory at the back where he mixes his medicines. You can talk to me. You look pale—are you all right?"

The girl's kindness made tears prickle Helen's eyes.

"I'm having dizzy spells and I feel terribly sick," said Helen. "I don't know if you have medicine for that."

"Let's see if we can work out why you're feeling that way, first." The girl touched her shoulder. "I'm Julia. Papa lets me help in his shop because he thinks it will cure me of my desire to be a nurse someday, but I think it's having the opposite effect. Please, sit down."

She retrieved a chair from behind the counter and tucked it into a private corner near the back, and Helen gratefully sank into it. Why were her feet so sore and swollen these days?

"When did this all start?" Julia asked.

"A few weeks ago, I suppose," said Helen, "but it's getting worse."

"I see." Julia paused. "Is it worse in the mornings?"

"Much worse," said Helen, "though sometimes I have dreadful heartburn at night."

"Oh... I see," said Julia. "Do you mind if I have a look at your tummy?"

Helen shook her head. Jerry was well-off, but not well-off enough for a proper crinoline and bodice, so Helen merely had to unlace her dress slightly for Julia's quick fingers to probe her belly.

Julia slowly sat back. Her gaze dropped to Helen's left hand and beheld no ring, but rose to her face with pity, not judgment.

"What is it?" Helen asked. "What's wrong?"

Julia bit her lip. "I might have startling news for you, Miss...?"

"Nicols," Helen croaked. "Mrs. Nicols."

"I beg your pardon." Obvious relief flooded Julia's face. "Mrs. Nicols, you're in the family way."

Helen's throat closed. "W-what?"

"Congratulations." Julia beamed. "You're going to have a baby."

Panic surged in Helen, white-hot in her veins. A small corner of her mind had known that this was possible, but the revelation was as shocking as falling into a pit of cold water. A baby! Jerry's baby! She had not been able to care for Beryl. How would she care for this child?

"Mrs. Nicols, are you all right?" Julia cried. "Should I get the smelling salts?"

"No," Helen rasped. "I'm fine." She rose to her feet, shaking.

"Here—I can sell you a tincture that will help for the nausea," said Julia.

"No. I don't want it." Helen swallowed.

"Are you all right?" Julia asked again.

Helen ignored her. She brushed past the young woman, making for the door, and paused with her hand on the knob. "One more thing, Julia."

"Yes?"

"How—" Helen's throat closed, and she had to clear it before she could speak again. "How far along am I?"

"About four months," said Julia, "if I've guessed correctly."

It could be; stress and starvation had made Helen's monthlies inconsistent for so long that she no longer kept track. She laid a hand over her belly.

She had thought that the small swelling she'd noticed there was from eating well, but now she knew that in a few more weeks, it would become impossible to ignore.

"Thank you," she croaked, then fled into the street.

Helen crouched and opened the wood stove a crack, peering at the roast beef slowly browning within. Jerry liked it very rare, but crispy on top, and it had turned perfectly golden brown. She took the dish from the oven and placed it on the stovetop, then spooned the beef's juices over it to make it extra tender.

Her heart thumped in her chest. In the past, she'd made Jerry his favourite dinner simply to curry his favour. Now, she knew that two lives depended on making him as happy as possible.

She covered the beef and left it to stew in its juices a moment longer while she attended to the caramelized carrots, using plenty of butter and sugar. With every step she took, she was painfully aware of the tiny life nestled within her.

The last time she had found out she was pregnant...

No. Helen froze the memory. It involved Adrian, and she barely allowed herself to think his name.

She could not think of the past, she reminded herself. She had to consider only one thing: her survival in the here and now. There was only one way to secure her future and the future of her unborn child, and it was marriage. She couldn't bring a poor little illegitimate baby into the world. They would live their life in utter shame.

The click of the opening door made her jump, dropping the wooden spoon to the floor with a clatter.

"Hello, my dear!" Jerry boomed. He laughed. "What makes you so jumpy?"

Helen snatched up the spoon and forced a smile as she rinsed it in a basin of warm water. "No reason at all. How was your day?"

"Perfect!" said Jerry. He flung an arm around her waist and kissed her with an abandon she couldn't grow used to. "They're planning our next voyage for the spring. It won't be a long one, though. Two months, then I'll be home for a while again." He boomed a laugh.

Helen forced a smile. "That's good news." She tried not to think of how much she enjoyed the months when he was gone and she had the tenement—and the money he left behind—to herself.

Jerry inhaled through his nose. "Oh, now that's wonderful. What are you making?"

"Your favourite," said Helen, uncovering the roast beef with a flourish.

Jerry's eyes widened. "You're a little beauty, you are." He dealt a swift tap to her posterior. "I'll wash up."

Helen's heart thudded as she sliced the beef and set the plates of food on the table with two glasses of the cheap mulled wine Jerry liked a little too much. She made sure to fill his glass to the top, then added an extra splash to hers. A little liquid courage was what she needed.

Jerry returned as she was placing the salt cellar on the table. His hair was slicked back, his friendly face grinning. Helen smiled back at him, thinking that there were far worse things than being shackled to a man like this. He was a fool, but he had never raised a hand to harm her. Few women could say that about their husbands.

Husband. It was not a word that seemed fitting for Jerry, but Helen told herself that she would have to grow used to it.

She slid into her chair as Jerry grabbed his knife and fork and tucked into his meat with exuberance. Even after nearly a year together, Helen had not yet grown used to the thought of eating meals without saying grace.

"You know, my dear," Jerry boomed, "I think it's time we got some Christmas decorations up, don't you?"

Helen blinked. "In our tenement?"

"That's right. I'll go looking for a good pine branch to be our Christmas tree. Will you make some bunting and paper chains?" Jerry asked. "Last time I had to buy them from street children."

Paper chains! It had been years since Helen had made one, but she nodded, eager to please him. "Of course. I saw one of the flower-sellers had holly and mistletoe, too. I could make a wreath for the front door."

"I'd love that." Jerry grinned.

Helen took a generous gulp of her wine. She waited until Jerry had finished most of his supper and all of his wine before she braced herself to ask.

"So, Jerry," she said, gripping her wineglass, "what... what do you dream about in... in the future?"

Jerry laughed. "I hardly ever dream, Helen. Except for the odd nightmare about that shipwreck off Portsmouth." He shuddered.

"No, I mean, what do you hope our future holds?" Helen asked.

Jerry grinned and held out his empty glass. "More wine."

Helen struggled to keep her frustration hidden as she obediently refilled the glass. "Do you ever hope that things might change for us one day?"

"I don't know, pet." Jerry shrugged. "Maybe it would be nice to have a bigger house someday if we get a few good voyages." He sipped.

"Don't you ever think about—" Helen paused. "About getting married?"

Jerry snorted, spitting mulled wine everywhere. Its spicy, alcoholic scent filled their tenement.

"Married!" he said, guffawing. "Married! Why would I want to do that?"

Sudden pain lanced through her chest.

"Well," she managed, "some would say that it's the decent thing to do."

"Oh, Helen, I don't have time for any of that silliness." Jerry waved a hand. "It's all made-up, anyway. What does it matter?"

Helen swallowed hard. Jerry was a man who lived among vulgar, swashbuckling sailors who thought nothing of him living with a woman he wasn't married to. It was a very different reality for her.

"It could make things easier," she said timorously.

Jerry shook his head. "I haven't set foot in a church in nearly thirty years," he said, "and I'm not going to start now."

"But—" Helen began.

Jerry held her gaze. "If you want to get married," he said, "find a man who wants the same thing." He spread his arms. "That's the beauty of our arrangement. If you don't like it, you can just leave."

Leave my only source of food and shelter? Helen didn't say it aloud, though the thought sent utter terror into her bones. "That's not what I'm saying," she said. "I don't want to go anywhere. I like being with you, Jerry." She put her hand on his.

Jerry was slightly guarded. "Good."

"More roast beef?" Helen offered.

Jerry grinned. "More roast beef. And pour yourself some wine, too!" He laughed. "You need to relax, Helen."

Helen poured the wine, but her hands trembled. The knowledge of the tiny life inside her made it impossible to relax.

Helen knelt on the cold stone floor, clammy sweat on her forehead. Her stomach heaved again, and she brushed her hair out of her face with one hand as she emptied it into the basin on the ground before her.

Snow hissed on the roof, and the kitchen smelled of the cinnamon rolls she was baking. Their scent was somehow repulsive to her now. She remembered, when she was pregnant with Beryl, that she had been suddenly able to stand tomatoes.

This time, it seemed, it was the same cinnamon rolls she'd endlessly craved during her previous pregnancy.

Another horrible retch arrested her stomach. When it was over, she sat back, wiping her mouth with a cool rag.

"Helen!" Feet clattered on the stairs.

"Don't come down, Jerry!" Helen pushed the basin underneath the table.

Jerry ignored her. He strode into the kitchen, his brow furrowed. "Helen, you're white as a sheet. What on earth is the matter?"

"I'm a little sick to my stomach, Jerry," Helen faintly croaked. "That's all."

"That's not right." Jerry seized his coat from its hook beside the pine branch waiting in the corner for its decorations. "I'll go for the doctor."

Panic clutched her. There would be no hiding from a doctor, not if little Julia had been able to tell...

"No, it's all right," she said. "Please, I don't need the doctor. I must have had a piece of bad fish, that's all."

"Better safe than sorry, pet," said Jerry. "I'll be back in a flash." He reached for the door.

"No!" Helen burst out.

Jerry turned, frowning. "Why not? What's wrong?"

There was no hiding it anymore. Helen tried to think of an excuse and found none. She had no choice.

Slowly, she rose, wringing the damp cloth in her hands. "Jerry, there's... there's something I have to tell you."

He stared at her. "What?"

Helen swallowed hard. "I'm... I'm enceinte."

Jerry blinked. "What does that mean?"

Euphemisms would not do, Helen realized. She spoke very quietly. "I'm going to have a baby," she whispered. "Your baby."

Jerry's jaw dropped. "Do you mean to tell me that you're *pregnant*?"

The vulgarity made Helen's ears sting, but why should it? Shame crashed down upon her as she realized that she had done this to herself. Why should the word appal her in comparison with the deed that had preceded it?

"How?" Jerry demanded.

Helen swallowed. "Well..."

"I know *how*," Jerry snapped. "But why did you do nothing to prevent this, Helen? I don't want a child!"

"I tried!" Helen cried. "There's nothing I could do, Jerry. Sometimes it just—it just happens."

Jerry turned away, fists clenched by his sides. "This is why you were talking about marriage."

"Please, Jerry." Helen edged nearer. "Think of your baby."

"*My* baby?" Jerry rounded on her. "I don't have a baby. I never wanted one, and I don't want it now."

"But we're having one," Helen whimpered.

"No, Helen. *You're* having one." Jerry's eyes flashed. "When you talked about getting married the other night, I thought perhaps it was because you were in love with me. Now I see that it's not true. You just wanted to make sure that I would have no choice but to care for you and that child."

Tears filled Helen's eyes. "Please—"

"You've never loved me," said Jerry passionately. "You only wanted somewhere safe and warm to sleep. Well, no longer."

Terror cut through her. "What are you saying?"

"I'm telling you to leave." Jerry shoved the front door open. Snow whirled into the living room in a bright eddy.

Helen stared at him in mute appeal, but the hardness in his eyes gave her no quarter. She would receive no mercy, she realized. Not even the father of her unborn child cared for her.

No one did.

She lowered her head and walked through the door.

"Helen," Jerry said, his voice breaking.

She looked up, but he was only holding out her coat to her. His hand trembled when she took it from him, and he didn't let it go. His eyes gripped hers.

"Do you love me?" he asked. "Do you truly, or did you really just come here for food and shelter?"

Helen knew it was useless lying to him. He would know.

"No," she whispered.

His eyes hardened. "I didn't think so." He released the coat.

Helen pulled it over her shoulders. She stumbled into the driving wind and swirling snow, and he slammed the door behind her.

Chapter Eight

A mass of children poured past Helen, giggling and laughing, clutching brightly painted Christmas cards in their chubby little hands. Their eyes shone in the morning sunlight, and they gazed at the slowly falling snowflakes with faces full of pure wonder.

"Where do we go next, George?" asked a little girl.

The boy grinned. "To Mrs. Wessex's house. Do you have her card?"

"I do!" said the girl. "She'll give us oranges!"

"And toffee apples," another girl chimed in.

The boy giggled. "Let's go!"

The children sprinted off, all rosy-cheeked and well-dressed, and Helen watched them go. Toffee apples and oranges! They had no idea how it felt to live on crusts of bread.

She stirred, rustling the newspapers she'd stolen from a rubbish heap to form a cushion when she sat begging. Her knees had long since gone numb, which meant that it was a good day. On a bad day, shopkeepers or bobbies drove her away before she could sit for long.

"Alms?" she croaked, extending a hand as a gentleman with a silver cane strode past. "Alms for the poor?"

The gentleman didn't look at her twice. So far, no one had. Helen's stomach felt shrivelled within her despite the steady nausea that still clutched her chest every morning.

She wondered if she would lose the baby from starvation. The thought filled her with dull horror.

"Alms," she croaked again.

It was impossible to tell how far she'd wandered through London. She knew nothing but the few blocks where she'd lived all her life; this place seemed as alien to her as another world. All she knew was that it was a very long way from the docks. Ever since fleeing Jerry, she'd moved steadily farther and farther away from the sea. She couldn't bear to lift her eyes to its grey waves.

Only the occasional carriage drove along this street. Most of its traffic was pedestrian; factory workers, warmly dressed but haggard, shuffled past in droves early in the morning and late at night. At this time of day, donkey carts were more common than horses. They rattled by, passing the little church with its well-groomed hedges, their foliage the only green thing in sight except for the church's decorations. It was all draped with mistletoe and ivy, and a gigantic holly wreath hung on the door. Though it was Wednesday, the organist seemed to be practicing; a rousing rendition of "Silent Night" echoed against its rafters.

Helen tried not to listen. Instead, she extended her hand as another well-dressed gentleman approached.

"Spare a penny for a poor soul, sir," she croaked.

This time, the man stopped. Helen blinked in surprise when a sturdy coin fell into her hand. A sixpence! Few people spared that much.

"Hello," said the man. "I haven't seen you here before. Are you new to the area?"

Startled, Helen looked up. Dismay flooded her when she realized that the man was wearing a vicar's white collar. He smiled, with warm, kind eyes that she could have trusted except for that collar.

She hurriedly jumped to her feet. "Yes, sir." She backed away.

"It's all right. I'd like to help you," said the vicar. "You seem—" He paused. "Like you need help." His gaze dipped to her belly.

How could he tell? She was barely showing. She cupped a hand over her belly, which only seemed to confirm his diagnosis. She saw it in his eyes.

"I'm quite well thank you," she sputtered, backing away.

The vicar extended a hand. "Please don't be afraid. My name is Reverend Samuel Weatherby. I'm not out to hurt you."

Not until you discover that I'm an unwed mother, not a widow. Helen backed away faster. "I'm tickety-boo."

"It's terribly cold this Christmas," said Reverend Samuel softly. "Let me help you."

She paused, studying the kindness in his eyes. Was it real? She doubted it. All the same, if she could trust it, then perhaps she would sleep somewhere warm this Christmas after all. Perhaps she would be able to have her baby in peace...

The thought of giving birth on the brutal streets made her eyes sting with tears. Her only other choice was the workhouse, the place where she'd been born and raised, a place filled with brutality.

"Come with me," said Reverend Samuel gently. "Let me help you."

For what? For him to judge her unworthy and throw her onto the street when he discovered how her unborn child had come to be?

"No!" Helen blurted out. She turned on her heel and strode away, passing the palisade fence of the workhouse on the corner. She dared not look up at its imposing walls.

It would be like looking her fate in the eye.

The vicar's sixpence was good enough for almost a week's food. Helen was careful, buying only stale heels of bread, slightly wilted carrots, and the odd piece of dried fish. She had no stomach for it much of the time; her appetite swung wildly between non-existent and desperate.

She had thought that being on the streets was the worst thing in the world. Yet, being on the streets as a pregnant woman was worse, and though she could hide it from almost everyone—Reverend Samuel had been a shocking exception. It would not be long before her lot would be more difficult than it was. It would grow much, much worse when she was showing. No one would look upon a street woman with a pregnant belly with anything but judgment.

Helen had spent her last penny on a bowl of piping hot bone broth. She could have gotten a few soft apples for half a penny, but she couldn't stomach them; only the bone broth held any appeal. She huddled in a doorway, sipping it slowly from the bowl, trying to relish every warm mouthful as it coursed down to her belly.

There was no way of knowing when she would have another meal. It had been days since she ran into Reverend Samuel, and she had scrounged only a few more pennies from this stingy crowd.

It was late, and brightly coloured candles shone in the windows of the few shops still open at this hour. The butchery was one of them, and they had set up a colourful Christmas tree in the window, its red and yellow ribbons shining in the candlelight. A blackboard in front of the shop announced, *Get your Christmas cuts! Tuppence off all geese until 25 December!*

Helen closed her eyes. It was all such foolishness, such wearisome foolishness. "Bah, humbug!" indeed.

She took another sip of the hot bone broth, and then she felt it.

Something stirred within her. Something that was intimately related to her, but not herself.

Helen sat up with a little gasp, her hands tightening on her bowl. Could it be? She had been five months along with Beryl before she felt it for the first time, but she had heard that women who had had a child before sometimes felt it earlier.

She placed a hand on her belly, feeling the goose-pimpled flesh through the soft cloth, and waited. A moment later, there it was again—a brisk, insistent stirring low down in her abdomen. The next kick was so strong that she felt it on her palm as well.

It was unmistakable. Her baby had quickened, and she could feel the unborn child moving within her.

"Oh!" Helen couldn't stop the smile that bloomed over her face. "Oh, hello, my little darling."

As if in response, the baby moved again, and tears filled Helen's eyes.

"There you are," she whispered. "I see you, my darling. I see you."

The tears spilled down her cheeks, first strikingly hot and then bitter cold when they cooled in the wind.

Helen set the bowl aside, wrapped her hands over her belly, and laughed as she sobbed with each wriggle of her unborn baby.

Memories flooded her. She remembered all the joyous times that she had felt little Beryl wriggling and kicking within her as she grew. It was certainly uncomfortable at times, especially as she approached her time, but every motion gave her a fresh reason to be overjoyed; it told her that the little one she carried was alive and growing. And it was true. Beryl came into the world a perfect, perfect baby, and a perfect, perfect child.

So would this baby. When this baby was born, Helen realized with stunning clarity, it would be just as beautiful and perfect as Beryl ever was.

Something flared in her soul. It was deep and fierce, as primal as the instinct that had kept her mud larking to stay alive, but it burned far brighter. Helen's hands tightened over her belly, and she lowered her head, speaking to the unborn child.

"I won't let you down," she whispered. "I won't let the same thing that happened to Beryl happen to you." Her teeth clenched with the intensity of her resolve. "I let my Beryl down. I won't do that to you, little one. I'll be better for you. I'll protect you, no matter what. I'll care for you, always. I promise."

Her tears stopped. Helen seized the bowl of bone broth and drank the rest in one gulp despite her queasy stomach. Then she rose to her feet and set off with bold strides, heading for the news board at the church, the one where jobs were always listed.

Helen had never read particularly well until the year she'd spent with Jerry. There, with nothing to do but tend the house and no friends to go out with, she'd spent hours curled up in an armchair, poring over books. It had been slow and frustrating at first, but Jerry was always happy to bring her more books or give her money for them, and soon she could fly through a Dickens or Melville novel like a real reader.

She had memorized the advertisement from the bulletin board and glanced up now at the street sign. This was Winchester Avenue, and the third house from the corner had the numbers *468* on the sign. It was the right house.

Maid of all work sought for middle-class home, the advertisement had said. Helen smoothed down her grimy dress, hoping that her bump wouldn't show too much.

"Come on, little one," she whispered. "This is for you."

She went around to the back entrance, following a narrow gate up to the back door of the stern old Georgian house with its blockish windows and bare garden. A wreath hung on the door and the firelight shone through green mistletoe in every window.

One day, I'll make sure Christmas is lovely for you, my darling, she whispered inwardly to her child. She raised a hand and knocked.

The door swung open a few minutes later to reveal a frowning woman with multiple chins.

"We don't give out alms. Go to St. Luke's if you have a need," she snapped.

"I'm not here to beg, ma'am," said Helen quickly. "I'm here about the job."

The woman looked her up and down. "What would you know about tending a house? You look like you've been on the streets."

Helen swallowed. "I've fallen on hard times, ma'am, but I once had a beautiful home of my own. I've been a washerwoman, too, and a seamstress. I'm great with mending and making things. I can cook—my best dish is roast beef with potatoes and carrots. I keep a spotless home, too."

The woman did that slow look up and down again. "I must say that I'm not convinced."

"Let me convince you, ma'am," Helen pleaded. "Let me cook something or mend something for you."

"And let you into my house? Not likely," said the woman.

"Please, ma'am." Helen stepped nearer. "I'll work for anything. Anything. Even room and board, I will."

That caught the woman's attention. She looked up, eyebrows rising. "Room and board, you say?"

"Yes, ma'am," said Helen quickly. She could work out ways of making extra money if she had to, perhaps doing mending for the neighbours. Room and board was a good place to start if she was going to nourish her growing child.

The woman studied her. "What happened that made you lose your home?"

Helen had her story ready to go. "I lived in a cottage by the sea with my husband, ma'am. He was a sailor." She swallowed hard, refusing to let any other memories reach the surface. "He was lost at sea, and... and now it's just me and the baby." She touched her belly.

The woman recoiled. "You and the *what*?"

Helen hesitated. "I'm a widow, ma'am. I'm—"

"You're enceinte?" the woman hissed, lowering her voice.

Helen gulped. "Yes, ma'am, but—"

"Get away from here!" The woman shooed at her with a dishtowel. "You'll bring scandal on my whole house standing here like this. Go! Shoo!"

Helen backed away a step. "Ma'am, but my husband—"

"Go before I tell *my* husband to set the dogs on you!" the woman cried.

Helen ducked her head and hurried away, heart pounding. She'd been so sure that her story of widowhood, partially true though it was, would secure her a place despite the pregnancy, but now she knew she was wrong.

Dismay threatened to flood her, but Helen pushed it down. She rubbed a hand over the tiny bump of her belly.

"We'll find another way, darling," she whispered. "Don't you worry. Mama will find another way."

Chapter Nine

The bustle of Christmas filled the market square. A magnificent Christmas tree presided over it from the middle, all draped with candy canes and oranges, wrapped with tinsel and ribbon. The snow fell softly and with no wind, dusting every surface with a layer of pure white. It sparkled on the pine needles of the tree and melted on the faces of the children skipping around it, playing games while their mothers hurried, laughing, from one stall to the next as they finished their last-minute shopping. A beautiful gold star stood at the tree's very peak.

Helen remembered learning about the Christmas star at the chapel in the workhouse in between dodging bullies. It was a symbol of perfect hope, but despite the laughter around her, hope seemed in short supply that night.

She knew that getting work on Christmas Eve would be impossible. Instead, she crouched on the street corner, holding out a hand to the bustling passers-by. Perhaps someone would feel a little generous this Christmas.

It had been two days since she had eaten. A full day since she had last felt her little one kick.

"Spare a penny?" she whispered.

The children running past didn't hear her. They carried paper-wrapped parcels with bright red ribbon and giggled with excitement. Their mother shouted at them to slow down as she bustled by after them, shopping basket on her arm.

"Someone will give us something, darling," she whispered to her baby. "Someone will have to. I'll keep you alive. I promise I will." She stirred, half hoping it would jolt the child awake, but nothing happened.

Had she already let this one down the way she'd done with Beryl?

The thought was terrifying, but Helen shoved it aside. Until it was proven, nothing would stop her from caring for this baby. She would do everything she could. Everything!

She extended a hand to an old man bustling by, but he crossed the square to avoid her and stopped at a stall selling expensive, turgid oranges, of which he bought six. Gifts for his grandchildren, she supposed. Everyone was doing such nice things for their children as she struggled to keep hers alive.

She couldn't let this one down, not like she had done with Beryl. Yet every place she enquired at for work turned her away when they discovered the pregnancy. The wild thought of trying to hide it crossed her mind, but she knew from having Beryl that she showed early and thoroughly. What good would it do to find a job for a month or two before they found out about her dishonesty and chased her away, calling her scandalous and unworthy?

Tears burned her eyes. Scandalous! Unworthy! They thought so even though she told them that the child was her husband's. How much more scandalous and unworthy the truth was, that she had traded away her morality for a warm place to sleep!

She hardly knew where the prayer came from. It spilled out of her almost unbidden.

"Oh, God!" she prayed. "I know I'm not worthy. I know I've done wrong. But Lord, my little one's done nothing to deserve this." The sob tore between her clenched teeth. "Please, God, save my baby!"

A cry jerked her from her reverie. Her eyes snapped open, and she saw a sea of fabric spilling onto the snowy cobbles. An old woman stood nearby, her hands red and chapped, a basket lying at her feet. Party clothes—bright dresses and handsome jackets—lay all over the ground.

"Oh, dear!" the old woman whimpered. "Oh, dear."

Her cheeks were pinched and nipped with cold, and her eyes watery. When she tried to bend down to pick up the fabric, she winced and cried out as though with bad rheumatism.

Helen rose to her feet almost automatically and grabbed a dress.

"No!" the woman cried, a pathetic, reedy sound. She reached out with a gnarled and trembling hand.

"It's all right," said Helen quickly. "I'm not trying to take it." She held the dress out to the woman. "I'm only helping you."

The old lady squinted at her with murky green eyes. Wisps of white hair clung to the sides of her face, damp with snow. Age and poverty had ravished features that must have been rounded and kindly once.

"Oh," she quavered.

"Here," said Helen, "let me help you."

She hardly knew why she was stuffing the items of clothing back into the basket; the old woman didn't look as though she carried any spare change. All the same, she found herself tucking the last jacket into the basket and returning it to the old woman's hands.

"You're such a dear," said the old woman. "Thank you ever so much." She took the basket, her hands shaking.

"Don't slip on the cobblestones, now." Helen gave her a brief smile, then limped back toward her square of newspaper on the pavement.

"Hold on a minute, lass," said the old woman.

Helen paused.

The old woman peered myopically at her over the basket. "You... you're not looking for work, are you?"

Helen's heart flipped in her chest. "I am," she croaked. Could prayer really work this quickly?

"Can you do washing?" the old woman asked.

Helen hastily nodded. "I used to be a washerwoman."

"Oh, wonderful," said the old woman. "Wonderful." She smiled. "Please, come with me. I'm desperate for someone to help. The other washerwoman around here died, God rest her soul, and now I have ten times the work I can do. It's not much money, but enough to feed two mouths, dear."

Helen froze. She glanced around, but no one else was close enough to hear.

"Please, dear," said the old woman, "all these clothes need to be done for a Christmas party tomorrow, and I'll pay you thruppence. There's room in my cottage. I need the help very much."

"I'm— I'm going to have a baby," Helen blurted out.

The old woman smiled. "I know, dear. You're not showing much yet, but I've a trained eye for such things. I helped many a woman birth a baby in times gone by."

Helen swallowed. "My husband died," she said quickly. "He was lost at sea."

"I've been widowed too, my dear," said the old woman. "I understand."

"But your customers..." Helen began.

"I don't need anyone the customers will see," said the old woman with steady kindness. "I only need someone who can wash clothes in the cellar. Can you do that?"

"Yes!" Helen cried. "Yes, I can. I certainly can!"

"Good." The old woman smile. "My name is Agatha. Come with me, lass. We have work to do."

She shuffled forward a few steps, clutching the heavy basket. Helen was frozen to her place with joy for a few moments before she could jump to her feet and take the basket from Agatha.

Helen paced in the tiny kitchen. Eight steps to the wall between the cabinet and the little stove. Eight steps to the opposite wall by the tiny table with its two rickety chairs. There wasn't much to the kitchen, but it was the largest room in the cottage, barring the laundry in the cellar below. Agatha's room was little more than a closet, and Helen's sleeping pallet rubbed shoulders with a ratty sofa in the tiny sitting room.

All the same, it felt like utter luxury to Helen. Coals smouldered in the stove, filling the room with warmth. She had had gruel for supper last night before many long hours bending over the vats in the laundry, then hanging the clothes by the boiler to cry. Even this morning, Agatha had given her a little bread and cheese before heading out to take the clean clothes to their customers.

The warmth and safety was wonderful, but still, Helen had not felt the baby kick for nearly two days now.

"Come on, little one," she whispered, touching her belly. "Please wake up. Please."

The door's creak allowed a burst of noise in from outside. Carollers passed by the cottage despite the early hour, filling it with their pure, piping voices.

"O holy night, the stars are brightly shining,

"It is the night of our dear Saviour's birth!"

The door shut, closing out the noise, and Agatha shuffled into the kitchen with shining eyes. She carried two large parcels wrapped in brown paper, and she was beaming.

"You won't believe it, Helen!" she said.

Helen stopped pacing. "What is it?"

"They were so surprised that we finished all the washing so early that they gave me fivepence extra," said Agatha. "So I've made sure we can have a little Christmas treat!"

She unwrapped the parcels, beaming, and showed Helen a modest spread: a whole rabbit to roast, potatoes, turnips, beets, a generous wedge of cheese, and two crisp red apples.

"We can make them into toffee apples," said Agatha, excited. "There's sugar in the cupboard."

"Agatha, this is wonderful!" said Helen.

The old lady beamed. "Oh, it *is* good to have company again." She shuffled to the cabinet. "You know, dear, I put tuppence away for you. Once we have a little more, we can buy you a new dress."

Helen flushed. "I don't deserve your kindness, Agatha," she said softly before she could stop herself.

"You've done right by me, dear," said Agatha. "Now come, let's get this spread ready."

They roasted the rabbit in the oven and Agatha retrieved a little flask of mulled wine that she'd been saving for Christmas. She had no decorations in the cottage, but she opened the window so that the carollers' music could come in despite the snowy chill, and lit a candle on the table as Helen set out the plates.

"Hark! The herald angels sing,

"'Glory to the new-born King!'"

Agatha smiled as Helen took the rabbit out of the oven. "Isn't that a lovely carol? I think it's my favourite. What's yours?"

A song about three ships filled Helen's mind with piercing agony, but she thrust it aside. "I don't have one," she lied. "Not yet, in any case."

Agatha sat as Helen carved the rabbit and set out its modest trimmings. There was a good slice of cheese for each of them, too, and the toffee apples rested on the table, gleaming with sugar.

"What a privilege," Agatha murmured. "How good to be able to celebrate Christmas." She smiled over the table at Helen. "It's good not to be alone."

"That's true." Helen reached for her knife and fork.

Agatha took her hand. "I'll say grace."

Sudden awkwardness filled Helen as the older woman bowed her head and murmured the familiar words. How long had it been? She wasn't sure whether to be angry or ashamed, so she said nothing and tucked into her Christmas supper instead.

"How long has it been since your husband was lost, dear?" Agatha suddenly asked.

Helen raised her head, panic thudding in her chest. Agatha's eyes held something knowing. *Five years*, she thought. *It's been five long years*. But she was only four months along, and she couldn't say that to Agatha.

"T-two months," she croaked. "It's been two months."

"The ship sank in October?" Agatha shook her head. "It's no wonder he was lost. What was the captain thinking, undertaking a voyage so late in the year?"

The roast rabbit turned dry in Helen's mouth. She gulped as though swallowing sawdust. "I don't know."

"You poor thing," said Agatha quietly. "Was he a good man?"

Helen's eyes stung with tears, but she refused to let herself remember his face or say his name. "The best," she croaked. "But I... I don't want to talk about him."

"Of course, my dear," said Agatha. "Forgive me for prying."

Oh, Agatha, Helen thought, *I should be the one asking you for forgiveness.* Her deception weighed on her shoulders as she ate the supper that this kind woman had provided for her, but she could not admit her lie. It would mean her unborn baby's death. Not even Agatha would be kind enough to keep her here if she knew how this pregnancy had come about.

"My husband's name was Joel," said Agatha softly. "He was a kind man, too. Gruff, of course, and always a little short with everyone around him. But he would have moved heaven and earth for me." Tears welled in her eyes. "It was my life's greatest sorrow that we never had children. I couldn't."

"I'm sorry," said Helen quietly.

"It's all right, dear. It was a long time ago, but I'll say that I'm very glad of your company," said Agatha.

Helen was about to respond when she felt it: the faintest fluttering deep in her belly. She gasped, almost dropping her cup, and pressed a hand to her abdomen.

"Helen, my dear!" said Agatha, alarmed. "Whatever is the matter?"

"Nothing," Helen gasped. "Oh, Agatha, nothing's wrong at all." Tears of joy and relief streamed over her face as the fluttering turned to a firm wriggle. "Oh, thank God!"

Agatha left her seat, the movement stiff and painful, and shuffled to Helen's side. "Are you all right?"

"I'm fine." Helen sobbed, cupping her belly in both hands. "It's—it's the baby. It hadn't moved in a long time, and I thought... I thought..." She couldn't say it out loud.

"Is it moving now?" Agatha asked, concerned.

"Yes." Helen raised her head, the tears of relief still streaming. "It's moving. It's alive. My little baby is alive."

"Oh, Helen!" Agatha wrapped her in a trembling embrace.

Helen bowed her head and wept with relief. Coals crackled in the stove and warm food filled her stomach as the Christmas carols floated through the open window, but all Helen had truly needed for Christmas was wriggling away inside her, alive and well.

Five Months Later

Despite springtime's chill in the air, sweat shimmered on Helen's skin. She sprawled on her sleeping pallet in Agatha's cottage, awash on a sea of familiar pain. A pot of water boiled on the coal stove.

Helen breathed hard, her fingers twitching in Agatha's gentle grasp.

"Oh, Agatha," she gasped, "your knees."

The old woman knelt on the floor beside her, and her legs trembled with pain and weakness, but fire flashed in her eyes.

"Don't you worry about me, duck," she said. "You have to concentrate now. You have work to do."

Another contraction gripped Helen's body. The pain and pressure crushed her, and she let out a roar of agony and determination as she pulled her knees up to her chest and pushed.

"That's right!" Agatha cried. "That's right, my girl. You're nearly there—nearly there!"

Helen's cry ended as the contraction faded, and she sagged against the hard pallet, breathing hard. Her body trembled with fatigue, but she forced the exhaustion aside. She had to bring this child into the world safely. If she did this right, she could hold her baby in her arms at last.

Agatha moved to the end of the pallet and hooked Helen's dress away from her knees. "You're almost there, love!" she cried, grabbing a clean towel from the table. "You're almost there. One more good push, duck. One more."

Helen fought back the weakness that threatened to swamp her. *One more push*, she told herself. *For your baby.*

That thought gave her limitless strength: the same strength she'd had as she laboured in the cellar day in and day out as her belly and ankles swelled, as the heartburn and nausea continued, as exhaustion made her dizzy every day. She kept working—she had washed a batch of laundry that very morning as the early pains gripped her—because she knew she had to, for her child.

The next contraction seized every part of her back and belly. Helen clenched her hands on her thin blanket and gritted her teeth over the cry that built up in her. Instead, she pressed that energy down into her body, her back rounding as she pushed with everything in her. She held her breath and pushed until dark spots swarmed in her vision, until every ounce of her strength had been spent, until it all suddenly stopped.

Pain and pressure vanished. Helen collapsed onto her pallet, her breaths coming in tiny gasps.

She heard Agatha's voice only dimly, crying her name, but she had nothing left. She lay with her eyes closed, her heart fluttering in her chest, until she heard it: a thin, wailing cry. The sound awoke her, ignited her, and opened a new reserve of strength that she hadn't known she had.

Helen sat up with a gasp, extending her arms, and Agatha beamed up at her. She cradled the towel-wrapped bundle in her arms. Tiny fists streaked with blood and fluid rose from the bundle, and Agatha moved the towel aside to expose the reddened, toothless, wailing face of Helen's infant.

"My baby," Helen croaked, holding out her hands.

"Here she is, Helen." Agatha gently placed the tiny bundle in her arms. "She's beautiful."

"She?" Helen croaked, holding the baby to her chest.

"A little girl," said Agatha. "She's perfect in every way. Why, look at those little arms!"

Helen gazed at the bundle, which, in that moment, contained her entire world. She had never seen anything as beautiful as the little screaming thing in her arms—except for the day that Beryl was born.

"Hello, little one," Helen croaked, happy tears burning in her eyes. "Oh, hello at last."

She bowed her head over the healthy, howling infant and cuddled her close, letting her feel the heartbeat that had fuelled them both for nine long months.

"She's perfect," Agatha whispered.

"She is." Helen raised her head, her face streaked with tears. "Oh, thank you, Agatha."

"Of course, duck." Agatha smiled.

The baby's cries slowed as she nestled in the warmth of her mother's arms. She opened her eyes, and they were warm brown.

"Oh, look that that," Agatha whispered. "She has your eyes."

Helen gently kissed the infant's forehead. "She's so beautiful."

"Have you thought of a name for her?" Agatha asked.

Helen caressed the baby's cheek with the back of her forefinger.

"She's a jewel," she whispered, the same words she'd said when Beryl was born. "She's my own little gem." Her throat closed. "Her name is Pearl."

"Pearl," Agatha whispered. "It's wonderful. I love it."

Helen closed her eyes against the sobs that threatened to overwhelm her and pressed her forehead to the baby's. In all the months she'd lived with Agatha, she had never told her about Beryl, so she made her next vow in silence.

I won't let you down, my darling, she whispered inwardly. *I will always be here for you, Pearl.*

Part Four

Chapter Ten

Ten Years Later

Eddie Mitchell ran ahead of the little group, his giggles filling the air like the snowflakes that tumbled thickly onto the expansive fields. Though Eddie liked to believe that he was terribly grown up, his laugh still sounded like that of a little boy.

Mabel Mitchell could almost believe that he *was* still a little boy when she heard that laugh; she could almost picture him as the chubby toddler he'd once been. But when she opened her eyes, her second-born son was a lanky figure, his dark hair bouncing beneath his knitted cap as he sprinted across the field.

"Eddie, wait!" Maggie's piping voice demanded. "Wait for me!"

A few years younger, the little girl struggled through the deep snow after her brother. Her voice grew plaintive when Eddie didn't slow down.

"Wait for me!" Maggie squealed.

Her boots stuck in the six-inch snow, and she fell onto her hands and knees with a yelp.

"Whoops!" Percy jogged ahead. "Don't you worry, poppet. You're all right."

Mabel smiled as her husband grabbed Maggie's arms and raised her quickly to her feet. Though the odd silver streak had begun to show in Percy's hair, he remained as spry and cheerful as ever as he dusted snow from Maggie's knees, chuckling.

"He won't slow down," Maggie complained.

"I don't think you need him to slow down." Percy winked as he took his daughter's hand. "I think you and me can catch up to him, don't you?"

Maggie giggled. "Yes, Papa!"

"Come on!" Percy broke into a run.

Mabel followed more sedately, smiling as her family ran across the field to the pine trees lining the lane at the end. She remembered toiling in this same field, struggling to weed her first husband's potatoes as she wrestled against the pregnancy she thought she hadn't wanted. Little had she known that that pregnancy would be the greatest miracle she'd ever experienced.

The grief came on her swiftly, as keen as it had been fifteen years ago when she'd lost her firstborn son. It pierced her soul. She touched her chest, walking slowly, feeling the keen pang of longing like a dagger in her heart.

"You all right, Mae?" Percy shouted.

Mabel forced a smile. "Right behind you," she called.

Eddie was jumping up and down at the foot of a handsome young pine tree when Mabel reached them.

"This one, Papa!" he demanded. "This one!"

Percy raised the saw in his hand. "It's a thick one, Eddie. Can you help me cut it?"

Eddie's eyes shone. "Yes, Papa, I can."

"What do you think, Mags?" Mabel took her daughter's hand. "Is it a good one?"

"It's a perfect one." Maggie beamed. "It'll look ever so nice in the parlour all strung with tinsel and ribbons and things."

"I think so, too." Mabel squeezed her chubby fingers.

Percy and Eddie laid the saw's blade against the bark and got to work. The clip-clop of hooves caught Mabel's attention as they sawed. She looked up as a pony trotted along the lane toward them, a pretty thing with a shaggy coat and bushy mane, its rider a scrawny boy who cheerfully kicked it along.

"Hello! Hello! Mrs. Mitchell!" he shouted.

"That's the postman's boy, isn't it?" Mabel murmured.

"That's right, Mama," said Maggie. "It's Bobby."

Mabel left the trees and approached the hedge. "Hello, Bobby!" she called. "Are you all right?"

"Yes, ma'am." Bobby touched his forelock as he halted the pony. "Road's too snowed up for Papa to get down here with his bad knee, so he sent me with your post."

"Oh! Thank you." Mabel smiled. "Pass it to me over the hedge, then you don't have to ride all the way down to the farmhouse."

The boy handed Mabel several envelopes secured with a rubber band, then turned his pony and trotted off.

Percy and Eddie were taking a break from their sawing when Mabel returned to them. Maggie and Eddie pointed up at the branches, telling each other about the decorations they planned.

"Got the post," said Mabel, waving it.

"Ah, good. Is there something from Mrs. Larchen?" Percy asked. "I'm waiting for her to send over the paperwork for her case."

"There is." Mabel extracted a fat envelope. "Also from the firm in London, and— Oh!" She froze.

"What is it?" Percy asked.

Mabel gulped. "It's from Mr. Goulding," she said.

"Mr. Goulding?" said Eddie, whirling around. "The man who's looking for Jack?"

"Oh, do you think he's finally found him, Mama?" Maggie asked eagerly.

Mabel sighed. Fifteen years of searching for Jack—with the investigator in London, Nathan Goulding, conducting the search for many of those—had taught her not to allow her hopes to rise too high. Yet it was so difficult not to let them soar, especially at a time like this. It was difficult not to picture her sweet Jack sitting beneath the Christmas tree with them all. Though she knew he must be a strapping young man by now—Lord willing!—she struggled to picture him as anything but the poor little boy she'd left in the workhouse so many years ago.

Oh, Lord, she silently prayed as she did every Christmas, *bring me my Christmas miracle this year!*

"Mama?" Maggie prompted.

"Maybe," said Percy, stroking the little girl's shoulder. "Maybe he has. Open it up, Mae. Let's see."

Mabel tore the envelope open, her hands stiff with cold and tension, and unfolded the letter.

"*Mrs. Mitchell,*

"*I apologize for the interruption to your festive season, however, I have excellent news.*"

Mabel's heart caught as she read the letter out loud.

"It says '*excellent news*'. Oh Percy, what if he *has* found our Jack!" Maggie cried.

Mabel had to clear her throat before she could keep reading.

"My trail has led me to a prosperous area in London, as I told you before. I ascertained that Jack worked for the Ashcroft family as a groom—again, as you know. However, my lengthy search has led me at last to one who might know where Jack went after leaving Ashcroft Manor.

"In interviewing servants at all of the surrounding houses, I finally stumbled upon the truth. I spoke with a housekeeper who remembered bringing hot dinners out to the young gentleman who drove a carriage belonging to a local doctor. She could not remember the name of the doctor, who frequently visited a member of the family she serves, but she remembered that the young man was the doctor's stablemaster. Crucially, she also remembered the young man's name."

Mabel's breath froze. She could say nothing for a few long seconds as her eyes dwelt upon the writing.

"What? What was his name?" Eddie cried.

Mabel swallowed. "Jack," she whispered. "Jack Finch." She lowered the letter, her heart hammering in her chest. "Oh, Percy, he's found him—well, almost. He's making enquiries about the doctor's name, but he believes he might find Jack before the winter is out. That's why he sent the letter so urgently. He's almost found him."

"A stablemaster!" Percy's eyes filled with tears. "He's safe, Mabel."

"He's alive," Mabel cried. She touched her trembling lips. "My sweet Jack-Jack is alive!"

Percy wrapped his arms around her, and Maggie and Eddie wriggled into the hug as well, their little bodies giggling and squirming as they were trapped between their parents. Mabel clung to her husband and wept tears of gratitude and joy.

Jack Finch strode across the stable yard, smiling as he ran his eye over the horses in their loose boxes. The gentle beasts wore warm rugs against the cold and watched the snowflakes fall with contented faces, blowing out jets of steam with every breath. Mistletoe hung on the stables' eaves and holly wreaths on every door. Jack's groom, Donnie, had spent the morning polishing the sleigh bells; he was sure Dr. Whitmore's grandchildren would want to go out with the pony and sleigh in the park.

But that would be tomorrow's concern. For now, Jack cast a last glance over his charges, then strolled into the cottage.

The delicious smells of nutmeg and cinnamon reached him as he stepped into the kitchen.

"Evening, my love!" he called. "Something smells wonderful!"

Footsteps clattered in the next room, and his beautiful young wife strode inside, smiling. Jack's breath caught at the sight of her the way it always did. The gas lamp shone on her scarlet hair, which was as rich and bright as the holly berries on the wreaths they'd hung everywhere. Freckles dusted her cheeks and her simple blue dress draped over an elegant frame, but the most beautiful part of her was her eyes. They were the brightest, most piercing blue Jack had ever seen.

"Hello, Jackie," she said, rushing to him.

Jack wrapped her in his arms. "Hello, my sweet Beryl."

Beryl nestled her nose against his neck and sighed with deep contentment. Their arms tightened around each other, and they held on for a moment longer, ever cognizant of what it had taken for them to be together like this in a warm home.

Jack kissed her forehead, then gently released her. "How was your day?"

"Wonderful," said Beryl, beaming. "I went to the market and bought some things—ribbons for the tree, candles for the window, and more mistletoe to decorate the house."

"We can put the ribbons on the tree together after supper," Jack suggested.

"Yes!" Beryl grinned. "I also bought a fruit cake from the baker. Last Christmas was before we were married, so I didn't have an oven to make my own."

Their life had changed so much in such a short span. Jack touched her arm, smiling, and offered up a silent hallelujah for the happiness they had now.

"How is Dr. Whitmore today?" Beryl asked.

Jack inclined his head. "Still not going out on calls. I took all the horses out for exercise myself, since I doubt he'll be going out in the next few days. Still, Mr. Popper says that he believes he'll be well by Christmas," he added, referring to the kindly butler.

"Poor old Dr. Whitmore. He's always healing everyone, and now he's ill himself," said Beryl. "I hope he feels better soon. He so loves celebrating Christmas with all his grandchildren."

"I polished the sleigh bells for them. I'm sure they'll come to visit as soon as he's well enough," said Jack.

"Do they know what's the matter with him?"

"He thinks it might be influenza or maybe just a bad cold. Either way, I told Mr. Popper to give him our best," said Jack.

"Thank you. I wish we could do something more to help. Dr. Whitmore has been so terribly good to us," said Beryl. "I don't know what we'd do without him."

"He has," Jack agreed. He kissed his wife's forehead. "What's for supper, my love?"

Beryl beamed. "I'm trying a new recipe. Roast beef."

"Sounds wonderful," said Jack.

"I don't think it's ready yet, but I'll just check on it." Beryl went to the stove and tugged it open, and a pungent cloud of black smoke rolled out.

"Oh, no!" Beryl cried. She pulled her oven gloves on and extracted a dish containing a charred black lump that might have been meat once. "Not again!"

"It's all right," said Jack.

"I don't understand," Beryl cried. "I keep doing this." Tears filled her eyes.

"Beryl, it's all right, darling," said Jack. "You were trying something new. You didn't know how long it should go in the oven."

"I thought it would be much longer than rabbit or chicken because beef is so much tougher." Beryl sobbed. "I'm so sorry, Jackie."

"No, darling, no." Jack hugged her tightly. "It's no matter."

"Of course it matters," said Beryl. "I'm your wife. I'm meant to feed you good suppers every night, but they keep going wrong." Her voice hitched. "I've wasted so much!"

"Shhh." Jack kissed her cheek. "It was by accident. Don't worry."

"I wish I knew how to cook." Beryl sobbed. "I'm so sorry. If only my mother had been around—" Her words dissolved into sobs.

"Oh, darling." Jack held her as she poured her sorrow into his chest, knowing that her pain had nothing to do with the burned roast and everything to do with that yawning absence in both of their lives. He closed his eyes and tried not to think of his own dear mother. So far, his efforts at finding Mabel Finch had been completely fruitless.

"I'm sorry," Beryl whispered as her sobs ebbed. "This is a happy time. I shouldn't be like this."

"You may weep over anything you like, my love." Jack brushed her flame-red hair from her face and kissed her forehead. "I know you must miss her awfully." He searched her eyes. "I think we should start looking for her again."

Beryl hung her head. "No... no. There's no point."

"But why not, my darling?" Jack asked.

Beryl sighed. "Jack, I thought my mother had lost me, but I know now that it's not true."

"What do you mean?"

"She would have called for me if she'd lost me. I never heard her call, and we were only separated for a few minutes when that man came up to me. He knew my name and knew my mother's name, Helen Nicols, and told me she had said to go with him." Beryl raised her head. "How else would he know that, other than if she'd—if she'd sold me?"

The thought struck a cold knife into Jack's belly. "Surely not."

"We were starving, Jack." Beryl's voice grew harsh and brittle. "She sold me to save her own skin."

Jack didn't know what to say. He squeezed her hands, fighting back fury and agony at the thought that anyone could have done this to poor little Beryl, who had been only four when they met.

"You know, darling," he said, "I think we should go out tonight."

Beryl looked up. "Out? Can we afford it?"

"It's nearly Christmas. We deserve a little treat." Jack grinned. "There's a lovely inn down the road—we can take Warrior in the trap. They make an excellent coq au vin."

"What's that?" Beryl asked.

"I have no idea!" Jack laughed. "But Mr. Popper tells me it's delicious. Let's go and find out."

Beryl grinned. "I'll wash my face," she said.

Her smile was everything Jack had ever needed.

Pearl skipped through the snow-covered street ahead of Helen, her petticoats flashing with every excited jump. They were cheap, ordinary, cotton petticoats, but they were warm and clean, and Pearl sang as she skipped.

"Deck the halls with boughs of holly, fa-la-la-la-la, la-la-la-la!"

Her piercing voice rose beneath the bare branches of the London plane trees lining this street, and Helen couldn't help smiling despite the considerable weight of the laundry sack on her shoulder. She balanced it with one arm and carried a smaller sack in the other hand, grateful that the washing business had begun to grow again. After Agatha's death two years ago, she had struggled to keep up with the constant demand and lost many customers. It was only now that Pearl was old enough to help that their business had recovered.

Still singing, Pearl skipped to the end of the street, and Helen raised her voice. "Pearl, darling! Slow down. It's time to be very quiet again."

Pearl obediently stopped at the end of the street. She knew that her penalty for disobeying Helen was staying at home when Helen made her deliveries and collections, and not out of choice.

"Quietly now, my dear," said Helen. "Take my arm."

"Yes, Mama," said Pearl.

"That's a good girl," said Helen. "Stay very quiet, now."

Pearl's little hand wrapped around her arm and Helen tugged her down an alleyway, avoiding the street that continued around a row of middle-class homes. The little girl made no sound at all until they had traversed the block and reached the little cottages where they lived.

"All right," said Helen. "You can go on now."

"Yes, Mama." Pearl released her arm, but instead of singing, the girl walked sedately beside her.

"Are you all right, darling?" Helen asked.

Pearl nodded, but her brow remained furrowed.

"What's the matter?" said Helen.

Pearl looked up at her. "Mama, why do you have to hide me sometimes?"

"Hide you!" said Helen, dismayed. "What gives you that idea?"

"When we make our deliveries, I always have to wait around the corner where no one can see," said Pearl, "and when we walk through a neighbourhood where we have customers, I have to stay quiet. You don't want them to see me."

Helen's mouth turned dry. She had thought that it would be another year or two before Pearl put two and two together.

"Are you ashamed of me, Mama?" Pearl asked.

Helen gasped, staring at the girl, who stared at her with deep brown eyes framed by silky blonde hair.

"No," Helen said fiercely. She took Pearl's hand and squeezed it. "No. I never could be, Pearl. Never."

"Then why?" Pearl asked.

Helen had crafted the story long ago, though it still tasted bitter on her tongue. Telling Pearl that her father had been lost at sea was easier than some of the other half-truths she'd spoken, like the one about her older sister being taken by child-stealers.

"There are dangerous people in the world, darling," Helen said gently. "And I want to make sure you're always safe with me."

She paused, watching Pearl's innocent face, and a pang of guilt twisted in her chest. "I don't want anyone thinking they can take you away," she added, her voice softer now.

Helen hated the lie, but she feared the truth even more. She knelt down, brushing a lock of hair from Pearl's forehead, her heart heavy with love and worry.

Pearl, in her innocent trust, accepted it with the unquestioning belief of a nine-year-old, but Helen's chest tightened every time she uttered those words.

"I understand, Mama." Her face brightened. "Can we make toffee apples tonight?"

Helen fondly smiled. "I think we have a few extra pennies for sugar."

"So can we?" Pearl begged.

Helen laughed. "Yes, darling. We can."

"Hooray!" Pearl ran ahead to the cottage, skipping with every step, her blonde braids bouncing on her shoulders.

Helen exhaled, trying not to feel the weight of this latest lie. The lies grew heavier at Christmastide, bringing with them the memory of the vow she'd made so desperately in that bleak tenement one Christmas—the vow to find Beryl.

Beryl...

Every year, thoughts of her grew more intense, yet Helen had to keep fighting to keep Pearl alive. This was the first Christmas in a long time that they would have the money for plum pudding and roast chicken; there had been many lean and starving Christmases leading up to this. Now, Helen felt as though she had merely blinked, and fifteen years had passed her by.

Beryl would be nineteen now, if she still lived; a young woman, old enough for a family of her own. Helen's heart fiercely ached for her. She had had so many wonderful moments with Pearl, moments that she would never have with Beryl.

I'm sorry, Adrian. The words slipped through her mind unbidden and brought with them an image that Helen had not asked for: a memory of Adrian sitting beneath the Christmas tree at Beryl's second Christmas, mere months before he had embarked on his last voyage. Helen remembered Beryl's laughter as the little girl unwrapped a package and found a doll waiting for her inside.

Thank you, Papa! Her tiny, piping voice resounded through Helen's mind. Adrian's deep, rich laugh came shortly after, echoing to the pit of her soul.

"Mama?"

Helen blinked her tears away and looked up. Pearl stared at her, worried. "Are you all right?"

"Yes, darling!" Helen forced a smile. "I'm perfectly all right. Come along, let's get this washing started—and then we'll make toffee apples while it dries."

Despite her worn, callused little hands, Pearl eagerly nodded. Helen tried to let Pearl's smile fill the hole within her, but it could not.

That space was reserved for Beryl alone.

Chapter Eleven

A sound roused Jack from his deep sleep. He stirred beneath his thick blankets and cotton sheets, struggling to rise from a confused dream about a chimney sweep and a gang of thieves. His outstretched fingers found his wife's silky nightgown and he rolled over to wrap an arm around her. She tucked herself closer to him, and he exhaled, the last tension from the nightmare leaching from his mind.

He was about to fall asleep once more when the sound tore the night, and this time, it was much louder: a woman's shriek of pain or terror.

Jack sat up with a gasp; beside him, Beryl shot upright.

"What was that?" she cried.

"I don't know," said Jack. "Stay here."

Beryl clutched the covers as he scrambled to his feet and pulled on his coat and boots. "Where are you going?" she gasped.

"I'll see what it is. Don't come outside, darling," Jack commanded. "Stay here."

Beryl remained frozen in place as another scream tore the stillness, clutching Jack's hand with a cold heart.

He rushed downstairs, boots clattering, and pushed outside into the stable yard. The horses were restless in their stables. A fine chestnut gelding reared, glorious despite the scattering of grey hairs on his face, and pounded the door with his front hooves.

"Whoa, Warrior!" Jack called. "It's all right, old lad." He hoped that it was. He prayed that it was.

He sprinted from the yard and ran toward the grand old house presiding over the beautifully groomed gardens that slumbered beneath their snow blankets. Another scream shattered the peaceful night and a chill sliced deeper than winter's cold into Jack's heart. He knew that sound; his hard life had led him to it often enough. It was the shriek of loss, of grief, of a pain far deeper and more serious than any physical sensation.

Jack ran to the front door, not hesitating even though he, as a servant, had never crossed its threshold. It was open a crack, and Jack flung it wide, making the holly wreath swing wildly.

"Dr. Whitmore!" he shouted. "Mrs. Whitmore! Are you all right!"

"Oh, Jack, thank Heaven!" Mr. Popper stumbled down the staircase into the entrance hall. The room's grandeur was lost on Jack in comparison with the usually impeccable butler's dishevelled appearance; he wore a gown and nightcap, his hair spilling from beneath the cap, and his eyes were huge.

"Mr. Popper, what's happening?" Jack cried.

"It's Dr. Whitmore," said the butler.

Terror bit deep into Jack's belly.

"He's—" Mr. Popper closed his eyes for a second, then croaked the words. "Jack, he's dead."

Jack froze. "N-no. It can't be. Surely—"

"He's dead," said Mr. Popper. "I saw him. Mrs. Whitmore woke beside him and... found him that way."

Horror drenched Jack in sympathy with the kindly old lady.

"Please," said Mr. Popper, "take that fine hunter of yours and ride to Dr. Gemford's house. There is nothing he can do for Dr. Whitmore, but Mrs. Whitmore is in such a state I fear she will become hysterical. Hurry, my boy. Hurry!"

Jack turned on his heel and sprinted from the entrance hall. He slammed the front door behind him, making the wreath fall to the ground, and sprinted across the snowy lawn back to the stable yard. Beryl was there, wide-eyed and clutching her coat around her body, as was Jack's young groom Donnie.

"Jack, what's happening?" Beryl cried.

"Donnie, saddle Warrior," said Jack. "Quickly, now, quickly."

Donnie nodded and ran for the tack room.

"Jackie?" Beryl croaked.

Jack reached out and wrapped her cold hands in both of his. "Go back inside, my love. It's freezing out here."

Beryl's eyes were huge. "Please tell me."

"I don't want you to be upset or frightened, my darling, so be brave for me now." Jack gently kissed her forehead. "Dr. Whitmore has died."

"What!" Beryl cried.

Jack kissed her forehead again. "Be brave," he reminded her. "I must go for Dr. Gemford for poor Mrs. Whitmore; she's in hysterics."

"Oh, the poor lady!" Beryl laid a hand over her mouth. "But Jack, what will happen to us now?"

The question bit deeply into Jack's heart, and he didn't know the answers. He put his arms around his wife and hugged her tightly.

"The Lord's will, my love," he murmured. "The Lord's will."

Warrior clattered into the yard, blowing steam and pawing the ground in a fine fury. Jack released his wife, seized the reins, and vaulted onto the grand old horse's back.

He leaned low over the animal's neck and whispered in his ear. "Fly, boy," he whispered. "You must fly now."

Warrior reared. When Jack released the reins, the horse charged as though truly taking wing.

Though her own work was back-breaking, Helen never envied the maids-of-all-work she met when she made her deliveries. Even though she knew that the Winslow's were kinder than usual, their maid, Penny, always looked red-eyed and tired when she accepted the clean washing from Helen at the back door to the nice middle-class home.

"Done early, as usual." Penny managed a tired smile. "Thank you, Helen, dear. Here's your payment."

Helen glanced at the few small coins in her hand. "There's a shilling too many, Penny."

"Oh, the master said to give that to you as a Christmas bonus," said Penny. "They're good folks, the Winslow's."

"They truly are." Helen beamed and lowered her voice. "This'll be a lovely gift for Pearl."

The employees at the Winslow's' house were happier than most, and generally kinder, too. They were among the few people who knew about Pearl. The little girl still hovered in the vegetable garden behind the hedge, where the family themselves couldn't see her.

"Oh, how nice. That's good." Penny smiled. "Thanks, Helen. Here's the next batch for you. Party clothes, too—can you believe it's nearly Christmas again?"

"A tiring time," said Helen, taking the bag of dirty laundry.

"That's true." Penny chuckled and withdrew into the house.

Helen shouldered the laundry and marched down the path through the vegetable garden, where Pearl sat on a bench, watching the Winslows' elderly gardener shovel snow from the path. Sam Harper moved slowly and with stiffness, but Helen was pleased to see that he had help today. A young man—perhaps twenty years old—worked beside him, flinging the snow from the path in white arcs.

"Morning, Sam." Helen paused. "How's the back?"

"Mama, he's retiring!" Pearl burst out, wide-eyed.

"What?" said Helen.

Sam straightened slowly, a hand on the small of his back. "Aye, it's true, Mrs. Nicols." He grimaced. "I'm not gettin' any younger, and the master's been good to me. He's set me up with a good pension, so he has."

"I'm glad to hear that, Sam, but I'm sorry we won't be seeing more of you," said Helen. "You've been very kind to me over the years, watching over Pearl when she was younger while I made my deliveries."

"It's no trouble to spend time with this sweet thing." Sam chuckled and pinched Pearl's cheek. "I know life is hard for widows in London. People always assume the worst about a single woman with a child."

The worst. Knowing it was the truth, Helen felt shame wash over her, but didn't let it show on her face.

Sam didn't seem to notice her discomfort. "Besides," he added, "I think you might be able to return the favour."

"Oh?" said Helen. "How so?"

"Let me introduce you to the new gardener." Sam smiled. "Finn! Come over here, boy."

A young man emerged from behind the garden shed. He was tall, but years of hunger and poverty had left their mark in the lines etched on his face and the pinched set of his shoulders. He looked perhaps twenty years old, a little older than sweet Beryl would be now, and there was something haunted in his green eyes. Charming freckles sprinkled across his nose beneath a mop of straw-coloured hair.

"This is Helen Nicols," said Sam, "the lady who does our washing. Helen, this is Finn Hargrove."

"Pleased to meet you, ma'am." Finn nervously tugged his cap.

"Finn's taking over my gardening work for me," said Sam. "You'll see Helen and her little one around once or twice a week, Finn."

"This is Pearl." Helen gestured at the girl.

Pearl neatly curtseyed. "Good morning, sir."

Something softened in Finn's eyes. "Morning," he rumbled.

"Have you finished turning the compost?" Sam asked.

"No, sir," said Finn.

"Go on, then. We'll get it done before lunch," said Sam.

"Yes, sir." Finn touched his forelock and trotted off.

"He seems a nice young man," said Helen.

"He is. Too nice for this world. Far too nice to have been lost on the streets," said Sam, "which is where I found him. Talked the Winslows into hiring him off the street if I could train him up in two weeks—they're kind folks, the Winslows are. He's shaping up well. I'm sure they'll hire him on permanently." Sam paused. "The boy's been through too much, Helen. Can you keep an eye on him when you come by, make sure he's doing all right?"

Helen smiled. "It's the least I can do, Sam, after all you've meant to Pearl and me over the past decade."

"Don't say that." Sam chuckled. "You're making me feel old."

He turned and shuffled off to help Finn, and Helen laid a hand on Pearl's shoulder to lead her into the snowy streets.

A holly wreath hung from the Winslows' back door when Helen returned a week later. Its bonny berries reminded her that Christmas was just around the corner. She glanced over her shoulder at Pearl as she approached the door, laundry bag in hand. The little girl tucked herself behind a rosebush, giggling. Hiding from their customers was a mere game to her.

It felt strange to be here without dear old Sam's reassuring presence, but as Helen knocked and waited for a response, the garden shed swung open and Finn emerged in the doorway. His hands were brown with potting soil. He waved at Pearl, who giggled and waved back.

Helen smiled. She handed the washing to the maid-of-all-work and accepted a new bundle, then turned to the garden shed. "Good morning, Finn!"

The young man withdrew a step as though she'd threatened him. "Hello, Mrs. Nicols." He turned to go back inside.

"Hold on a minute," Helen called.

Finn froze. She'd barely glimpsed him in her last two visits to the Winslow house; he always hovered on the periphery, keeping half an eye on Pearl, but never approaching. Today, Helen was ready to change that. Sam had done so much for her. She felt that it was her duty to honour his request.

She strode across the snowy lawn, her feet crunching, and paused a few feet from the shed. Finn held his hands in front of him as though ready to protect himself.

"Do you have family nearby, Finn?" she asked.

"I don't think I have family at all," said Finn quietly.

"Then you're on your own for Christmas."

"I suppose."

Helen smiled, tilting her head. "This year has been kind to me, young man. I have more washing clients than ever and I have a little to spare. I'm trying a plum pudding recipe for this Christmas tonight. Would you like to come and try some? I live only a few blocks away."

Finn blinked. "I... I have nothing to bring you," he admitted. "Nothing."

"You don't have to bring anything except yourself," said Helen. "We have enough." The words seemed like magic to her. "The Lord has been good," she added.

The words magically melted Finn. A shy grin spread over his face, lighting up his eyes. "I'd like to come after work," he said. "If that's all right. I finish at five."

"We'll see you at six," said Helen.

Finn arrived with great punctuality as the church bell struck the sixth hour.

"He's here, he's here!" Pearl bounced up the cellar's steps. "It must be him!"

"Wait a moment," Helen called, wringing out one more sheet, her hands aching with the work. "I'm coming."

Pearl danced with impatience at the top of the steps as Helen hung the sheet in front of the boiler and then laboriously climbed to their little living room. Her knees ached with the effort; she realized with a pang that she was getting no younger, either. She ignored the feeling and opened the front door.

"Evening, ma'am," said Finn. He wore a clean shirt and carried a little wreath twisted together from bits of mistletoe and the odd sprig of holly. "This's for you."

"A wreath!" Pearl gasped.

"Hang it up over the fireplace, dear," said Helen.

Finn's eyes softened as he handed the wreath to Pearl, who sprinted off to hang it on the wall.

"Come inside," said Helen. "Supper's only soup, but there's enough."

Finn shuffled in, looking lost, and sat at their table. Pearl made tea while Helen ladled soup into their bowls. She couldn't afford meat for three, but she'd added bone broth and made it hearty with plenty of parsnips and potatoes, and Finn smiled as she set it before him.

"Thank you very much, Mrs. Nicols," he said politely.

Helen chuckled. "You were raised right, young man."

Finn's smile grew thin, but he said nothing.

Pearl and Helen took their seats. The little girl extended her hands. "Time to say grace," she announced.

Helen had taken her to Sunday school; Pearl took it seriously. The child grasped Helen's hand firmly and wrapped her small fingers around Finn's, giving him no opportunity to pull away. She bowed her head and recited the little prayer, then released him.

Finn's shoulders relaxed. He sipped the soup and told Helen that it was excellent.

"It's good to have a full belly of hot food." Helen smiled. "Isn't it?"

Finn ducked his head. "It is, Mrs. Nicols."

"We didn't always have that privilege, Pearl and I," said Helen.

"You always made sure I had food, Mama," said Pearl. "You went without sometimes when I was little. I remember."

The little girl's sharp dark eyes pierced Helen, reminding her that little Pearl was growing up. *How much more grown-up is Beryl by now?*

"It's hard to go without," Finn murmured.

"We almost had to be on the streets after Agatha died," said Pearl. "Have you ever been on the streets, Finn?"

"That's a very personal question," Helen chided.

"No, no. It's all right." Finn lowered his spoon and inhaled. "There... there are things you should know about me as you've been so kind to invite me into your home."

"Things like what?" Pearl demanded.

Helen shushed her.

"Yes, Pearl, I used to be on the streets," said Finn. "In fact, I spent all my childhood there. I ran away from home when I was five or six years old. I might have died if not for Liz, who was kind to me, but she was also..." He paused. "She was a criminal. A thief."

Helen raised her eyebrows. "A thief?"

"Yes." Finn lowered his head. "We all were. We were a gang of child thieves, stealing whatever we wanted, and we did bad and wrong things while living an easy life with everything we thought we needed. I lived with them for years."

"Are you still a thief?" Pearl asked.

"Pearl!" Helen hissed.

"It's a very good question, Pearl," said Finn, "and I'm glad you ask such things; I'm glad you test the people around you to see if they're good or bad." He paused. "I haven't been a thief for years now. I left the gang about seven or eight years ago."

"Why?" Helen asked softly. "Why did you leave? Did you find work?"

"No," said Finn. "In fact, I found only a few odd jobs in all this time, and begged for much of it. But I left because one of the boys in the gang showed me that what we were doing was wrong. His tone softened. "His name was Jack Finch, and I'll never forget him. At first I rejected him because of it, but after he had left, I realized that he was right. We were in the wrong and I didn't want to live like that anymore." He paused. "I left. I tried to find Jack, but never did. I don't know what became of him."

"You never went back to stealing?" Helen asked.

Finn shook his head. "Never. I've repented of that." He hesitated. "But I understand if that makes it impossible for you to trust me. I'll leave if you like."

Helen froze, but Pearl smiled widely. "You stopped, so why wouldn't we trust you?"

Pride flooded Helen's chest as it so often did these days. Her child was growing up into everything she'd dreamed Beryl might be someday; kind, accepting, clever, and loving.

"Pearl's right," said Helen. "You didn't have to tell us everything. I... appreciate that you confessed it all." Her belly clenched. There was so much that she had never confessed to anyone, not even to Pearl.

Finn's smile blossomed over his face. "Thank you, Mrs. Nicols."

"Not at all," Helen managed.

"We've lived here all my life. I don't have a story to tell you," said Pearl. "I had a big sister named Beryl, but somebody stole her. And I had a papa named Adrian but he was lost at sea."

"Oh." Finn blinked. "I'm so sorry to hear that."

"Finn doesn't want to know everything, Pearly." Helen laughed. "Go and fetch the plum pudding from the oven—that's what he's really here for. Don't let it burn, now."

"Yes, Mama," said Pearl, jumping up.

Finn turned gentle eyes on Helen. "I truly am sorry," he said quietly. "You must miss them very much."

"Yes," Helen murmured. "I do."

Yet it was not her longing that settled like a great burden over her shoulders, but her terrible shame. Even Pearl could never, never know how she had come about, or that her father was not the kind and wonderful man that Helen had always told her about.

Pearl could never know that she was not legitimate.

Chapter Twelve

Beryl's shoulders trembled under Jack's arm. He tightened his gentle embrace as he led her through the front door of the cottage where they had known such brief years of such tremendous happiness. She was shaking as he steered her to a seat at the kitchen table, but she resisted when he pulled out the chair.

"N-no," she croaked. "No, I need to make us a pot of tea."

"Tea sounds wonderful," Jack murmured.

She stepped away, and Jack helplessly watched as she stoked the coals in the fireplace and hung the kettle above the rising flames. She wore black clothing, a veil covering the flame-red of her hair, and moved stiffly as she prepared the teapot and leaves. It was as though his pretty young wife had aged a decade in mere days.

The mistletoe and candles all around the kitchen seemed lame and pointless at that moment. Their undecorated branch was propped in the corner of the living room, visible through the open door; a box of decorations stood untouched at its feet.

"The funeral was very nice," Jack offered to break the silence. "I thought the vicar gave a wonderful message."

"It was very good. I'm sure it brought great comfort to Mrs. Whitmore," said Beryl, "but it doesn't change the pickle we're in now, Jack." Tears filled her eyes.

The silence returned as Beryl made the tea. She retained her composure until she placed the cup at Jack's elbow and sat; then she covered her face with her hands and wept.

"Oh, my love, my dear, please don't cry." Jack rubbed her back. "It'll be all right, you'll see. It'll all be all right."

"Oh, Jackie, how can it be all right?" Beryl cried. "You heard Mrs. Whitmore. She's selling the house and moving to her sister's all the way out in Essex... and she'll sell all of the horses... everything. Even the cottage. We have nowhere to go! We have nothing!"

"She'll give me a very good reference," Jack reminded her, "and Dr. Whitmore even left us a little money, remember?"

Beryl raised her head, tears still streaming, but managed a little smile. "He was so very kind, even to the end. Who ever heard of someone leaving money to their stablemaster?"

"Dr. Whitmore was the kindest master anyone could ever hope for," Jack agreed.

Beryl's smile vanished. "Oh, Jack, we'll never find another one like him. Even with the best references in the world, even if you find another job, where will we find a man who'll treat us with the kindness that Dr. Whitmore did? I'm sure there's not another one like him in all London."

Jack thought of the few pounds he'd been left and squared his shoulders. "Well, Beryl, maybe we shouldn't stay in London."

Beryl stared at him.

Jack reached over and wrapped his hands around hers. "Do you remember how we used to dream when we were little children?" he asked softly.

"How we used to talk about living on a farm in the country, with fields and trees and all sorts of animals?"

"Yes." Beryl's smile flickered. "Your mother had a farm, you said, before your father died. You said that she'd find us someday and we'd all go live there together." She managed a small laugh. "It was a wonderful dream."

"We haven't found Mama; Lord only knows if we ever will. But what if we can have part of that dream?" Jack asked softly. "What if we move to the pretty seaside town where you stayed with dear Annabel?"

The mention of Beryl's late mistress made tears well up again, but she gave a wistful sigh. "It's a beautiful place, but I doubt there are many opportunities there for a stablemaster."

"No," Jack murmured, "but do you know what the town also doesn't have?"

"Pollution?" Beryl asked.

Jack laughed. "Yes, that, but it also doesn't have a livery stable."

Beryl blinked. "A place where people can hire horses and carriages?"

"Precisely," said Jack. "Beryl, my dear, what if we start one?"

Beryl's blue eyes widened. "You mean... a livery stable of your own? Run your own business?"

"We might not have much," said Jack, "but if I could find a place to rent in the village, I could use the money Dr. Whitmore left me to buy a few horses and carriages. Perhaps I could even make Mrs. Whitmore an offer on the horses and equipment here. She's terribly attached to some of them; she might be willing to let me take them for a good price as she knows I'll look after them."

Beryl blinked. "She... she did say that she dreaded selling the horses when you were helping her into the carriage after the funeral..."

"We could even take the horses and tack instead of the money Dr. Whitmore promised," said Jack. "Since Mrs. Whitmore won't be needing them anymore; she could use the money herself instead."

"Jack, that's a wonderful idea." Beryl's lips trembled into a smile. "We'd have no master—if it works. But if it doesn't..."

Jack bit his lip. "If it fails, we'll lose everything, my love. We could be back on the streets."

They both shivered at the thought.

"I could search for other work," said Jack quietly. "It would be less risk."

"No." Beryl gripped his hand, sudden ferocity in her eyes. "No, Jackie, I trust you. More than that, I trust the Lord. He's been with us all this time and He'll be with us now."

Jack smiled. "Then that's what we'll do, my love," he said. "I'll start searching right away."

"You'll have no choice," said Beryl, "as Mrs. Whitmore said that she already had a buyer for the house, and she wanted to be with her sister by Christmas."

Jack swallowed. "Then I'll simply have to search quickly."

He gave her a bold smile, trying his best to hide the tell-tale sting of worry deep in his belly.

The soft crackle of roasting chestnuts filled the living room in the grand old farmhouse. Mabel dozed in a chair with her feet up, her stomach and heart both equally full.

The Christmas tree stood splendidly in a corner, colourful with ribbons and tinsel, and a glittery homemade star stood at the very top.

Percy sprawled in his armchair beside Mabel's, open-mouthed and gently snoring, his book lying on his chest. The children paid their sleeping father no mind as they hung their stockings over the fireplace.

"Mine's bigger than yours," said Eddie.

Maggie tossed her head. "No, it's not. Mama knit them both. They're the same."

"She loves me better than you, so she made mine bigger," said Eddie.

"Children!" Mabel scolded. "I love you all three with all my heart."

"All three, Mama?" said Eddie.

Maggie elbowed him. "Jack, you, and I, you big fool."

"If you two keep on fighting," said Mabel mildly, "then Father Christmas will put coal in your stockings."

Eddie and Maggie exchanged a wide-eyed look and immediately stopped arguing.

They turned their attention to the chestnuts on the fire, and Mabel was about to drift off herself when there was a quiet knock at the door. Their sheepdog barked, making Percy sit up with a snort.

"Who could that be at this hour?" Mabel wondered.

"I'll go and see." Percy stood and shuffled to the door, the dog close by his side. A moment later, he called, "Mae! Get over here. It's from Mr. Goulding!"

Excitement lanced through Mabel's heart, almost as painful as grief. She tried to hold it back as she scrambled to her feet and rushed to the door. It was Bobby, and he was wide-eyed and breathless.

"Here, Mrs. Mitchell!" He held out an envelope. "It didn't come in the post; it came by a horseback messenger, very fast. They said to bring it to you right away. They said it was urgent."

Mabel felt suddenly sick. Was Nathan rushing to tell her that he'd found her son, and it was too late? Her knees felt weak.

"Thank you, Bobby." Percy gave the boy a penny. "Off you go."

"Thank you, mister!" Bobby grabbed the penny and fled.

"Well, go on, Mae." Percy shut the door. "What does it say?"

"I don't know," said Mabel faintly. "I can't read it. Please—you read it. I can't bear it."

Percy took the envelope and pressed his lips delicately to her forehead before opening it. His eyes widened as he read, and Mabel's heart squeezed. Then a grin spread over his features.

"What?" Mabel cried. "What is it? Is it good?"

"Oh, Mae, it's wonderful!" Percy laughed. "The best news we could hope for!"

Mabel clutched his arm. "Did he find him?"

"Yes," said Percy, beaming. "Yes, Mae. He found Jack, alive and well."

Mabel's knees gave way. She sank to the ground, sobs and laughter vying to escape her first as tears of joy poured over her cheeks.

"Oh, Lord!" she prayed. "Oh, God, thank You! Percy, where is he? Is he all right? Is Mr. Goulding sure it's him?"

"Mr. Goulding hasn't seen Jack with his own eyes yet," said Percy, "but he's found out that Jack Finch is the stablemaster for Dr. Charles Whitmore. Someone who used to work at Ashcroft Manor identified him. It sounds like our Jack, my love. Mr. Goulding is sure it must be him. He wrote to us right away; he wants us to come to London so that you can identify Jack when he goes to see him."

Mabel pressed her fingertips to her lips, a sob escaping her. "We're going to see Jack?"

"Yes, my love," said Percy. "We'll take the overnight stagecoach and be in London by morning."

"By morning. Tomorrow morning." Tears poured over Mabel's cheeks. "The morning of Christmas Eve. It is our Christmas miracle after all, Percy."

"It really is my love." Percy smiled. "I'll arrange the stagecoach right away. I think we should leave the children with my sister as we usually do; they can meet their brother once we're sure."

The logistics seemed so distant and abstract to Mabel, but she knew she needn't fear. Percy would have control of it all; he would make sure that all was well with their younger children.

For now—for once—Mabel could concentrate only on the child she'd lost all those years ago, on her Jack-Jack, her firstborn. She was on the brink of her Christmas miracle, after all. In mere hours, she could be holding her child in her arms again.

The thought was more wonderful than she could bear. She could not stem the flow of joyous tears as she sank to the ground, hands covering her face, and Percy strode to the living room to talk to Eddie and Maggie.

Chapter Thirteen

Helen's hands ached and trembled with weariness as she pulled one more garment from the washing line by the boiler. The pretty dress, all chiffon and tulle, belonged to one of the young Winslows. Helen knew she had chosen it for the Christmas party their neighbours hosted every year, and she took extra care inspecting it for any spots or wrinkles before hanging it up and wrapping it in a garment bag.

"Is that the last one, Mama?" Pearl asked.

Helen buttoned the bag. "It is, my dear. I think we're all ready to take the Winslows their things."

Pearl beamed. "We're early, too."

"We are." Helen chuckled and touched the little girl's cheek. "All because I have a wonderful helper."

Pearl's eyes brightened. "Are these the last things we have to hand in before Christmas?"

"They are," said Helen, "and the Winslows gave us half-a-crown to spend as we please last week, so on our way home, we'll get a chicken to roast and a little extra sugar for the plum pudding."

"Oh, goody, Mama!" Pearl clapped her hands. "Can we invite Finn for Christmas this evening?"

Helen tilted her head. "You'd like him to join us for Christmas Eve?"

"Oh, can he, Mama?" Pearl begged. "It was so nice when he visited last week. He's so very kind."

Helen smiled. Finn *was* kind and held a gentleness within him that didn't match his past. She and Pearl had struggled on alone for long enough that Helen knew having a male guardian in Pearl's life—a sort of older brother—could be nothing but beneficial, if he was as gentle as Finn.

"Of course we can invite him," she said. "You take this bag, it's the shortest. I'll take the others. We'll ask him right away when we go to the Winslows."

"Hooray!" Pearl reached for the hanger.

Helen winced as the child took the garment bag from her, noticing how red and chapped Pearl's knuckles were, her skin worn away and dried out from hours spent in hot, soapy water as she helped Helen with the laundry. If only Pearl could have the soft white hands of a schoolgirl! But Helen supposed that having a friend over for Christmas and an extra helping of plum pudding was the best she could hope for. It was more than she had dreamed of, she admitted to herself, during her long, frightening months on the streets.

"Come on, Mama!" Pearl danced at the top of the steps with relentless excitement. "Let's go!"

Yes, everything was far more than Helen had ever dreamed of... except that she still hadn't found Beryl. The thought weighed painfully on her chest as she climbed the steps and followed Pearl out into the snow.

Finn's face glowed with pride when he arrived at their cottage that evening, having joyfully accepted their invitation to spend Christmas Eve with them. His face was bright pink, as though he had thoroughly scrubbed it, and he had attempted to plaster his straw-coloured hair to his scalp. Several bits endearingly stood up near the back.

When Helen answered the door, she had the fleeting thought that Beryl would be only a couple of years younger than Finn was now. She wondered if her little girl had grown into a beautiful young woman, if she had caught the eye of someone like Finn... or someone very different to him.

Finn's smile slipped. "I'm sorry," he said. "It's not much."

"What do you mean?" said Helen.

Finn raised a little bundle wrapped in paper. "I thought I should bring something. I wish I could have afforded more, but I've only had my second week's wages now."

Helen blinked down at the bundle. She folded back a piece of the paper, revealing a tiny wedge of real fruit cake. Dried fruit and raisins speckled the hearty cake, and the sweet smell of rum rose from it.

"Oh, Finn!" Helen laughed. "This must have cost you a small fortune!"

Finn beamed. "Pearl said the other day that she'd never tried fruit cake before. I thought she might like a piece."

"Is it really fruit cake?" Pearl bounced at Helen's elbow. "It looks wonderful. Oh, thank you, Finn!"

"Come inside," said Helen. "The chicken is almost ready."

Finn beamed with pride as he strode into the cottage and Pearl fussed over him, taking his coat and pouring him a cup of tea. The young man seemed almost at home as he took a seat and sipped his tea.

"Well, look at that." Helen slid the piece of cake onto a tin plate and gave it pride of place in the middle of the table. "Two different sweet things on one night! Aren't we ever so lucky?"

"We really are, Mama," said Pearl. "We have milk for your tea if you want it."

"I haven't had milk in my tea for years." Finn held out his tin cup. "That would be lovely."

He sipped his tea, watching in bemusement as Pearl and Helen set out a glorious feast for them: a whole roast chicken with a golden-brown skin, a roast potato apiece, carrots, a wedge of cheese, a handful of roast chestnuts, and the plum pudding, which Helen set beside the fruit cake.

"Wow." Pearl's eyes popped. "Look at all this! Nobody has a feast as nice as this in all England tonight, I think."

Finn chuckled. "Do you think you're eating better than Queen Victoria tonight, Pearly?"

Pearl paused. "Is it true that she has roast swan and hare curry for her Christmas dinners?"

"I think it is," said Finn.

Pearl laughed. "All right, maybe our feast is the second nicest in England, then."

"I don't think so," said Helen, pouring eggnog.

"Why not?" Pearl asked.

Helen smiled at the little spread and at the earnest young man who gazed up at her with wide eyes. There was something trusting in his expression, something she'd seen before in Beryl and Pearl. He was looking at her the way her children did.

It made her longing for Beryl ease just a little, and the exhaustion that weighed down her tiring joints and the corners of her eyes lightened, and the worry over paying next month's rent eased.

"Because being with people we love is far more hearty and delicious than any amount of roast swan or hare curry," said Helen. "I would much rather be here with the two of you than in any king's palace. Christmas doesn't have to be a grand feast or people in pretty clothes. It can be just... this." She gestured around them. "Just us."

Finn's eyes filled with tears. He rapidly blinked them back as he raised his eggnog glass. "Hear, hear!" he said.

Pearl swung her teacup with enthusiasm. "Hear, hear!"

Tea slopped on her dress, and Helen and Finn burst out laughing. Their mirth filled the cottage with brightness and warmth until it felt as though Helen's heart might pop at the seams.

It had been a long time since Jack last fed and mucked out a whole yard full of horses on his own. His hands stung from splinters left by the pitchfork as he shouldered the cottage door open and stumbled inside.

The gloom within did little to lighten his mood. Every home he'd passed on his route through the village after fetching something for supper had been bright and cheery, with decorated trees shining in the windows, wreaths hanging from every door, and every house brilliant with candlelight. In comparison, Jack and Beryl's new cottage seemed like a cold, dark cave.

A few coals smouldered in the pot-bellied stove. Beryl crouched beside it, soot streaking her dress, hopelessly scrubbing at the floor.

"Beryl, darling," said Jack, "what are you doing?"

Beryl raised her head. Tears glimmered on her cheeks. "Oh, Jackie, I'm sorry. I know it's Christmas Eve and everything is just so bleak and horrible." She choked back a sob. "We didn't have money for decorations this year, so I— I thought we could at least make the place clean…"

Jack's heart ached. He placed their simple supper on the table—bread, cheese, and two fat red apples—and hurried across the kitchen to wrap an arm around his wife's shoulders.

"Come now, my dear," he said gently. "Come and sit down. Let's eat."

Jack gently guided her to the table. Beryl wiped away her tears and rummaged in a wooden crate for a breadknife, which she used to cut the bread.

"I haven't any butter for you," she said faintly. "I'm so terribly sorry."

"There's no need for you to be sorry," said Jack.

Beryl's lower lip trembled. "But look at this, Jack." She gestured helplessly at the simple meal. "It's Christmas Eve, and this is our dinner… and the house is so dirty… and I forgot to bring candles." She gulped.

"Beryl, my dear, everything happened far more quickly than we expected." Jack smiled. "Don't you think that it's pure providence that we found a yard to rent so soon, and that Mrs. Whitmore agreed to give us a few of the horses, and that we didn't have to wait around for a solicitor to give us our inheritance?"

Beryl's lips twitched. "It worked out far better and more quickly than I expected."

"We've only been here a day," said Jack, "and this place was abandoned for months. I didn't expect you to make it perfect in a mere day, my love." He brushed her tears from her cheeks.

"I'm scared, Jackie," Beryl admitted. "It feels... it feels like we have nothing again. We know all too well how that feels."

"No, darling," said Jack. "We don't have nothing. We have four beautiful horses standing in that yard, a little old perhaps, but still very serviceable. We have paid one month's rent for this cottage and yard. We have a carriage and a wagon, and saddles for them all. We have enough to put food on the table for another week, if we eat simply. There's hay in the loft and a little oats in the feed room."

"And what about next week?" Beryl whispered.

Jack took her hand and squeezed it. "By next week we'll have our first customers. We'll be all right, my dear, you'll see—for no matter what, there's something that we also have, something far more enduring than any amount of riches."

Beryl's blue eyes searched his. "What's that?"

Jack squeezed her hand. "We have each other."

A smile flickered over Beryl's face, and her fingers twitched in his. "Yes, we do," she said quietly. "Always."

"Always," Jack echoed.

Her tears dried up, and they ate together, smiling and laughing over their simple meal. Though it was a strange and dark and frightening Christmas, still their love shone bright as the Star of Bethlehem, and it was all the light that Jack needed.

It was nearly midnight when the hansom cab drew to a halt outside the estate.

The sight of it made Mabel's breath catch in her chest. During the long journey from the farm to London, she'd envisioned all sorts of horrible situations for poor Jack-Jack; she'd imagined a run-down stable yard without any money, accommodations with draughty walls and a leaking roof, and her son scraping up a living. But it was immediately obvious upon seeing the Whitmore estate that this was not the case here. Snowbound lawns glimmered between beautifully maintained hedges and rows of evergreen trees. A beautiful house presided over the lawns, its windows all intact, its paintwork glowing and fresh.

"Oh, Percy." Mabel clutched Percy's hand, struggling to hold back tears of relief and joy. "My boy has been *here*, Percy. Not a common stable lad, but a stablemaster for a place like this. He'll have had a full belly every night. Oh, my dear, it's better than anything I prayed for."

Percy smiled. "You must be so ready to see him."

Mabel gulped her tears back. Oh, she was so ready. She couldn't wait to fling her arms around him, to tousle his hair as she used to when he was a very little boy, to look into his friendly eyes and know that her son was safe and alive and by her side again. Her heart had longed for this moment for so many years. She could barely believe that it had finally come.

"Aha!" said Percy. "Here comes another cab. It must be Mr. Goulding."

Another hansom pulled up beside their own, the horse's flanks steaming in the cold night. The athletic form of the investigator jumped from the cab and rushed over to them. Mabel gathered herself and followed Percy onto the pavement, gasping at the air's frigid cold. The sky was clear above them, the stars themselves like bits of frost on the dark sky.

Mabel had always hated how few stars one could see through London's smog. Now, she'd never seen anything more beautiful. It was beneath this sky that she and Jack would at last be reunited.

Nathan Goulding was grinning from ear to ear as he strode toward them, his scarf stirring in the breeze. He briskly shook Percy's hand and smiled at Mabel.

"Mr. Goulding, we can't express our gratitude," said Percy.

"You found him," said Mabel. "You really did find him."

"Nothing brings me greater joy than doing so, Mrs. Mitchell. You have been longing to see your boy for such a very long time. It is my greatest pleasure to bring you this moment at last," said Nathan. "Now come, come! Let's waste no time. He'll be in the stable yard, I'm sure."

A church bell tolled as they walked around the estate, avoiding the tall main gates and making for the horse gates instead. Mabel didn't count the rings, but it seemed Percy did.

"Midnight!" he said. "Why, we'll wake the whole house."

"It's Christmas Eve, Mr. Mitchell. I'm sure everyone will be up and enjoying their feast," said Nathan. "Besides, I doubt your wife—nor her son—wish to wait another half-day to meet at last after all these years."

"No," Mabel cried, "I can't wait another moment. Not another second." Her entire body ached with excitement and yearning.

"You don't have to," Nathan told her.

She felt a pang of panic as they approached the horse gates, but they were not locked. Nathan pushed them open and led them into a stable yard so beautiful that Mabel could barely hold back her tears.

"Percy, look at it," she croaked.

The loose boxes looked onto a broad, cobbled yard, which was covered with snow but showed no signs of straw or dirt; it had been swept spotless. Mistletoe and holly hung from the stables' eaves. These people decorated even their stable yard... and best of all was the cottage at the end. It was small and charming and in perfect repair, with ivy climbing over the stone walls. This was her Jack's home, a beautiful place where he was safe and warm. It was everything Mabel had prayed for.

"Oh, the lights are out," she whispered. "We'll be waking him."

"Not to worry," said Nathan. "He won't mind once he sees you." He beamed, excitement shining in his eyes.

Mabel's heart thudded wildly as she followed Percy and Nathan to the bright blue front door. Nathan was the one who knocked, the sound reverberating around the quiet yard.

There was a long silence but for the pounding of blood in Mabel's ears.

"He's a deep sleeper," said Nathan, smiling. He knocked again, and the sound echoed and echoed.

A pit of worry opened deep in Mabel's stomach. She swallowed, her mouth suddenly very dry.

"That's odd," said Nathan. "Perhaps he's out for the evening."

Disappointment was a swift kick in her belly, but she supposed it would be quite normal for a young, single man to visit friends over Christmas.

"What will we do?" she asked, struggling to hold back tears. "Come back in the morning?"

"Perhaps someone at the main house will know," said Nathan encouragingly. "Wait here. I'll go there and see."

Percy's arm encircled her shoulders. "Not to worry, Mae," he said as Nathan hurried off. "You'll see him tomorrow, even if he's off with friends somewhere."

Mabel tried to smile at the thought of Jack enjoying himself with friends at Christmas Eve. *Next Christmas Eve, you'll have family to be with*, she thought. *We'll spend it together.* The idea was cheering, but as she and Percy stood in the quiet yard, the unsettled feeling spread through her body and sucked her bones dry of their strength. The wind seemed very cold, and the yard very dark. Mabel shivered and Percy pulled her nearer.

"Something's wrong," Mabel whispered.

"No, no," said Percy, "not necessarily. Don't go worrying before it's needed, my love."

"No. Something *is* wrong," said Mabel, her voice as hollow as her heart felt. "I can feel it. I know it."

The night was very black. The wind blew straight through her as though she had lost her substance. A troubled furrow appeared between Percy's brow, telling her that he, too, knew something was wrong.

It was when they heard the thud of Nathan's footsteps returning that Mabel realized what was troubling her.

"Horses," she croaked.

"What?" said Percy.

Mabel clutched her hands to her chest. Her heart pounded against them, relentless as a blacksmith's hammer.

"There are no horses here, Percy," she whispered, "not one."

"No... no. They're asleep," said Percy, "or—"

Mabel tore away from him and rushed to the nearest stable. She looked inside and saw exactly what she expected: not a well-kept, shining beast resting on golden straw, but heart-breaking emptiness.

There was no hay in the rack and no water in the trough and no oats in the manger. The cobblestones had been swept clean. There was nothing here.

"No horses," Mabel whispered. "No stablemaster."

She did not have to rush to the other stables to know that the same would be true of them. The silence told her so. No hooves stamped and no heads peered over the doors. This yard was as empty as the cottage.

She looked up as Nathan reached them, and the set of his mouth told her everything she needed to know. Percy came and gripped her hand hard as Nathan spoke. His words seemed distant and jumbled compared to the throbbing agony in Mabel's heart. She heard only their gist: that the house was locked and empty, too, utterly abandoned; that he had looked through the windows and seen no furniture; that not a sound stirred on all of the Whitmore estate.

"I'm so sorry, Mabel." Nathan's voice cracked. "I don't know what's happened, but there's no one here. Someone must know where Jack went. I'll find him. I'll find him."

Mabel tried with all of her heart to believe him, but she could not. There was no hope in that silent stable yard.

There was no miracle.

Part Five

Chapter Fourteen

One Year Later

Sea Crescent Livery bustled with activity. Jack's feet already ached, and it was not yet lunchtime, but he could not keep the smile from his face as he proudly strode from the stable, holding a pair of supple leather reins. The little Welsh pony strutting beside him was a new addition, fresh from the mountains, with a perky head and a blue roan coat that made him look like a freshly polished bit of blue slate.

"I think he'll suit your daughter nicely, sir," he said.

The man in the yard held one of Jack's hunters and beamed from ear to ear at the sight of the pony. "Oh, yes, perfect!"

"What's his name?" the little boy beside him asked.

"Blueberry," said Jack.

"Oh, it suits him!" The boy giggled. "Papa, let's go! I want to take him hunting!"

"You're a bit small for that yet, little chap." The father chuckled. "Maybe hound exercise before next season."

The little boy pouted, but once Jack had boosted him into the pony's saddle, his joy returned.

Jack watched the hunter and pony head off together, their haunches rippling with fitness; they went out every day with one client or another.

"Hello!" A fat man bustled into the yard. "Hello, I've booked a horse and carriage!" He waved a banknote. "I'm in a great hurry!"

"The horse is harnessed, sir," said Jack. "Mind you watch the ice on the roads, please."

"Yes, yes, I will," said the man.

Jack brought out his carriage horse and hitched it to the trap. Two hot, sweaty horses waited for attention in their stables as he handed the reins to the fat man and accepted the banknote.

"Thank you very much, sir," said Jack fervently.

The man softened. "I should be thanking you, boy. Your livery's all but saved my business. Can't afford to keep a horse for the odd trip to London, can't afford not to go." He scrambled onto the carriage. "I'll be back by nightfall, as usual."

"Thank you, sir," said Jack.

He glanced at the banknote, his stomach flipping at the amount written there. It was difficult to believe that his little business could bring in what amounted to a fortune compared to what he had once earned, even with Dr. Whitmore.

Jack thrust the note into his pocket and hurried to the stables to attend to the hot horses. He walked them, one in each hand, until they stopped blowing. Then, with quick and tender hands, he sponged the sweat from their flanks with warm water and covered each with a blanket. Straw tucked beneath the blanket helped them to dry off.

One of them, a gentle old grey he'd inherited from Dr. Whitmore, nudged his shoulder as he topped off the water bucket.

"Yes, old fellow, your mash is coming," Jack promised. He patted the horse's neck and hurried to the cottage.

When he set foot in the kitchen, Jack froze in place and gasped with joy. Every surface of the room was filled with beauty. Strings of garlands hung all around the walls and bunting stretched across the window. Bits of holly, chequered ribbons, and braided twigs lay all over the kitchen table, where Beryl sat at its head, weaving a wreath.

She looked up. "Jackie! You're finally inside. I've brewed some tea."

"No time for tea, my love. I'm just here for the bran mashes," said Jack.

Beryl rose and touched his cheek. "You're half frozen, you poor thing. Here—drink this cup while I scoop out the mashes for the horses."

"You're an angel," said Jack, meaning it.

Beryl handed him a cup—real china, albeit the rough, cheap kind—and ladled the warm, boiled, and salted bran into two buckets. Jack thirstily slurped the hot tea.

"The kitchen looks wonderful, my dear," he said. "Is this wreath for the front door?"

"It is." Beryl smiled. "One of the church ladies showed me how to make it."

"It looks very promising to me," said Jack. He chuckled. "You're getting ready early."

"Oh, Jackie, the first snowfall always puts me in the mood for Christmas." Beryl smiled. "Besides, last Christmas was so bleak and dreary. I want to make up for it this year."

Jack smiled. "I don't need a thousand decorations for this Christmas to be glorious, my dear. We've been richly provided for. Oh, I know that the first few months were very, very hard on this little livery yard."

Beryl laughed. "Do you remember when we picketed the ponies on the common and let the carriage horses graze on the vicar's lawn? He said it was in exchange for manure for his roses, but I know he was helping us."

"He helped us indeed, my love, and now at last our yard flourishes." Jack beamed. "That's all the Christmas I need."

"Well, we can have a bonny, bonny Christmas," said Beryl firmly, "not like last time. We'll have decorations and roast beef and fruit cake. I brought that fruit cake along from the cottage, you know, the one I started making last Christmas. It's been in its tin all this time."

"We'll enjoy it on Christmas Eve, then." Jack smiled. "We have everything we want."

Beryl's hands fluttered over her lower abdomen. "Well… not quite everything, not yet."

Her bottom lip trembled. Jack abandoned his tea to wrap her in his arms.

"Someday, my love," he murmured, kissing her hair. "Someday our little family will be complete."

Beryl hid her face in his neck for a moment, then withdrew, her eyes damp but smile wide.

"Someday," she agreed.

Jack slurped the last of his tea. "I'd better get outside. Mr. Gardiner is coming to hire the tandem pair at eleven."

"Poor thing! You've barely had time to breathe all day." Beryl handed him the buckets. "Don't you think it's time you hired a stable lad?"

"I do," Jack agreed. "I love you, my dear."

"I love you, too." Beryl paused. "And merry Christmas, Jackie."

Jack beamed. "Merry Christmas."

Snow had not yet fully come to London. Instead, slush slopped around Helen's feet as she tried to avoid the gutter, dodging pedestrians and bustling carriages as she made her way through the city.

"Stay close, Pearly," she called.

The little girl stayed on Helen's heels, her arms wrapped around a heavy bag of dirty laundry that smelled of cigarette smoke and urine.

"Are you all right with that bag?" Helen asked.

"Ugh, it's so smelly," said Pearl, "but it's not heavy."

"You can rest when we get to the Winslows," said Helen.

Pearl smiled, the expression brighter than the candles in the windows. A few of the business they passed had already begun hanging sprigs of mistletoe over their doorways, though Helen saw no Christmas trees yet.

"Can we ask Finn to dinner again tonight?" she asked.

Helen laughed. "Land's sakes, child, don't you think poor Finn is sick of us yet?"

Pearl frowned. "Not at all. I think Finn loves us both, Mama. He's my big brother," she added earnestly.

Helen smiled. "I'm only joking, dear." She paused. "You know that we'll have nothing but bread and butter tonight if he comes, don't you? He hasn't much to go around himself."

"He might bring us jam," said Pearl, "and it'll still be nice even if he doesn't."

Helen laughed. "You're a good girl, Pearly." She said those words so often. "Of course we can ask Finn."

They reached the Winslows' house a few minutes later and found Finn digging over a last bed in the vegetable patch before the deep freeze came. Helen waved to him and Pearl stayed at the garden gate, chatting, while Helen went up to the back door. Pearl was old enough now that she no longer needed to hide. Helen covered her auburn hair with a headscarf and told her customers that Pearl worked for her; so far, they had accepted the lie.

She exchanged clean washing for dirty at the back door and returned down the garden path. Finn leaned on his turning fork, smiling. The dark earth he'd overturned in the vegetable patch filled the air with its rich smell.

"Finn says he'll come," said Pearl.

Finn nodded. "Last of the Brussels sprouts are in, and it was a good harvest. Mrs. Winslow told the housekeeper to let me have some. She says the garden was better than ever this year."

"Poor Sam was getting so old. I'm sure you're doing a wonderful job," said Helen.

"Brussels sprouts?" Pearl cried. "I love them!"

"Then I'll bring my share tonight," said Finn, "and you can roast them for us, Helen."

"Perfect." Helen laughed. "I'll do that. Here, Pearly, this bag's not so heavy. Give me that smelly one."

"Thank you, Mama!" Pearl took the bag. "Oh, look, there's Mrs. Avery selling fresh bread from her cottage again. They're always cheap, Mama. Should I get some?"

"Good idea." Helen gave her a couple of pennies. "Two loaves, my dear, then there's enough for Finn."

The girl scampered across the street, her bag bouncing in her arms.

"She's grown so much," said Finn. "It hardly seems possible that only a year's past since we met."

Helen touched his arm. "Isn't that true." A sigh escaped her. "Beryl would be eighteen now. A young woman."

Finn tilted his head. "Jack knew a little girl called Beryl years ago. He hardly ever spoke of his past—he never said where he'd grown up or what he'd done before joining us—but he mentioned Beryl a few times."

Helen's heart thumped. "Maybe it was my Beryl."

"It's a common enough name, I suppose," Finn murmured.

"Did he say what she looked like?" Helen asked.

Finn shook his head. "No. Never. Nor where they'd met or how he knew her."

Helen's heart sank. "It might not have been my Beryl at all. Even if it was... well, how would we ever find out more?"

"I shouldn't have said anything," said Finn. "I'm sorry."

"No... it's all right." Helen swallowed. "I'll find her someday." *I'll make good on my promise yet.*

"May I ask you something, Helen?" Finn asked.

She nodded. "Of course."

"Why didn't Beryl and Pearl's father ever help you to find Beryl and get her back?"

Helen froze.

Anger blazed behind Finn's eyes. "Surely he should have done whatever it took to find Beryl."

He would have. Helen almost cried the words. It had been so long since she'd allowed memories of Adrian to bubble to the surface, but she knew with everything in her soul that he would have done anything—anything in the world—to have Beryl in his arms again. He would have scoured every inch of London to find her.

She tried hard not to weep, but could not stop a few tears from spilling over.

"I'm sorry," said Finn quickly.

Helen frantically tried to remember what she had told Finn about Adrian's disappearance and Beryl's kidnapping. She had only ever spoken of Beryl as a small child, yet she was seven years older than Pearl. How could she explain that gap? Would it expose her lies?

"I shouldn't have asked," said Finn. "I understand it must be terribly painful to think of. Let's not talk anymore about it. Let's think of dinner together instead."

Helen forced a smile, but the disapproval in Finn's eyes made her heart sting. Not that she feared he disapproved of *her*—it was Adrian's memory to which his anger was directed.

She had dishonoured her late husband in so many ways already, yet this latest one stung most bitterly of all. How would she ever escape the layers of lies her life had become?

And when she found Beryl, how would she convince her daughter not to tell Pearl that "their" father had died five years before Pearl was born?

Jack's feet throbbed despite the warm water lapping over them. He wriggled his toes, enjoying the Epsom salt soak that Beryl had drawn for his sore, tired feet.

"You're an angel, darling," he said.

Beryl chuckled. "You've said."

Jack smiled. The fire crackled, its flames leaping extravagantly high and filling their cottage with bright warmth. Beryl's first wreath hung over the mantelpiece, its holly berries bright. Jack didn't mention that it was slightly lopsided. The imperfection made it all the more charming.

"Are your poor feet feeling better?" Beryl asked.

"They are, dear, thank you," said Jack. "Did you make up another batch of that poultice for old Warrior?"

"I did," said Beryl. "How is his leg?"

"It feels the cold a little, but once he's had half a mile's slow trot, he's as sound as ever," said Jack. "He likes your poultice. He told me to thank you for it."

Beryl laughed. "Oh, so Warrior talks now, does he?"

"Always has." Jack winked.

Beryl shook her head and returned her attention to the novel in her lap. Its edges were well-worn from much reading over the years. Jack thought of the present he'd ordered her—a brand new copy of *Great Expectations* by Charles Dickens. Beryl adored Dickens, but they'd never been able to afford brand new books. She'd read only his oldest works.

Jack smiled. She would love the book. He couldn't wait for it to come in the post so that he could wrap it in brown paper and tuck it beneath the Christmas tree.

He turned his own attention back to the newspaper in his hand. Slowly, word for word, he skimmed through every single line. The work was endlessly tiresome as he combed through advertisements for lithograph exhibitions, expert carpentry, and those new-fangled toilets that cleaned themselves with flushes of water.

Jack had no interest in any of the words on the paper. It was a specific name that he sought: Mabel Finch. His mother. Though they'd been separated for years after entering the workhouse, and Jack had little hope he would find her, he could leave no stone unturned.

Beryl yawned and lowered her book. "I think I'm going up to bed. Are you coming, love?"

"Not yet." Jack smiled and raised the paper. "Still have a page to finish."

Beryl smiled. "You don't have to finish a whole paper each day, Jackie."

"I might miss something," said Jack. "I might miss *her*."

Beryl rose and rested her hand on his shoulder. "We'll find her someday. You told me to trust the Lord when we moved out here, and look how much it paid off. Keep trusting Him with your mother, too."

Jack closed his eyes and leaned his cheek on her hand. "You're always wise, my love."

"I know," Beryl teased. She kissed his head.

Jack tilted his head back to gaze at her. "What about yours?" he quietly asked.

Beryl looked away. "Your mother had no choice but to go into the workhouse. Mine sold me. I want nothing to do with her."

"Perhaps she had no choice either, my love," said Jack.

Beryl firmly shook her head. "She did. She had the workhouse."

Jack shuddered. "It was not easy either."

"I know." Beryl fixed him with a cold glare. "I spent more time in one than you did, and I still would have preferred that over being sold like an old pair of shoes."

Jack ducked his head. "I'm so sorry, my dear. I didn't mean to upset you."

Beryl sighed and wrapped an arm around his shoulders. "It's all right. It's not your fault. You're not the one who sold me." She pressed her cheek against his hair. "You're the one who found and kept me."

"Forever," Jack murmured.

Beryl hugged him tightly. "Forever."

"I'll be up in a minute," said Jack.

Beryl kissed him again and then climbed the stairs to their bedroom as Jack returned his attention to the paper. He understood that Beryl might not be interested in finding her mother now, but all the same, he kept an eye out for the name Helen Nicols. Just in case.

Chapter Fifteen

Early Christmas decorations hung on several businesses in the streets that the hansom cab passed. Though Mabel tried not to allow her heart to feel troubled, it was difficult to feel anything but dismay on a snowy London evening one year after that devastating Christmas Eve.

Her head leaned against the window, bumping on the glass as the hansom rattled across the cobblestones. Percy's arm tightened around her shoulders.

"Come on, Mae," he said. "Try to be cheerful. It's a good thing that Mr. Goulding's found someone who used to work for Dr. Whitmore. Maybe she'll be able to tell us about Jack!"

"Maybe." Mabel sighed. "Oh, Percy, what use is it? It's been a year. All we know is that Dr. Whitmore's widow moved to Essex and died before the winter was out. Jack could be anywhere... just as it's been all these years."

"It's all the use in the world, Mae. We're going to find our boy and bring you two back together," said Percy.

"We've been saying that for so many years… fifteen? Sixteen?" Mabel sighed. "I can hardly remember, only that it's been a lifetime." She finally spoke the words she'd spent her life hiding from. "Percy, what if we never find him?"

"We can't stop trying," said Percy gently.

Mabel closed her eyes. She knew she couldn't, and she hated the part of herself that wanted to. It would be so much easier to grieve her son and mourn his loss than to suffer this terrible, heart-wrenching hope every time Nathan came up with a tiny lead.

The hansom rattled to a halt before the investigator's office. Percy paid the driver extra to wait and they climbed the stairs to the nondescript office, where they found Nathan sitting behind his sturdy desk. A woman sat opposite him. Though her face was youthful, younger than Mabel's, her gnarled and knotted fingers testified to many, many hours of work.

"Mr. and Mrs. Mitchell, it's so good to see you." Nathan rose. "Thank you for coming so close to the holiday season."

"It's no trouble, Mr. Goulding." Percy shook his hand. "Mabel and I were in London tying up the last of our business before Christmas in any case." He glanced at the woman. "Is this…?"

"This is Miss Josie Spinner," said Nathan. "She used to work as a maid for Mrs. Whitmore."

"I knew Jack," said Josie.

Mabel's heart clenched, and she realized that this was the first time she'd spoken face-to-face with someone who had known her son in the past fifteen years. "You did? Do you know where he is now?"

Josie hung her head. "Sorry, ma'am. I don't. If I did, I would tell you, so I would. Jack used to talk about his mother so often and with such great fondness."

Tears flooded Mabel's eyes. She fought them back, but a tightness of more than a decade suddenly eased in her chest. *He knows. He understands that I wouldn't have left him in that workhouse if I had had any other choice*. She had spent all these years fearing that Jack felt she had abandoned him wilfully, that he thought she didn't want him, when the opposite was true.

"Is he all right?" Mabel croaked. "Is he— is he—" She hardly knew how to ask.

Josie smiled from ear to ear. "Oh, Mrs. Mitchell, he's a fine young man." She giggled. "*Very* fine! The maids don't talk much to the men who work outside, you know, but we all knew who handsome Jack Finch was. We used to watch him working with the horses, talking to them all gently, petting them."

"He got that from his mother," said Percy, smiling.

"Was he happy?" Mabel whispered.

"We were all happy with Dr. Whitmore, Mrs. Mitchell. He was a good, good man, so he was. Paid us well, treated us well. Jack too." Josie paused. "Well, I suppose he was. Like I say, we didn't talk much. I only knew who he was from watching him through the window and from hearing the other maids talk. Everyone liked him, but of course, he would never pay any of us any attention."

Mabel frowned. "Why not?"

"Oh, of course. You wouldn't know," said Josie. "Jack's married."

Mabel's heart fluttered. "M-married?"

"To a pretty girl with red hair," said Josie. "I don't know her name, but I know that he only had eyes for her."

Mabel covered her mouth with her hands. Her dear Jack, working for a good man and married to a pretty redhead! It was wonderful, glorious. She'd seen the Whitmore estate. She could imagine him being happy there with his little wife.

"Please," she croaked, lowering her hands. "Please, don't you know where he went?"

Josie's face fell. "I'm so sorry, ma'am. Mrs. Whitmore only took her lady's maid with her when she moved to Essex. Everyone else found other work. I wouldn't know where to begin to look for them, and they're the only ones left who might know where Jack went. I certainly don't."

"I've thought of asking people who knew Mrs. Whitmore what might have become of him," said Nathan quietly, "but I'm afraid my few attempts were not well-received. It would not be ladylike for a well-bred woman such as she to discuss her stablemaster with others."

"I understand," Mabel croaked, cursing their arrogance. "You're sure you have no idea, Miss Spinner?"

Josie shook her head. "I'm sorry. None. He could be anywhere."

The words sank deep into Mabel's soul, stabbing like icicles. Jack had been happy, yes. But now...

He could be anywhere.

Adrian's eyes shimmered as the candles in the window by the Christmas tree reflected in them. He sat cross-legged amid a pile of torn brown paper wrappings, gazing up at the stars, Beryl curled up in her lap. It was only her second Christmas, and even in her sleep, she clutched her new ragdoll with fierce joy.

Helen came in with two cups of eggnog. She handed one to Adrian and sank down beside him, smiling.

"Christmas only gets more beautiful," Adrian murmured. "Seeing it again through the eyes of a child... it's magical."

"I know." Helen pillowed her head on his shoulder. *"You make it magical for both of us."*

Adrian smiled. She felt the prickle of his beard as he kissed her forehead. Helen leaned against him, wishing that this moment could last forever.

"Then why did you sell her?" Adrian asked. "Why haven't you found her?"

Helen opened her eyes. "What?"

Adrian stared at her, his smile still in place. "Helen, you sold our child. Why haven't you been looking for her?"

"Adrian, she's right—" Helen stopped. Adrian's lap was empty.

"Where is she?" he asked.

"I don't know!" Helen cried. She scrambled to her feet and staggered back as the cottage walls melted and fell around her, replaced by the cold, icy streets of London in winter. "I don't know where she is!"

"She was my child, your last link to me," said Adrian, "and you lost her."

"I'm sorry, Adrian," Helen sobbed. "Please..."

"Did you stop loving me, Helen?" Adrian sat beneath the tree; it was all that was left the cosy scene. The London streets swirled and vanished, replaced by the crashing grey waves of the sea, boiling and breaking around him in pale foam. "Did you stop caring?"

"No!" Helen cried.

"Did you forget?" Adrian whispered.

"Adrian, no!" Helen screamed.

She tried to run toward him, but an inexorable force dragged her backward. No matter how fast her legs moved, they could not close the distance between them. She tried to cry out, but no sound came. She could not warm him, she could not save him.

She could do nothing as the grey wave broke over his head and engulfed him, Christmas tree and all.

Helen sat up, a gasp ripping from her lips. Cold sweat shimmered on her skin.

"Mama!" Pearl lifted her head from the pillow beside Helen's. "What's wrong? Are you all right?"

Helen's heart pounded as she wrapped an arm around Pearl. "Shhh. Everything's fine, my dear. It was only a dream."

Pearl lowered her head, and soon her breathing returned to the slow rhythm of sleep. But Helen stayed awake for a long time after that, watching the flicker of Christmas candles in the window, knowing that it was not only a dream.

Adrian was right. She had forgotten him.

The washing bag felt a hundred times heavier than usual, weighing hard in Helen's arms as she plodded up the garden path to the Winslows' back door. Lack of sleep and sheer exhaustion burned her eyes as she approached.

"Here, Mama." Pearl held out her arms. "Let me take it."

"No, it's all right," Helen mumbled.

"Mama, I can see you didn't sleep well. You seem so tired." Concern shone in Pearl's eyes. "You sit here on the bench in the sunshine for a minute. I can carry this. I'm strong."

Helen sighed. "Yes," she said. "Yes, you are."

She gave the bag to Pearl, who strode between the frozen vegetable patches to the back door. Despite the unseasonable, bright sunlight pouring from the sky, it was too cold for last night's snow to return to slush. Instead, the sunshine made the pure white surface sparkle.

Helen sagged onto the bench by the garden wall. *Oh, Adrian.* It had been so long since she allowed herself to remember the smell of his beard and the colour of his eyes.

The greenhouse door nearby opened. "Hello, Helen!"

She raised her head, smiling. "Good morning, Finn."

Finn shut the greenhouse door and brushed soil from his hands as he approached her. "Are you all right? Usually Pearl waits here while you take the washing to the door."

Helen knotted her hands in her apron. Grey stains from endless hours bent over the vats marred the pale fabric. She thought of the vow she'd made all those Christmases ago—a vow to find Beryl—and her throat knotted.

"Oh, Helen!" Finn sat beside her. "What's wrong?"

"It's Beryl," Helen croaked.

"I'm so sorry. Is it what I said?" Finn asked.

Helen shook her head. "No... no. It's... I just miss her, Finn. I miss her more with every passing year. Each time I see Pearl grow up a little more... I see what I missed with Beryl."

Finn rubbed his chin. "There must be a way to find her."

"I don't know," said Helen faintly. "It's been so very long. Maybe she's—" She wouldn't let herself say the word *dead*.

"We have to start somewhere," said Finn firmly. "You used to live by the docks, didn't you? That's a long way from here. We don't have much chance finding her looking around here."

"No," Helen murmured, "we don't. We'd have to search all London. It's impossible, I'm telling you."

"Maybe not." Finn beamed. "I learned to read a little—the housekeeper here is helping me—and I read the papers sometimes. There are stories and advertisements in there from all over the city."

Helen raised her head. "What are you saying?"

"Well," said Finn, "why don't we put something in the paper asking about Beryl?"

Helen blinked. "Something like what?"

"We could put everything in it that you remember about her," said Finn. "It's a shot in the dark, isn't it? But it's not impossible."

Helen's hands shook at the thought. What if she placed the advertisement and never heard anything?

Or what if she *did* find Beryl? What would she tell her? Beryl would know that Pearl wasn't Adrian's child. She would reveal everything...

"I know it'll cost something," said Finn, "but we'll find a way to afford it, I know we will. I can see how it's eating at you, Helen. I want to help you if I can."

Helen squeezed her eyes shut. Adrian's words from her dream rang through her mind. *She was my child, your last link to me, and you lost her.*

A sense of duty stung deep in her chest. The dream was right; she owed it to the man who'd loved her so deeply to find his daughter once more.

"All right," she croaked. "All right, let's do it."

Finn beamed. "All we have to do is find out what it costs and how to afford it."

"How to afford what?" Pearl asked, striding up to them with a bag of laundry.

Helen inhaled, doubting for a second, but spoke knowing that she was doing the right thing—perhaps for the first time in a long while. "Finn had the good idea of putting something in the paper to help us find Beryl."

Pearl's eyes lit up. "Oh, Mama, that's a wonderful idea! It would be so, so good to find her. I've missed her all my life even though I never knew her. I would love to know my sister."

Half-sister, Helen thought, and her lie seemed heavier than ever. "I want her back, too, pet. But it'll cost money to put an advertisement in the paper. We barely have enough to go around."

Pearl tucked the bag under her arm. "We have to find a way to make a little more."

"How?" Helen asked. "We hardly have room for all our laundry."

"Not with laundry." Pearl grinned. "Mama, can we buy a little extra flour, butter, and sugar if we have only bread for supper tomorrow?"

"We could," said Helen, "but why?"

"Because I'll bake gingerbread men and ice them." Pearl raised her chin. "We could sell them in the market or to the housekeepers when we bring the washing. I saw the baker was selling a dozen gingerbread men for thruppence."

"You *do* make the best gingerbread men," said Finn.

"Pearly, my dear, that's a wonderful idea." Helen took the laundry bag. "We'll do that on our way home. I'll help you to bake and ice a batch tonight."

"If we get thruppence for a dozen, we can buy more flour and make more," said Pearl, excited. "We'll soon have enough money for the paper, Mama, you'll see."

She skipped away, singing in time with her footsteps. Helen's heart felt almost unbearably full. She gave Finn a quick smile, then followed Pearl onto the street.

The little heap of coins glimmered on the kitchen table in Helen's cottage. Despite the late hour, Pearl's eyes glowed with excitement as she gazed at them.

"Two pennies, a sixpence, and a ha'penny bit," she said. "That's enough for the advertisement."

"All thanks to you, Pearly." Finn ruffled her hair.

"It's true." Helen placed cups of tea in front of everyone and sat at the table. "You did a wonderful thing, pet. She was up every night icing gingerbread men until late, Finn. Why, this poor child hardly slept more than a few hours a night for a whole week."

"It's worth it if we can find Beryl," said Pearl firmly.

Helen had spent her last half-penny on a bit of paper and a stub of pencil from one of the scruffy street sellers. She spread the slightly rumpled paper on the table and raised her pencil.

"What should it say?" she murmured.

"Everything you can think of it that could help to identify Beryl," said Finn. "What she looked like, perhaps, and her whole name and where she came from."

Helen slowly and painstakingly scribbled the words.

In search of Beryl Nicols, 18. Lost near docks 14 years ago. Red hair, blue eyes.

"She sounds beautiful," said Pearl softly. "Her hair must have looked like yours, Mama."

"It was brighter." Helen struggled not to cry.

"Do you know anything else?" Finn asked.

Yes. I know that I sold her to a man named Simeon Cragg. The shame made a tear spill over.

"Oh, Mama, please don't cry," said Pearl.

Helen cleared her throat. "I'm sorry. It's a hard thing to think of."

"Of course it is," said Finn gently. "Let's not talk about the time she was stolen from you."

Stolen! I sold her. The weight of Helen's deception made her want to scream.

"Instead, let's put in anything you've heard about her since," Finn added.

Helen stroked her hair, thinking. The lie came with an ease she hated. "I heard rumours once about a girl her age with red hair working for a chimney sweep."

"That's good, Helen!" said Finn encouragingly. "Do you know which one?"

Helen squared her shoulders. "Smudge Blackwood." She paused. "I tried to ask him about her, but he chased me off and beat me." That much was true, at least.

"Oh, Mama," said Pearl, her voice filled with compassion Helen felt she didn't deserve.

"Put that in," said Finn. "It could help."

Helen bent over the advertisement and laboriously scratched out the words. *May have worked for sweep Smudge Blackwood*. "That's all I have," she said. Her voice softened. "Oh, it seems like so very little."

"It's a start, Helen." Finn stood. "Quickly, give it to me. The paper might still be open. I'll run and give it to them."

"I'll come with you," said Pearl.

Helen shook her head. "No, Pearly, you stay inside out of the cold. We can do this tomorrow."

"No!" Finn grinned. "If I give it to them now, they could print it for tomorrow's edition. We'll get answers even sooner then, Helen." He held out his hand. "Let me take it for you quickly."

Helen blinked back tears of gratitude. She thrust the paper and money into Finn's hand, and he paused to pat the top of Pearl's head, then swept out of the door and into the snow before she could thank him.

She sent a prayer after him instead, a brief and timorous one. *Lord, I know I don't deserve it. But please, please, help us to find Beryl.*

Pearl gripped her hand. "We'll find her, Mama."

Helen wrapped her arms around her little girl and could only hope that it was true.

Chapter Sixteen

Despite the few happy years Jack had spent working for Dr. Whitmore, returning to London town always sent a shiver down his spine. The tall mare beside him felt his nervousness and blew loudly, steam rolling on her breath.

He tightened his grip on the reins. "Now, now, old lass, no need for that."

The mare shook her ears, but steadied. It was her calm eye that had caught Jack's attention at the sale.

"Beryl will like you," Jack told her. "She'll give you a name, don't you worry. You'll work hard, lass—that's why I came to buy you; things are getting too busy for my others around Christmastime—but you'll have all the hay and oats you can eat and an apple from my wife every Sunday."

The mare bobbed her head as though she understood him.

Jack smiled. "Good girl." He rubbed her neck, feeling a strange mixture of gratitude and awe swelling in him. Who would ever have thought that Sea Crescent Livery would have all its stables filled only a year after he'd started it?

He reached the inn and handed the mare to a stable lad before going inside to warm his hands at the fire. A holly wreath hung over the hearth, not lopsided like Beryl's, which only made him miss his wife more than ever. He'd hired a boy from a local farm to look after the horses while he was gone for a night, but he knew Beryl would be out there helping him to toss hay and wrap legs anyway.

He would buy her something nice on his way out of London tomorrow, he thought—something in addition to the book. Perhaps a chocolate bar if he could find one. They were wonderful, new, exotic things and she loved them.

Jack climbed the stairs to his room at the inn, where mistletoe draped the doorway. A young maid scurried past with a mop and bucket. She paused when she saw Jack.

"Mr. Finch, sir," she said, "I found the papers you asked for. They're on your pillow."

"Thank you very much, Rose." Jack gave her a penny.

The maid hurried off, grinning, and Jack entered his room. He'd asked for a stack of London papers to go through in search of his mother—and, secretly, Beryl's. They lay on the pillow, crisply folded, and Jack pushed them aside to sprawl on the bed and feel the ache of a long day in his legs.

He turned the gas light on, picked up the first paper, and started reading the first page. An insert tumbled out of it onto the covers.

"Whoops," said Jack. He picked up the insert and went to put it on his nightstand when his eye caught on a name: *Beryl Nicols*.

Jack laughed at himself. He missed his wife so much that his mind was playing tricks on him. "Silly," he chided. But he couldn't resist looking over the page just in case, and his breath hitched.

There it was, plain as day, his wife's maiden name in print: *Beryl Nicols*.

Jack flung the other papers aside, his blood pounding so hard that he felt his pulse in his fingers as he read the block of text surrounding her name.

In search of Beryl Nicols, 18. Lost near docks 14 years ago. Red hair, blue eyes.

"Red hair," Jack whispered. "Blue eyes." It sounded just like her, but he was not absolutely certain until he read the last line: *May have worked for sweep Smudge Blackwood.*

Jack shot to his feet, the other papers falling, forgotten, to the floor. Smudge Blackwood! The name was a dreadful bolt from his past—so awful that he'd never spoken it to anyone, not even to Finn Hargrove, his best friend from the gang of thieves in his misspent youth. It was the name of the chimney sweep where he and Beryl had worked when they were tiny children.

There was no name at the end of the advertisement, only an address across London. Jack didn't care how late it was. He knew that someone was searching for his wife, and he had to find out why—and whom.

He ran down the stairs, ignoring a cry of surprise from Rose as he shouldered on his coat and rushed to the stables. The lads panicked at the sight of a guest, but he ignored them as Warrior neighed over the stable door to him. Jack seized his saddle from the rack by the door and flung it onto his horse's back. In moments, Warrior was charging down the street in a fine temper, nostrils flared, hooves clattering on the cobblestones.

Perhaps the person looking for Beryl was some cruel figure from her past, one whom Jack would crush rather than allowing anything to happen to his wife.

But perhaps this advertisement was the answer to Jack's heartfelt prayer of the past two weeks: that they would find Beryl's mother.

Helen hung the last piece of laundry with hands that trembled in weariness. She stretched her raw, chapped fingers, the skin pulling painfully over her knuckles.

"All done," said Pearl cheerfully, placing a basket upside down on the floor to dry. "We'll fold it up and iron it tomorrow morning before taking it to the customers."

"You're an angel, Pearly." Helen wrapped an arm around her shoulders and kissed her cheek. "Come on, let's have supper. I'm ready for bed."

They went upstairs, leaving the laundry hanging by the boiler. Helen's back ached from bending double over the vat and scrubbing. She put the kettle on and Pearl fetched a loaf of bread from the cupboard and began to cut it.

"I'm afraid there's no butter," said Helen, "only cheese." They'd spent everything they had on making the gingerbread men that had funded today's advertisement. Finn had used his own money to bring them a copy of the paper that morning before work; it lay on the corner of the table, Beryl's name in print for all to see, but Helen doubted anything would come of it.

"I don't mind, Mama." Pearl brilliantly smiled. "If we find Beryl, none of it matters."

If, Helen thought. She offered a silent prayer that this would be the case.

A knock at the door made her jump as she prepared the tea. "Who might that be?"

"Finn, I suppose," said Pearl. "I'll go." She lowered the knife.

"No, it's all right," said Helen. "We can't be sure. I'll answer it."

She left the tea and went to the front door. When she pushed it open, at first she saw only a stranger, and a gasp of terror wrenched from her. She grabbed the door to slam it in his face, but something about his voice made her freeze.

"Good evening. I'm sorry to have startled you," he said.

Helen stared at him. It was not his words that made her hesitate, but the way in which he delivered them. His tone held tremendous gentleness. When she met his eyes, they, too, were deep and warm, filled with kindness. He reminded her of Finn.

He was a handsome young man, perhaps Finn's age, with well-kept dark hair. Though his clothes were plain, they were sturdy and appeared new. Helen's experienced eye picked out no mends and noted that the seams were strong and the fabric thick—far better than anything bought from a slopshop. Leather reins hung over his arm, attached to an elderly chestnut horse with fiery eyes. Snow trickled from the sky, settling in white flakes on his mane.

"Who are you?" Helen asked, keeping a firm grip on the doorknob.

The young man removed his cap and held it in front of him. "My name is Jack Finch. I'm sorry to disturb at this late hour, but I'm leaving London tomorrow morning and I had to know..." He paused. "I'm here about the advertisement regarding Beryl Nicols."

Helen froze as though the cold had turned her into a pillar of ice. She stared into the young man's eyes, drenched in emotion; it was so intense that she could not tell if she felt terror, joy, or both.

"You know Beryl?" she croaked.

"Yes, ma'am," said Jack.

"Is she all right?" Helen stumbled through the door and clutched his lapels. "Is she still alive? Is my little girl still safe?"

Jack's eyes widened. "Are you—"

"Helen," she cried. "I'm Helen Nicols, her mother."

Jack's grin glowed like the star atop a Christmas tree.

"I'm her husband," he said.

Helen snatched her hands back and clutched them to her mouth as she stared at him. Could it be true? Could it be that this sweet young man had married her Beryl?

"Mama, who's that?" Pearl called.

"Stay inside!" Helen barked. She backed away. No, no! She couldn't trust him, not like this. "You married my daughter?"

"Oh, Mrs. Nicols, I'm so glad to finally meet you," Jack cried. "My sweet Beryl has missed you all this time. She seldom says it, but I know she does."

Helen clutched the door for support. "How can I be sure you truly know Beryl… *my* Beryl?"

Jack smiled. "Firstly, because I can describe her to you. She has more than red hair and blue eyes. Her hair is as red as fire, as red as a coal, and her eyes—they're like jewels. They pierce you. She has freckles, too." His eyes searched hers. "I can see the resemblance in you, Mrs. Nicols. She told me that her mother's name was Helen."

Helen said nothing. He had yet to prove anything; she had given him her name.

Jack's tone softened. "And her father's name was Adrian."

Adrian. Helen's heart leaped within her at the sound of that name. It resounded to the deepest part of her, rattling her bones, making her breath freeze in her lungs. Oh, Adrian! She had seldom mentioned his name to anyone but Pearl and Finn; she had neglected to put it in the advertisement.

It was true. This young man was married to her daughter. Adrian's name lit the way, a lighthouse in the darkness, guiding her in death as he had done in life.

Helen realized that she had plastered her hands over her mouth and tears coursed over her cheeks. "She's all right?" she burst out.

"Beryl is perfectly all right, Mrs. Nicols. She's warm and safe in our cosy cottage with everything she needs," said Jack.

The news made Helen's knees buckle. She clung to the doorframe to keep from falling. "Oh, Jack—oh, Jack!"

He stepped forward and steadied her with a hand on her arm. "Thank God! I can't believe we finally found you." His eyes were misty. "We live in a village by the sea near London. I wish to take you there right away, Mrs. Nicols. I want Beryl to have her mother home for Christmas."

Christmas with Beryl in a village by the sea! The notion was so overwhelming that Helen could barely breathe. What would she do? What would she tell her? What would she say when she realized that Pearl could not possibly be Adrian's daughter? But the thought of seeing Beryl again swept all the frightening possibilities from Helen's mind. She would come up with something, she would spin a story about Adrian coming home after Beryl was "taken" and then returning to sea to drown. She would lie. She would do whatever was necessary to be with her daughter that Christmas.

"Mama?" Pearl called. "Who is it?"

"Who is that?" Jack asked.

"That—that's Beryl's sister," said Helen. "Pearl."

Jack's eyes widened. She wondered if Beryl had told him everything, if he realized that Pearl was illegitimate, and panic gripped her head. But perhaps he thought that she had been widowed again. At any rate, he made no comment except to say, "Pearl must come with us, too."

"I haven't any money," Helen confessed.

"That's all right." Jack smiled. "I'll pay for everything. I'll take you there, not to worry."

"You will? Oh, Jack—how can you be so kind?" Helen cried. It was a genuine question; she barely believed her ears.

Jack smiled. "I'm leaving in the morning. Does that suit you?"

"I—" Helen was flustered. "I'm a washerwoman... I'll need to speak to my customers. Perhaps the other washerwomen can look after them for a day or two. I'll need to get back to my business shortly..."

"Don't worry. I'll bring you home as soon as you want," Jack promised.

"All right." Helen gulped. "I'll speak to them tomorrow morning."

"Then I will be here tomorrow at lunchtime to bring you to Beryl." Jack beamed. "Don't worry, Mrs. Nicols. All will soon be well."

Looking into his gentle brown eyes, Helen could almost believe it.

"God rest ye merry, gentlemen! Let nothing you dismay," Jack sang against the backdrop of clattering hooves. "Remember Christ our Saviour was born on Christmas Day to save us all from Satan's pow'r when we were gone astray. Oh tidings of comfort and joy, comfort and joy!"

The merry clatter of the black mare in harness felt like Providence to Jack. He had purchased her as an all-rounder, but it seemed she truly shone in the brougham he had hired for the occasion.

She flung out her toes with a fine spirit, red and green ribbons in her flowing mane to celebrate the occasion. Warrior, tied to the side of the cart, appeared deeply peeved.

"Sorry, old boy." Jack laughed. "But wait till you see Beryl's face when we come around the corner with her family!"

He briefly wondered how Pearl had come about. Helen had said that the girl was Beryl's "sister", not "half-sister." But he supposed it was not his place to ask. He was far too happy about finding Beryl's mother to worry about such details, and, after all, it would be indelicate to ask.

All that mattered was making Beryl happy—and he knew that seeing her mother again would be the best Christmas gift she could have dreamed of.

He slowed the mare to make the turn onto the narrow street where Helen lived. Children peered from the cottage windows in awe as Jack drove past. This place reminded him of the neighbourhood where he'd swept chimneys with Smudge Blackwood as a child. The memory sent a shiver down his spine, but he still admired the wreaths on all the doorways and the blankets of snow sparkling on the rooftops. Christmas made even London beautiful.

He halted the horses outside Helen's little cottage, noticing the broken pane that was boarded up. Poor Helen—life had not been easy for her. But he could make it much, much easier soon. He secretly hoped that she would stay in the village with them. There had to be work for a washerwoman in the village, or perhaps far more decent work, something that Helen could do in the warm without hurting her back. He would work something out. The Lord would provide.

Jack tied the mare to a ring on the wall and strode to the front door, whistling the Christmas carol. He briskly knocked on the door and stepped back, waiting for Helen to answer it.

The door swung open, but did not reveal Helen. Instead, Jack had to tip back his head to look into a familiar face that he thought he would never see again. His heart thumped sharply in his chest.

He thought perhaps that he was dreaming. Maybe he had dreamed all of it, from finding Helen to this strange moment.

"Finn?" he croaked.

The burly young man's green eyes filled with tears. "Jack!" he cried. "Helen said it was Jack Finch, but I—I couldn't believe it until I saw you, and— it's you. Jack, it's really you!"

Jack had last seen Finn as a street thief, but he didn't care. He flung his arms around the taller young man and embraced him, laughing.

"How?" he cried. "How are you here?"

"I'm friends with Helen... well, she's become more like a mother to me," said Finn. "She came to me this morning asking if I could go with her to see Beryl; she wished for a male companion to protect her, you understand."

"Of course." Jack nodded. "I am a stranger to her, after all."

"She said the young man's name was Jack Finch and I remembered that you talked about a girl called Beryl, but I never dreamed... you married her?" Finn cried.

"I did, but Finn, tell me about you!" Jack gasped.

Finn shook his head. "Oh, Jackie, I'm so sorry for how I treated you when you left the gang. I soon realized that you were right and left myself not long after that. I had many hard times, but now I work as a gardener for a kind family nearby. They were content to give me one day off since it's winter and there's little to do in the garden. They're terribly good people."

"Then I'm delighted you're coming to Sea Crescent with me," said Jack. "Finn, this is wonderful. I can't tell you how happy I am to see you so well and happy."

"The straight and narrow road has been harsh at times, but I know it's the right one," said Finn, "all thanks to you."

Jack had to swallow his tears. "Oh, Finn, this is an even better Christmas miracle than I could ever have hoped for!"

Helen appeared behind Finn. She was smiling, but worry lined her face, surprising Jack. He wondered why she appeared so anguished. Why would Beryl be anything but delighted to see her? Helen could at last tell the full story of what happened, and Beryl would realize that she had been taken, not sold. Helen would not have advertised looking for her daughter if she'd sold her, after all.

"Is it your Jack then, Finn?" Helen asked.

Finn beamed. "It is! Come on, Helen. Let's go!"

A little girl of about ten or eleven appeared in the cottage doorway. She had deep auburn hair, but her brown eyes were unfamiliar. "Hello," she said. "I'm Pearl, Beryl's sister."

Jack smiled and bowed to her. "It's wonderful to meet you, Pearl. Have you ever ridden in a carriage?"

Pearl giggled. "Never."

"Then you're in for a real treat," said Jack.

He held the door for his passengers and climbed onto the driver's seat with a light heart. It was as though the black mare understood the joyousness of the occasion, for when she set off, she flung her feet so high that her jingling harness bells sounded like they could have belonged to a whole team of reindeer.

Chapter Seventeen

"Here we are!" Jack called. "The next turn takes us to my yard."

Helen was aware that her mouth hung open in shock as they drove down the street, but she couldn't help it. Sheer joy made her heart flutter at the sight of the little village slumbering among the foothills. Warm yellow light spilled from the windows beneath the grey day, casting golden shadows upon the deep banks of snow that lay between the houses. Dark streaks of smoke rose from the chimneys and put her in mind of bubbling kettles and crackling fires. Everywhere she looked, the cottages were bright and ready for Christmas. Every door had a holly wreath and every window a candle. A great Christmas tree stood in the market square, its decorations now half-buried beneath snow.

The snow was still coming down swiftly as they clattered down the street, moving slowly as the carriage wheels crunched in the snow. Helen could hardly believe that this place was her Beryl's home. This was beyond anything she had ever dreamed of or dared to pray for.

Any minute now, she would look into the jewel-bright eyes Beryl had inherited from her father. The excitement she felt was almost unbearable.

The carriage turned down a short driveway leading between bare oak trees, their branches gnarled and empty, and they drove toward a small, cobbled yard with stables on either side and a charming cottage at the back. Mistletoe hung everywhere and candlelight flickered in the cottage windows.

"Oh, Jack," Finn cried through the window. "Is this really yours?"

"We're renting it for now," said Jack, "but I hope I can buy the property in the next few years. The business is mine, and all the horses." He whistled, and horses popped their heads over the doors and whinnied to him in welcome.

"Oh, look at them, Mama!" Pearl clutched her arm. "They're all so pretty!"

This was a place of perfect love, joy, and peace. Helen hardly knew how to feel. She was delighted that Beryl lived here, of course... but already she felt like a blight upon the place, the only stain upon the white fabric of this happy home.

She was rooted to the seat with fear when Jack stopped the brougham. A young lad, perhaps a little older than Pearl, bustled from the feed room.

"Master Jack!" he called. "You're home early."

"I made good time. We found a nice one, lad," said Jack, patting the mare's neck. "Rub her down well, and Warrior, too. Don't forget the liniment for his legs, and then you can run along home."

"Yes, guv," said the boy.

"Where's the missus?" Jack asked.

"She's in the cottage, guv," said the boy.

Jack turned to Helen, eyes shining. "Come on! I can't wait to tell her who you are."

Helen's heart panged with terror as Finn disembarked from the brougham. Jack was already at the front door, knocking and calling his wife's name.

"Beryl! Darling! You'll never guess who I've brought with me!"

Helen had imagined a dozen lies on the journey from London, lies that would make Beryl accept her, not reject her as so many had done when she sought work while pregnant with Pearl. She ran through her falsified story in her mind, making sure that she would make no mistakes when telling it.

"Beryl!" Jack called.

Footsteps clattered behind the door.

"Come on, Mama." Pearl nudged her. "I want to get out."

Helen had no choice but to move. She slid from the brougham and shuffled to the door as it swung open.

All the lies in Helen's mind evaporated the instant she laid her eyes upon her daughter and realized how much she had truly lost when she had sold the child in her desperation. Beryl had grown into the most striking young woman Helen had ever seen, but it was more than her flame-red hair and brilliant eyes that made her breath-taking. It was the warmth of her smile and the deep kindness that lay beyond it. Flour coated her hands to the elbow and charmingly streaked across her cheek. She was the most beautiful thing Helen had ever seen, in so many different ways.

"Jackie!" Beryl hugged him, keeping her floury hands from his clothes. "You're home early!"

"I brought you something, my darling." Jack beamed and stepped back.

Beryl's bright eyes landed on Helen, and she froze.

"Hello, dear," Helen croaked.

Tears flooded Beryl's eyes. "M—Mama?"

The crack in her tone stabbed deep into Helen's chest. She stepped forward. "Yes," she whispered. "It's me."

"What are you doing here?" Beryl croaked.

"Your mother didn't sell you, Beryl. It's like I said," said Jack, beaming. "I was in London when I saw an advertisement in the paper. She was looking for you. She's been looking for you all this time, I'm sure!"

His words sent a deep pang of guilt through Helen.

"Is... is this true?" Beryl whispered, turning to her.

Helen's lie lay ready. She could tell it effortlessly, spinning a story that would make Beryl love her, and yet not a single word would pass between her lips.

She couldn't lie to Beryl, she realized. She had done enough wrong to her. Lying was one injustice to which she could not stoop.

"I was looking for you," Helen croaked. "I have been for a while... I always wanted you back."

Beryl slowly wiped her hands on her apron, a tear spilling over. "You didn't mean for me to be taken away?"

"Go on, Helen," Finn urged. "Tell her!"

Helen squeezed her eyes shut. The weight of her lies had become far too much for her.

"I'm sorry, Beryl," she whispered. "I thought I didn't have a choice." She opened her eyes.

Jack's head snapped around to face Helen. Finn emitted a strangled gasp.

Beryl's face darkened. "Tell me the truth, Mama. Was I taken? Did someone kidnap me that day in the marketplace?"

Helen could not hold the truth back for a moment longer. She couldn't lie to Beryl.

"No," she croaked. "A man gave me money to take you away to Mr. Blackwood."

"What?" Jack cried.

"Helen, you said—" Finn began.

Helen didn't care about either of them; she focused only on Beryl, hating the terrible cold in her daughter's eyes.

"Please, darling, you must understand," she cried, stepping toward her. "You have to know that I thought you would starve and die on the streets with me. I did it to save your life. I wanted you to live! I thought Mr. Blackwood would treat me well!"

"You thought a *chimney sweep* would treat me well?" Beryl cried.

"It was better than dying on the streets!" Helen gasped.

"Please, darling." Jack laid a hand on Beryl's shoulder. "Hear her out. It was a very, very long time ago. She's searched for you now. She thought she was saving you."

A shudder ran through Beryl. She struggled with her emotions, and Helen held her breath. Maybe, just maybe, Beryl would forgive her.

Pearl shuffled forward. Helen could tell from the look on her face that she did not understand what was happening, but she extended her hand to Beryl.

"Hello, Beryl," she said softly. "My name is Pearl. I'm your little sister."

"My—my sister?" Beryl's eyes widened and grew soft. She stepped forward, then hesitated. "Half-sister, I mean." She turned to Helen. "Mama, I'm glad you remarried."

"No, no," said Pearl. "I'm *your* sister, Beryl."

Beryl's eyes narrowed.

"Tell her, Helen," Finn urged quietly.

His loyalty despite knowing she'd lied about selling Beryl made tears spill over Helen's cheeks.

"I'm sorry. I'm so sorry," she burst out. "It made it easier for Pearl if she—if she thought that Adrian father to both of you—but— I never remarried, and—"

"You had a child out of wedlock?" Beryl cried.

Finn took a swift step away from Helen as though she had become suddenly contaminated.

"Why would you do such a thing?" Beryl shrieked.

"What does that mean?" Pearl asked, confused.

"I'm sorry," Helen cried. "I'm sorry about all of it."

"We can talk about all this," Jack pleaded. "Let's go inside, and—"

"No." Finn turned away. "She lied to me... all this time, she's been lying to me."

"I don't understand," Pearl cried.

"Please forgive me, Beryl," Helen pleaded. "I did what I thought I had to do to survive and protect you and Pearl. I had no choice!"

Beryl raised a hand to her face; her cheeks were ashen. Jack's arm tightened around her.

"Please go away," Beryl croaked.

"Beryl—" Helen stepped forward.

"I told you to get out of my sight!" Beryl shouted.

Helen had heard those angry words many times from people on the street or housekeepers she had approached for work, but this time was different. Her own daughter's rejection cut deep into her heart. No, they felt more like they sliced into her belly, eviscerating her.

"Beryl, darling..." Jack began.

Beryl wrenched from her husband's arms. "Leave me be!" she cried, and rushed into the cottage, sobbing.

Helen turned to Finn for help, but one look at his face told her that he was as angry and hurt as Beryl.

Why should he not be? She had lied to him all this time. He had looked up to her as a maternal figure in his life, and Helen had disappointed him in the deepest way possible.

"I'm sorry," she whispered.

Finn recoiled. "How could you?"

"Don't talk to my mama like that!" Pearl yelled.

Pain flooded Finn's features. Pain surrounded Helen, and she knew that she was the cause of it all.

"Come, Pearl." She grabbed the girl's arm.

"Mama, what's happening?" Pearl cried.

"Mrs. Nicols—" Jack began.

"Pearl, *come*!" Helen cried.

She yanked on Pearl's arm and ran across the stable yard, tears flying over her cheeks and freezing in the cold air. She heard Jack call after her, but she ignored him, and no one followed her out of the stable yard and into the cold, unfamiliar streets.

Jack's heart felt as weighty as a cannonball in his chest. He thrust his hands deep into his pockets as he trudged across the market square, clutching a tray of the plum pudding from the local baker that Beryl loved so much but did not yet know how to make. It would be their dessert this Christmas Eve to go with the fruit cake she'd made.

Perhaps it would make her look at him with warmth again, and not the cold distance he'd felt between them for the past few days—ever since he'd brought Helen back from London.

The golden light of Christmas candles tucked into the boughs of the tree at the marketplace's centre fell around Jack, bright as a halo. He stopped to gaze up at the paper angel perched at the tree's very top, her wings trembling delicately in the gentle breeze.

Oh, Lord, he prayed silently, *what have I done?*

"Any luck?" Finn called.

Jack looked up. His tall friend stood on the other side of the marketplace, rubbing his hands and tucking them underneath his threadbare scarf. Finn had no idea that Beryl had already helped Jack to purchase a new, thick scarf for his Christmas gift.

"None." Jack strode up to Finn. "I've asked everyone around here and no one remembers seeing Helen or Pearl."

"They're strangers in a small town," said Finn. "Someone will find them eventually." He sighed. "Unless they've tried to get back to London on their own."

"Did Helen have the money to do that?" Jack asked.

Finn shrugged. "Helen's business is good; sometimes she has a few pennies to spare."

Pennies! Jack could only hope that Helen hadn't taken the train to London, where the lowest-class passengers crammed like cattle into a windowless car. His heart ached at all the mistakes he had made this Christmas.

"Jack..." Finn sighed. "I'm so sorry."

Jack lifted his head. "Finn, why would you apologize?"

"I didn't know about Helen. I believed her when she told me that Beryl had been taken and that Pearl and Beryl had the same father." Shame made Finn's cheeks flush scarlet. "Otherwise, I would have warned you."

"Oh, Finn, nobody blames you," said Jack gently. "Not even Beryl... and I know that she blames me."

"You were only trying to help," said Finn.

"I was, but in the process, I stopped listening to her," Jack admitted. "She told me that she wanted nothing to do with

Helen, and I ignored her. I should have given her some warning, at least, that I'd found her." He shook his head. "I should have known that Helen was lying about Pearl. Instead, I've hurt and angered my wife, and now Helen and Pearl are stranded here in a town they don't know. I'm afraid for them, Finn. I know Helen has made mistakes, but I fear they're all alone in the cold. We have to find them before something happens to them because of me."

"Don't say that," said Finn. "You did nothing wrong. In fact, you—" He paused, awkward. "You changed my life yet again when you offered me work at the livery."

Jack grinned. "One good thing has come of this Christmas, at least." His smile quickly faded. "Oh, Finn, do you think she'll ever forgive me? Will I ever be able to undo the harm I've done to my sweet Beryl?"

"Of course she will," said Finn. "She loves you, Jack. She knows you didn't mean to hurt her." He clapped Jack's shoulder. "Come on. Let's go down to the Higgins farm; perhaps they're staying there."

The taller young man set off with a jaunty step. Jack followed more slowly, head hanging, heart heavy. This was far from the joyous, miraculous Christmas he had dreamed of.

"I don't understand, Mama," Pearl whispered. "Why are we hiding again? I don't think Jack wants to take me away from you."

"Shhh!" Helen hissed.

They crouched in the gloom of an abandoned cottage, listening to the wind moaning and whistling through all of the holes in the roof and cracks in the floor. The door was too waterlogged to close fully, and Helen peered through the crack as Jack and Finn strode from the marketplace.

"I think they want to help us," said Pearl. "Why else would they be asking people if they've seen us? Maybe they want to give us food." She touched her belly, hunger in her eyes.

Helen sagged against the cold, damp wall. The cottage's interior was all shadows and cobwebs; none of Christmas' cheer had reached this place. It was all she could do to stop herself from tearing out her hair and screaming at their situation.

Bitterness rose in her belly like vomit. Why had she ever placed the advertisement in the paper to look for Beryl? She, Finn, and Pearl had been happy in their lies. They had been a little poor, but there had been food on the table and a cottage to call their own.

Now, she assumed that her business was falling apart, that the other washerwomen in the area pounced on the chance to take in all of her good customers.

"What are we going to do, Mama?" Pearl tearfully asked. "Why won't you let Jack help us?"

Helen gritted her teeth. She couldn't admit the real reason to Pearl: that the sight of Jack filled her with terrible shame. Though she tried to hide it with bitterness and anger, the emotion she truly felt was boundless guilt over all she had done, especially her lies. She had lied to everyone she loved, and she saw that betrayal in the eyes of the young man who had been so kind to her.

"We won't accept his charity," said Helen sharply. "We don't need it."

"But I'm so hungry," Pearl whispered. "We haven't had anything since supper yesterday, and that was just bread."

Pearl had grown up with two or three meals a day. To Helen, eating once a day had long been a luxury.

"A little hunger won't kill you," said Helen. "We need to save our money as much as we can until the day after Christmas."

"But why?" Pearl asked. "Will we go home then?"

Helen thought of taking the train back to London, returning to her old life, and trying to pick up the pieces of her business. She was not yet late on her rent at the cottage. They had only been gone for a few days; perhaps she could salvage it all.

It would be best for Pearl, she thought, if she left all this business behind them and returned to London. They could pretend that none of this had ever happened.

But when she closed her eyes, she saw only Beryl's face, and the agony in her pale blue eyes. Eyes that were so very like her father's. She felt a tug deep inside her heart and knew that, no matter how angry they both were, she could not leave Beryl behind again. Not even for Pearl.

"Why is everyone so angry with you, Mama? Why does Finn hate us so?" Pearl began to cry. "I don't understand. Why has everything gone so very wrong?"

Helen opened her eyes and gripped Pearl's hands. "Pearl, darling, you must listen to me very closely now."

Pearl blinked and stared into her eyes.

"Your mama made some very big mistakes," Helen began. "I'll tell you all of them when you're a little older. They're not right for a little girl to understand yet, but I promise that I'll tell you everything when you're ready. All you need to know now is that I did some wrong things. Beryl and Finn are angry with me about them, but they won't be angry forever."

Pearl swallowed. "Was it because of me that you did the bad things, Mama?"

"Oh, Pearly." Helen gently brushed the girl's auburn hair from her face. "Of all the mistakes I've made, I will never count you. You are perfect, darling. God made you, not me. He doesn't make mistakes." She kissed Pearl's forehead. "Don't worry, and don't be afraid. I brought my sewing kit with me from London and we have a few pennies left. When Christmas is over, we can start washing and mending clothes for people again. We'll soon have the same business we had in London."

"But we're not going home?" Pearl asked.

"No, my love. We're not going home," said Helen. "I have to stay here, close to Beryl, even if she doesn't want me. Perhaps one day she will."

I can't walk away, she thought. *I can't disappoint Adrian again.*

"I'm scared, Mama," Pearl whispered.

Helen wrapped her arms around the girl. "Hush, Pearly. Everything will be all right."

The little girl sobbed into her chest. Helen silently hoped that her words would come true.

Part Six

Chapter Eighteen

One Year Later

The sun set so early at this time of year. It was dusk as Helen trudged through the village, carrying a heavy bundle of laundry on her back. Though Sea Crescent had fewer homes than her neighbourhood in London, nor did it have any other washerwomen, and Helen found that many of the increasingly prosperous homes in the growing village were happy to employ her to do their washing and mending.

She had been happy about this at first, as she and Pearl had first started trying to eke out their existence here almost a year ago. But now, the bag on her back felt like an impossible weight to carry to her cottage, never mind washing, mending, ironing, starching, and pressing all before the following evening.

Exhaustion made her hands tremble as she strode past. A few people still moved about in the market square, from the young lamplighter—this village still had old lanterns for streetlights—to a gnarled old farmer leading a team of heavy horses toward his barn. He touched his cap to Helen, startling her. Had no one learned of Pearl's scandalous origins yet?

The girl emerged from a shop on the market square's corner, the brisk wind tugging at her skirt and pressing it around a figure that had begun to show the promise of womanhood. Pearl's auburn hair snapped over her scarf. Eddies of snow blew around her feet as she crossed the square.

"Did you get the thread, darling?" Helen asked.

Pearl nodded. "I did."

"Good." Helen exhaled. "We'll start the mending first thing in the morning."

Pearl said nothing as they crossed the square. Helen knew her daughter was as tired as she was from a long day's washing. The bag seemed leaden on her back.

A clatter of hooves caught Helen's attention, accompanied with the cheery jingle of harness bells. Pearl turned around, and her eyes widened.

"Look, Mama!" she cried. "It's—"

Helen's head snapped around. "Hush!" she cried. "Hush, pet!"

She seized Pearl's arm and thrust her into an alley between two houses.

"But Mama—" Pearl began.

"*Hush!*" said Helen.

They remained between the stone walls in silence as the trap rattled merrily toward them, drawn by a black mare with red and green ribbons plaited into her mane and a little holly wreath hanging from her breastplate. Jack and Beryl sat in the front seat, smiling and laughing; Jack had a holly sprig in his buttonhole and Beryl wore a cheerful red scarf.

Suddenly, Helen longed to burst from the alley and cry out to her oldest daughter, but shame kept her rooted to the spot. She could not bear the thought of seeing hatred in those blue eyes again. So she remained silent and unmoving as the trap rattled by, and neither Jack nor Beryl glanced in their direction.

"Oh, Mama, she's so pretty," said Pearl. She sighed heavily as they stepped from the alleyway. "Why won't you let us speak to her? I know she was angry with you, but that was a long time ago."

"You won't understand, Pearly. We just can't speak to them, all right?" Helen snapped.

Pearl shook her head. "I'm twelve years old, Mama. I'll understand. I know I will."

"Not yet," said Helen. "These are indelicate matters. They're not appropriate for you to know about."

Pearl sighed. "I wish we could know Beryl, that's all. I know they'd help us."

"I'm not so sure," Helen murmured, "and I think that's enough of that. We won't talk about it anymore, is that clear?"

Pearl nodded and hung her head.

In silence, they followed a street that went from pavement to cobbles to frozen mud after a few yards. It led them to a tumbledown cottage on the corner, its neglected garden now hidden by snow. It was the only home Helen had seen all day that bore no Christmas decorations; the angry, elderly woman who lived upstairs and owned the cottage could barely summon a kind word, let alone even an inkling of Christmas spirit.

They avoided the front door, where the old lady often watched them come and go, and took the back entrance instead. The garden gate hung drunkenly from one hinge and threatened to collapse when Helen pushed it open. She let it hang open instead—she could not afford to replace it if it collapsed, and their landlady would undoubtedly blame her for such a disaster—and Pearl silently followed her as they descended the rickety back stairs to their cellar home.

"I'll light the fire," said Pearl.

Helen dropped the heavy bag on the floor and fell into a chair.

Soon Pearl had brought yellow flames to life in the grate and stoked the boiler so that it bubbled and hummed, giving off a red glow, and Helen gazed at the space that had been their home for almost a year. It was painfully bare compared with the cottage in London. Their vats for washing and rinsing water stood against one wall and washing lines crisscrossed most of the cellar, with their living quarters crammed into the other side. There were two sleeping pallets with straw mattresses and worn blankets. A coal stove stood beside the fireplace with a worn cabinet containing their kitchenware. The little table by which Helen now sat could barely accommodate the two of them.

I wish we'd never left London, Helen thought, not for the first time.

"I'm glad we have plenty of work tomorrow," said Pearl.

"It's because we're so close to Christmas. Everyone wants their best clothes mended for their Christmas parties," said Helen.

Pearl nodded. "I remember how it used to be in London. Sometimes—" Pearl stopped. "Sometimes it's hard to think of London. It was lovely there."

Helen stared at her. "Do you want to go back?"

Pearl gave her a wide-eyed look, then hastily turned away. Her silence was an affirmative response, Helen knew.

She rubbed her face. Perhaps it was time for her to think of saving money and going back to London. The thought instantly terrified her. Building up her business in Sea Crescent had been hard enough with no competition from other washerwomen. Going back to London... As much as Helen longed for her old life there, she knew it was impossible.

Pearl opened the cabinet. "We have plenty of bread, Mama, and there are some apples. Should I cook the fish?"

"As you wish, Pearly," Helen mumbled.

She was too tired to care. She pried off her shoes and stumbled to her pallet as the sizzle of frying fish filled the room. Hunger and exhaustion briefly fought in her mind before exhaustion won and she tumbled into a weary sleep. And the nightmare that followed was far simpler and more brutal than before.

Beryl's bare feet dug into the deep grass at their picnic spot outside the city. She moved with two-year-old wobbliness, her little hands held high, blue eyes wide with pure wonder as she followed the small white butterfly across the grass.

"Look at that!" Adrian laughed, his arm tightening around Helen's shoulders. "Go on, Beryl. Catch it! Catch the butterfly!"

Beryl stopped when the butterfly perched on a nearby daisy. The tiny flower bobbed beneath the insect's weight. Beryl giggled, her laughter musical, then looked up at her parents.

"Buh-uh-fly," she said.

Adrian gasped. "Did you hear that?"

"I did!" Helen laughed. "She said 'butterfly!'"

"Buh-uh-fly," said Beryl again, giggling.

Adrian released Helen's shoulders and clapped his hands. "That's right, darling. Butterfly! Butterfly!"

Beryl squealed with pleasure and clapped her chubby hands. The butterfly took flight, and Beryl stumbled after it, her little giggles filling the air.

"Oh, she's so perfect, darling," said Adrian with a happy sigh.

Helen smiled up at him. She caressed his cheek, feeling smooth skin and prickly beard.

"Yes, she is," she said softly.

Adrian turned to look at her. "So why have you made no efforts to talk to her?"

Helen blinked. "What?"

"You've lived in that village a year, Helen, and you've never spoken to Beryl—not since last Christmas." Adrian frowned. "Why haven't you tried to reconcile?"

Helen looked away, her throat tight with sorrow. "How can I? I'm too ashamed. You know what I did. I betrayed her... I betrayed you. How can I face her? I want to go home to London, Adrian. I want to forget all this." She paused. "I want to forget you."

He touched her chin, forcing her to meet his eyes.

"You can never forget me," he murmured, "and you can never leave Beryl. Never."

He leaned in and kissed her, and though she knew it was only a dream, Helen felt that kiss sink into her soul.

Helen woke with a gasp, her hands pressed over her lips, as though she could trap Adrian's kiss there.

"Mama?" Pearl called from the stove. "Are you all right?"

Tears burned Helen's eyes, and it was all she could do not to give in to them and sob hopelessly.

"I'm fine, darling," she croaked. "Let me help you with that fish."

She staggered to her feet and walked to the stove as though all was well, but inside, her heart felt as though it was being ripped in half. Shame on one side and duty on the other threatened to tear her apart.

Adrian was right. As much as she longed to leave the village, she could not.

But nor could she face the shame of speaking to Beryl again.

Finn strode into the cottage, cheerfully whistling "Silent Night" as he wiped horsehair from his hands with a damp rag. A bright wreath bumped on the door as he shut it behind him, sealing in the heat from the crackling hearth fire. Three knitted stockings hung from the mantelpiece.

"Right on time, Finn," said Beryl, pouring tea from a pot. "Where's Jack?"

"He'll be here in a minute," said Finn. "He's finishing his last check of the horses for the evening. You know how he is."

"Fanatic about those horses." Beryl chuckled as she brushed her hair from her face. "I shouldn't complain. It's his care that's made our livery so successful—and yours, Finn. You make his life much easier by working for him. I truly appreciate it."

"You're the ones who changed my life," said Finn, taking a seat. He took his meals in the cottage with Jack and Beryl, but slept in a comfortable flat above the tack room. "The Winslows were very kind to me, but I was so lonely there. I love working here with friends."

"You've taken to the horses like a duck to water, Jack says." Beryl smiled. "I'm sure you know that, of course. Why, I can hardly believe it's been almost a whole year since you joined us. It feels like yesterday." A troubled shadow crossed her face. "At least one good thing came out of that terrible day."

"I'm sorry about that nasty business," said Finn quietly.

Beryl's smile quickly returned. "Oh, Finn, you're like my husband! Always apologizing for that day when none of it was your fault—or Jack's. I know I was angry with him at the time, but Jack acted in pure love. I could never have stayed angry with him about that. As for you, you had no idea. You did nothing wrong."

"I'm pleased you've forgiven Jack for that whole affair. He truly was only trying to make you happy," said Finn.

Beryl smiled. "I know. Jackie always does. Of course I forgave him. Who could stay angry at a man like that?"

Finn laughed. "You and Jack have made a beautiful life for yourselves here. I'm glad to be part of it."

"I'm glad you're part of it, too," said Beryl. "I'm glad it all happened. I'm only sorry that my mother is a liar and a cheat." Her face shut down.

"Helen has been through some terrible things," said Finn gently.

"I see your good heart, Finn, but I'd be pleased if you never mention her name under my roof again," said Beryl crisply.

Before Finn could protest, the door swung open and Jack entered, shaking snow from his shoulders. Beryl rushed to take his coat and kissed his cheek, exclaiming about how cold he was.

"I'm quite all right, my love." Jack kissed her. "This kitchen smells wonderful! What's for supper?"

"I'm testing recipes for Christmas lunch," said Beryl. "Tonight we're having chestnut stuffing with our chicken. I hope you'll tell me honestly what you think."

They settled around the table for the delicious meal, and Beryl and Jack's happy banter made Finn smile. But when he glanced through the window and saw the snow falling quickly, a deep tug at his heart reminded him that not everyone he loved was safe and warm in this cottage with him.

Chapter Nineteen

Helen dusted a last bit of starch onto the tight shirt collar. Unwelcome memories crowded her thoughts as she hung the shirt and carefully covered it with a cloth bag: how she'd bought a high collar for Adrian once and starched it to perfection for him to wear to church, only for him to refuse to keep it on for more than ten minutes. He hated it. The open-chested shirts he wore at sea were more to his taste.

Stop thinking of Adrian, Helen ordered herself.

She checked the bag of clean laundry and drew its string closed. "Pearly!" she called. "Where are you?"

Pearl opened the front door, carrying the empty coal-scuttle; she had been dumping the ashes outside. "Here I am, Mama."

"Oh, Pearly, what were you doing outside?" Helen chided. "You already have a cold. I don't want you setting foot out of this cellar."

"I'm not so bad, Mama," Pearl protested, her voice raspy.

"No, but if you go out there, you'll get worse," said Helen.

"I can't let you do everything on your own today," said Pearl. She hovered in the open doorway. "It's not right."

"You can carry on with the mending I didn't finish last night," said Helen. "It's all right."

Pearl sighed. "If you're sure you'll be all right."

"I'll be fine, darling," said Helen.

A distant voice called, and Pearl stiffened. "Oh, look! It's dear Finn!"

Utter shame swamped Helen, crushing her under its weight. "Pearl, get inside," she ordered.

Pearl sighed. "Mama, why won't you let me speak to him? I miss him so much."

"I told you to get inside," said Helen.

Pearl hung her head and returned to the cellar as Helen strode up the steps. She shut the door behind her and turned to face Finn, who approached down the street with a cautious smile on his face. He wore a new coat, Helen noticed; it was made of lovely leather and lined with sheepskin. It must have cost a fortune.

"Good morning, Helen," he called.

She folded her arms, fury bubbling in her chest. He had rejected her last Christmas. How dare he speak to her with such friendliness in his voice? He kept coming to her home every week or two, trying to be friends with her again, but she couldn't allow him near her daughter. If he rejected Helen, he would reject Pearl. After all, Pearl was the product of the mistake for which Finn had judged her so heavily that day.

"I've brought you some things," Finn added. He held out a parcel wrapped in brown paper. "The bakery had lovely fresh bread and a few beautiful gingerbread men. I know how much Pearl loves gingerbread, so I brought a few." He hesitated. "There's some money in the parcel, too. I want you to have it."

Helen raised her chin. "We don't need your charity." They were the same words she'd used every time he came to her with bits of food and money—except when she was truly desperate. She did not want to admit to herself that Finn's generosity had carried them through the hardest times.

"It's not charity," said Finn. "It's simply a gift from a friend." He held out the parcel.

The tantalizing smell of gingerbread made Helen's heart cry out. Pearl would be so pleased... But no. She would not let Finn worm his way back into their lives only for Pearl to experience such painful rejection.

"You weren't our friend the day we came here," said Helen coldly.

Finn's shoulders sagged. "Oh, Helen, I've tried so hard to apologize for that. I was shocked... I never meant for any harm to come to you."

"So you say, but harm did come to us. We're stuck in this village now," said Helen.

"Jack has always tried to reach you and help you," said Finn.

"Ha! I'm not good enough for that man's wife. Why would I accept anything from him?" Helen asked bitterly.

Finn sighed. "Beryl's still your daughter."

I know that. I know! Helen wanted to scream at him, but she pressed her lips together instead.

"It's been a year," said Finn gently. "Won't you come to the livery and try to talk to Beryl again? Perhaps she'll let bygones be bygones."

"She will, will she?" said Helen bitterly. "Does she ever talk about me, Finn? Or about Pearl?"

Finn looked away.

"I thought not," said Helen, her tone ice cold. "Please leave us alone."

"I want to help you," said Finn.

"We don't need the help of the likes of you," said Helen angrily. "You've already decided to find us wanting, so leave us alone."

"Helen, it's not like that," Finn protested.

"It's exactly like that," said Helen icily. "I won't let you harm Pearl with your judgment."

"Helen, please—" Finn began.

"Leave us alone, Finn," Helen ordered.

Finn hung his head. He crouched and placed the parcel on the ground, then turned and walked away with his hands in his pockets.

Helen stared at the parcel for a long few seconds. Then she tucked it into the snow, hoping that Pearl still believed in Father Christmas, and hurried into the cellar to finish preparing for the day's work.

The snowy fields were beautiful on this unseasonably sunny day. Though the sky was clear, the bitterly cold wind prevented the snow from melting, and so the fields glittered in the sunshine like pieces of a patchwork blanket with the walls and hedges running around their edges like seams. Farmhouses with slanting roofs and wisps of smoke escaping from their chimneys made the scene all the more idyllic.

Mabel could hardly bear to look at them. She trained her eyes on the horses' haunches instead, watching the big muscles ripple beneath their hairy coats as they trotted along the country lane. Her hands were sore where they rested in her lap; she had spent the past few weeks knitting new jumpers for the children for Christmas. Eddie was growing uncontrollably.

His voice had broken over the summer, and Mabel knew that soon his jumpers would be too big for his father.

"Here we are, Mae," said Percy. "There's Sea Crescent."

Mabel raised her head and glanced at the village, which clustered around its market square in the low hills by the sea. The sea glittered a cold, beautiful blue. Even from this distance, Mabel could see the Christmas tree at the square's heart, its decorations sparkling in the sun.

She quickly looked away.

"Oh, Mae, please try to smile," said Percy. "I know Christmas is terribly hard for you ever since that time at the Whitmore estate…"

"We nearly found him, Percy," Mabel whispered. "Now it's been nearly two years and we still can't find my sweet Jack. I…" Tears almost escaped her eyes before she blinked them back. "I don't know if we ever will."

Percy didn't know what to say. He reached over and squeezed her hand. "There's a lovely little inn by the sea," he said after a few minutes' silence. "They make the best rabbit pie you'll ever taste. We'll have that for lunch after I've finished the last of my business here before the holiday."

Mabel silently nodded. She knew that Percy had brought her along to make her feel better, but nothing could ease the pain in her chest.

Suddenly, the carriage slowed. One of the horses' heads bobbed in pain.

"Whoa! Easy!" Mabel pulled the reins, bringing them to a halt.

"I'll hold them," said Percy, taking the reins. "You see what's the matter."

"It's old Polly." Mabel scrambled from the seat and hurried to the chestnut mare's side.

"Oh, poor old girl. Maybe she's getting too old for these journeys." The thought made her heart ache. She'd named Polly after her dearest friend, and she and the mare had spent many hours toiling in the fields together before they could afford farm hands.

But when she lifted the plate-sized foot, she realized that the problem was simple. Polly's metal shoe had twisted at an awkward ankle. The clench dug into her foot, causing pain with each step.

"It's all right. It's only a loose shoe," said Mabel. "She must have trodden on it when they came down the hill. Could you pass me the pliers under the seat?"

Percy descended from the seat with the pliers. "I can do it."

"No, darling. Your arm is still sore from that little accident with the stable door," said Mabel. "I've pulled many shoes in my day."

She tucked Polly's hoof between her knees and grasped the back of the shoe, pulling forward and down, but it refused to budge. The nails had bent at an odd angle, making it harder than usual.

"Perhaps I can walk into town and find a farrier," said Percy.

"In this cold?" Mabel grimaced.

"I don't have a choice. She can't walk on that foot," said Percy.

Hooves rang merrily on the road in the bright rhythm of a brisk trot. Mabel looked up and saw a handsome chestnut hunter moving toward them. He had pricked ears and a shiny coat despite the grey hairs leaving a sprinkling of age around his eyes. A handsome young man with dark hair and friendly brown eyes rode on his back.

"Hello!" he said, halting the hunter. "Do you need help?"

"Can you pull a shoe?" Percy asked. "Our mare's loosened one."

"Oh, that's rather awkward. I'm sure I can help." The young man dismounted from the hunter and handed its reins to Percy. "Here, let me see."

"Thanks ever so much," said Mabel, stepping back.

The young man lifted Polly's foot and pulled the shoe with a single, swift movement.

"You've done that before," said Percy, laughing.

"Oh, I have a livery yard in the village. Horses are my life." The young man winked and handed Mabel the pliers and ruined shoe. "There's a lovely blacksmith by the square; he'll have this shoe fixed and back on in no time. Go slowly and she'll be all right without it until you reach the village."

"Thank you," said Mabel. "Your hunter is lovely."

The young man's eyes lit up in a smile that seemed vaguely familiar. "He's a wonder, old Warrior is." He vaulted into the saddle. "Travel safely!"

Mabel and Percy piled back into the carriage as the chestnut named Warrior trotted away with his rider.

"What a nice young man," said Percy.

"Very nice," Mabel agreed, staring after him as their team set off. She watched until Warrior disappeared into the distance.

Tumbledown though their cottage was, the sight of it was one of the few truly cheering things Helen had seen all day. It was dusk as she laboured up the road with a heavy bag of dirty washing on her shoulders. She'd missed Pearl for every moment of this day as she hurried to and fro with the laundry, and her delivery to the Thompson farm always took hours—it was a terribly long walk. They paid her extra for it, though, so she had no choice but to make it.

Snow fell steadily, settling on Helen's eyelashes and stinging her bare hands as she approached the cellar. Bitter cold rose from the frozen earth and poured from the grey sky. She couldn't wait to get into the cellar and escape it for a moment.

"Pearly," she called, "I'm here!"

She pushed open the cellar door and blinked, confused, at the dark interior.

"Pearl?" she called, dropping the washing bag inside. "Where are you?"

A flash of anger ran through her. If Pearl had decided to go looking for Finn…

Then she heard a quiet groan from the back of the room, and panic made her heart turn over. She lit a match with shaking hands and glimpsed Pearl's form lying on her sleeping pallet.

"Pearl!" Helen hastily lit a candle and rushed to their sleeping area. Pearl lay on her side, arms wrapped around her body, which was wracked with painful shivers of fever. Sweat shone on her forehead and upper lip. When Helen touched her, Pearl was burning up.

"Oh, my darling," said Helen. "My poor darling!"

She'd thought that the girl looked pale that afternoon before she'd left for the Thompson farm. Guilt wrenched her belly. She should have stayed here to care for her, but then again, how would she earn money?

It seemed that no matter what Helen did, she always made mistakes.

"It'll be all right, dear." Helen grabbed a blanket and wrapped it around Pearl's shoulders. "You'll be all right."

"No," Pearl groaned, pushing the blanket away. "Too hot."

"I'll sponge you down in a minute, darling. You'll be all right," said Helen.

But the blue pallor around Pearl's delicate lips made her heart pound. She frantically prayed as she fetched a bucket of clean water and a rag, then gently sponged her daughter's skin, which blazed like coals.

"You'll be all right," Helen whispered. "I know you will."

Pearl's ragged breathing echoed through the cellar, denying Helen's words.

Chapter Twenty

Dawn was frigid and grey in the cellar's tiny, high window, but it felt like the depth of night to Helen's wounded heart.

She cradled Pearl in her arms, tears rolling over her cheeks. All night, she'd fought to keep herself from crying. But now that Pearl was finally asleep—a terrifying, deep sleep, one from which Helen feared she wouldn't wake—she could allow the tears of utter fear to flow.

"Come on, Pearly," she whispered, her voice raw with pain and terror. "Please, please get better."

She touched her daughter's forehead. The fever blazed on, unabated despite Helen's endless efforts at sponging her down. She knew that Pearl needed medicine to live, but Helen didn't have the money. The few pennies Finn had left for them had gone straight to paying the rent.

Pearl emitted a quiet cough, then a deep groan. Helen kissed her forehead, terrified by the blazing heat against her lips, and ran the damp cloth over her skin once more. She was almost surprised when the water failed to sizzle like fat in a pan. The child's fingernails were blue, her face utterly pallid. Her breaths came in tiny, painful gasps.

"I don't know what to do," Helen sobbed out. "Oh, God, help me. I don't know what to do!"

She wrapped her arms around Pearl's blazing body and wept, terror making her tremble. The thought of losing Pearl was interminable. She could not lose both of her daughters. She would not!

An idea flashed through Helen's mind at the thought of Beryl, but she recoiled from it at once.

Finn would help them, but if she asked him, he would involve Jack and Beryl. It would mean that she had to face her oldest daughter once again and see the judgment and rejection in her eyes. The thought sliced her deeply.

"Oh, I'm not brave enough," she whimpered. "I could never be brave enough!"

The memory came from deep in her heart, where she had hidden it so deeply that she had never remembered it before. But at that moment, it felt like yesterday.

Helen's first labour pains with Beryl came upon her while she was washing the dishes in her home. She had felt the vague pangs of discomfort all night, but the first true pain came in terrifying fashion, gripping all of her abdomen with its intensity. A scream burst from her and she dropped her finest cup as she grasped the basin for support.

"Helen!" Adrian ran in from the living room, paper in hand, shirt unbuttoned over the strong muscles of his chest. "What's happened?"

Helen clutched her belly and sobbed through the long contraction until it eased. "Adrian, I—I think it's my time," she cried.

Joy and excitement sparkled in Adrian's eyes. "I'll go for the midwife." He shrugged on his coat.

Helen seized his arm. "It hurts," she cried. "I'm scared. I don't know if... if I'm strong enough."

Adrian crouched to look her in the eye. His eyes were the cool blue of a pool of water in the desert.

*"You are strong enough, Helen," he murmured. "You are strong enough to do anything—*anything*—for your child."*

Helen looked into his eyes and believed him.

Tears rolled down Helen's cheeks and splashed on Pearl's bleached dress. Adrian had been right that day; she *did* have the strength to deliver Beryl. She had the strength to do anything in the world for her child, even this.

Thank you, Adrian, Helen thought.

She gently kissed Pearl's forehead and lowered her to the sleeping pallet. After tucking blankets tightly around the girl, she turned and hurried outside.

The sheer cold snatched her breath. Snow poured down thickly upon her as she rushed from the cellar and into the street, her feet crunching and slipping in the thick layer that already covered the road. The grey sky and early light made it difficult to see, and she squinted against the driving wind, shielding her eyes with one hand as snowflakes whipped across her skin with bitter cold. Yet she knew the way.

She hurried into the village square, where the Christmas tree's top whipped and bucked in the wind, the angel clinging bravely to its summit. The houses slumbered, their windows not yet candlelight, their wreaths and bunting blowing. Helen rushed across the village square, her hands and feet numb with cold now, and took the lane to her right to the livery yard.

Though the rest of the village still slept, Sea Crescent Livery seemed to be waking. Golden candlelight spilled from the windows of the main cottage. Curious horses looked out over their doors as Helen stumbled into the yard and greeted her with enquiring whinnies, wondering if she'd brought carrots or oats. They looked wonderfully snug in their cosy blankets with holly wreaths on every door.

Helen froze, staring at the cottage. Would Finn be there? Then she heard a deep voice coming from a closed door on her right—Finn's voice singing.

"I saw three ships come sailing in

"On Christmas Day, on Christmas Day,

"I saw three ships come sailing in

"On Christmas Day in the morning!"

Oh, if only! Helen thought. *If only!* That would have spared her all the torturous worry and fear that now clung to her. She hastened to the door beside the tack room and knocked.

Finn kept singing, oblivious to her presence.

"Finn, please!" Helen cried. "Please!" She knocked again, much harder.

The singing stopped and footsteps shuffled to the door. Finn pushed it open. His green eyes widened when they landed upon Helen, and he retreated a step, as though unsure of her intentions.

"Helen?" he said. "What are you—"

"Finn, forgive me, please," Helen begged, "or be angry with me still; only please, please help my poor little Pearl. Please, she's never done a thing wrong in her life. None of this is her fault." She struggled to hold back tears. "You have to help her. You can't blame her for what—"

"Helen." Finn gently gripped her shoulders and searched her eyes. She beheld terror in his face. "What's happened to Pearl?"

"She's ill," Helen cried. "She's so very ill. Her fever won't break. She can barely talk."

The colour drained from Finn's face until his cheeks appeared the same shade as the snowy sky. "Come quickly," he said, grabbing Helen's arm.

She did not resist as he hastened to the cottage; she knew that this was inevitable. All the same, fear pounded in her belly at the thought of looking into Beryl's blue eyes—the eyes so much like her father's—and seeing hatred and rejection in them. It was like seeing Adrian's hatred, and made all the worse by knowing that she had wronged his memory as much as she had wronged Beryl.

Finn hammered on the door. "Jack!" he cried. "We need help!"

The door opened at once, and Jack stood in it, his brow furrowed with concern. He paused when he saw Helen. "What is it?"

"Please, Jack, I know you owe me nothing, I know I've wronged you," Helen cried, "but it's my sweet Pearl. She's so ill, and I don't know where else to go. Please, hate me all you like, but help my little girl!"

"Oh, Helen." Jack's eyes softened. "I don't hate you."

"Is that—" Beryl appeared in the doorway and froze. Her baleful eyes gaze cut through Helen like a lance, and she knew

Finn was wrong. Beryl had no designs to ever forgive Helen. The knowledge burned her.

"My love," said Jack quietly, "it's Pearl."

"I heard." Beryl looked away. "You must bring her here, Jackie."

Jack nodded. "Yes. We must."

"I'll prepare a room," said Beryl, vanishing into the cottage.

Helen didn't understand. She knew Beryl was furious with her; why would she be kind enough to lend a room for Pearl?

"Finn, I have to start the horses, but you must go and fetch Pearl," Jack ordered. "Bring her here, where she'll be warm and safe. Hurry!"

Finn spun on his heel and ran out of the yard, feet hammering on the cobbles.

"Helen, go for the doctor," said Jack.

Shame made more tears spill over Helen's cheeks. "Jack, I'm sorry. I... I have no money for the doctor."

"Don't worry about that now. Tell him I sent for him," said Jack. "Go, quickly!"

Helen's breath caught. "Oh, Jack, thank you."

"Don't waste time," said Jack with a quick smile. "Go!"

Helen turned and ran as Finn had done, her heart pounding with agony and hope in her chest. Her gratitude for Finn, Jack, and Beryl's help overflowed, but she could not forget the way her oldest daughter had looked at her.

Beryl had stared at her with the horror and disdain of one beholding their greatest disappointment.

Beryl sat at the kitchen table with her head in her hands.

All was ready. The cottage had two spare rooms; one lay quiet and empty beside Jack and Beryl's, awaiting a child who had still not appeared even after years of marriage. Beryl could not bear to open its door. Instead, she had placed clean linens on the small bed in the guest room, filled a bucket with clean water, and retrieved extra blankets from the cupboard in her bedroom.

Now all she could do was wait—and question her own actions. Why, why, why had she agreed to let them bring Pearl here?

The pain of what her mother had done throbbed deep inside her chest. Protest though she might that she had done it to save her, Helen had sold Beryl like a piece of unwanted furniture. Tears stung Beryl's eyes, and she fought them back. As if that was not enough, Helen had then turned and betrayed Beryl's father, no doubt with a man to whom she was not married.

Beryl only vaguely remembered her father. She remembered his rough beard tickling her face when he hugged her and that he smelled like the sea. But she knew that he was a good, kind, wonderful man, and that everything had changed when he died. What Helen had done flew in the face of everything Papa used to be.

Beryl fiercely rubbed tears from her nose and rose to her feet. She would go upstairs and continue making the bunting she wished to hang all around the stable yard for Christmas. They could nurse Helen's child in her house if they so desired, but Beryl wanted nothing to do with it.

Footsteps clattered outside.

"Beryl!" Finn cried. "Open the door!"

Beryl hurried to the front door and pulled it wide. Finn stumbled within, snow showering from his shoulders, breathing hard. Their doctor—a gentle old man named Dr. Jennings—followed him into the kitchen.

"Where shall I put her?" Finn asked.

Beryl looked down at the child in his arms, and her heart turned over.

The girl was painfully thin. Her collarbones jutted against her grey skin between the sleeves of her worn and faded dress, which was so old that its colour was indiscernible. Sweaty strings of auburn hair fell over her face, and her breaths came in painful rasps.

The sight of Pearl—of her own sister—sliced deeply into Beryl's heart.

"Upstairs," she said. "I've made the bed ready."

She hurried up and led Finn to the guest room, then stepped aside as he laid Pearl on the bed. The little girl groaned with pain as Dr. Jennings bent over her.

"Thank you, Mr. Hargrove," said Dr. Jennings. "You may go."

Finn glanced at Beryl, who touched his arm.

"Don't worry. I'll stay with her," she said.

"You will?" said Finn, shocked.

"Yes." Beryl nodded. "I promise."

Finn hurried away, and Beryl stood beside the bed as Dr. Jennings examined the bone-thin girl. Pain throbbed in her as she gazed at Pearl's sleeping face. How different would this child's life have been if Beryl had only heard Helen out instead of condemning them to the streets?

"How is she, doctor?" Beryl quietly asked.

Dr. Jennings extracted a glass syringe and a sharp metal needle from his back. Beryl had never seen such a thing before, and she watched in utter horror as he filled the syringe with fluid and then pressed the needle into Pearl's skin. The girl's brow furrowed, and she whimpered.

"This should break her fever," said Dr. Jennings, replacing the syringe in his bag. "But I'm afraid she should have been seen days ago, Mrs. Finch."

"What's the matter with her?" Beryl asked.

"It's the cold," said Dr. Jennings. "It has caused disease to invade her lungs."

Beryl's heart stuttered. "Like consumption?" The dread disease had taken her dearest friend, Annabel, in this very village.

The doctor shook his head. "No, no. This is a far more acute illness. If she survives this, she will do well." He paused. "But I must tell you that she is very, very ill. You must keep her fever down, Mrs. Finch. If she becomes well enough to sit up, you must ensure that she drinks hot milk or broth as often as possible. She is already very weak; we cannot allow her to become weaker."

Beryl nodded. "Yes, doctor."

"Good luck," said Dr. Jennings, "and merry Christmas."

He left, and Beryl pulled up a chair beside Pearl's bed. She dipped a clean cloth into the bucket of water she had drawn and gently wiped it over Pearl's hands and arms. A red spot marked the place where Dr. Jennings had applied the needle.

"I'm sorry, Pearl," Beryl whispered. "I'm so very sorry."

Pearl gave a quiet moan, the way Annabel had often done when her consumption gripped her at its worse. Beryl struggled to fight back tears.

There as was a gentle knock, and Jack popped his head around the door. "Are you all right, darling?"

Beryl looked up. "Yes, thank you."

"Finn says he will care for Pearl if you like," said Jack, "and of course, Helen would be glad to do so."

Beryl looked away. "I don't want Helen in here," she said sharply.

Jack inclined his head. "I understand."

"But she could make hot broth for Pearl," Beryl quietly added. "She needs to get her strength back."

"Yes, dear. I'll tell her," said Jack, about to retreat.

"Jack..." Beryl murmured.

He paused. "Yes?"

Beryl raised her head to meet his eyes. "Tell her that I'm here with Pearl," she said quietly, "and that she should get some rest. I will care for my sister until she's well."

Hope flickered in Jack's eyes. "Well done, darling."

He hurried away, leaving Beryl alone in the room with her illegitimate half-sister. Yet looking at the groaning, suffering child, Beryl saw nothing at fault with her. She saw only the features they shared; the same freckles, the red hue of their hair. Deep inside her chest, a frozen place began, at last, to melt.

Chapter Twenty-One

"Beryl?"

The tiny voice gently pulled Beryl from a deep, deep sleep. She raised her head, blinking against the bright sunlight.

Sunlight? Beryl thought, and sudden panic gripped her. It had been very dark when she'd fallen asleep. She glanced at the candle on the nightstand and saw that it had only burned down a little; sleep must have taken her shortly before dawn.

"Beryl?" Pearl whispered. "Is it really you?"

Beryl stirred. Her limbs ached from sleeping in the chair beside Pearl's bed, and her neck stung from the awkward angle at which it had been twisted to rest her head upon the mattress. Pearl lay with her head on the pillow, her nose only inches from Beryl's, staring at her with soft brown eyes.

"Pearly, darling." Beryl gently brushed auburn hair from the girl's face. "Are you feeling better?"

Her fever had returned late last night even though Dr. Jennings had given her another injection yesterday evening. Beryl had battled it all night, trying to coax Pearl to take sips of milk in between sponging her trembling, blazing body.

Pearl smiled. The unnatural brightness had left her eyes; in fact, there was a gentle flush on her cheeks.

"I do," she said. "I'm just very, very hungry."

"You're hungry?" Beryl cried.

Pearl nodded.

"Oh, Pearly, how wonderful!" Beryl straightened and looked around, finding a cup of milk on the nightstand. "Do you think you could sip this?" She handed it to the girl.

Pearl raised the cup to her lips and drained it. "Thank you," she said, giving Beryl the empty cup.

Beryl couldn't believe her eyes. She'd fought for hours to get half the cup into Pearl last night. "Would you like some more?"

"Is there more?" Pearl asked carefully. "Will there be enough for everyone?"

Beryl's conscience burned her deeply. She rested a hand on Pearl's arm. "Don't worry, Pearl. There's more than enough for everybody here. You may ask for anything you like." She smiled. "Would you like a piece of toast with butter and jam?"

"Butter *and* jam?" Pearl's eyes lit up. "Oh, yes please, Beryl."

"Then you'll have it," said Beryl firmly.

She rose and turned to the door, but a knock stopped her. Expecting Jack, Beryl flung it wide, and instead looked up at Dr. Jennings.

"Mrs. Finch!" said Dr. Jennings, a little startled.

"You're here early, doctor," said Beryl.

"Well, yes. I— I feared the worst," Dr. Jennings admitted, "when I saw how the girl looked last night. But the twinkle in your eye tells me that she is better."

"I'm much better," Pearl declared. "Please don't stab me with that big needle again."

Beryl laughed. Dr. Jennings chuckled as he went over to Pearl, felt her forehead, and listened to her chest.

"I certainly won't stab you again, young lady," he said. "You've no need of it. All you need now is plenty of rest, sunshine, fresh air, and good food."

Pearl smiled, but her eyes were cautious. "That sounds nice."

"Doesn't it?" Dr. Jennings smiled. "Now, I would like to speak with your, ah—" His eyes darted from Beryl to Pearl and back again as he tried to discern their relationship. "Your benefactor," he said.

Pearl looked mystified, but Beryl gave her an encouraging smile before stepping into the hallway and shutting the door.

"Will she get well again?" she asked quickly, before Dr. Jennings could enquire as to why she'd taken in this scruffy urchin.

"She will be perfectly well once she has convalesced, Mrs. Finch, and in very large part thanks to you," said Dr. Jennings. "The return of her appetite is an excellent sign. Give her nothing too rich for the first few days, but if her stomach tolerates it, she may return to her usual diet."

"Thank you, doctor," said Beryl. "Jack will pay you; I believe he's in the yard."

"Thank you, Mrs. Finch." Dr. Jennings doffed his hat. "And Merry Christmas."

Beryl followed him downstairs and froze at the sight of Helen. Dr. Jennings let himself out, to her relief. She couldn't move as she stared at her mother sitting by the kitchen table, her head down, her fingers interlaced in desperate prayer.

The word *Mama* sprang to Beryl's mind. She didn't know what to do with it, so she cleared her throat and said quietly, "Helen?"

Helen raised her head. The terror and hope in her eyes made Beryl's heart ache.

"B-Beryl," she stammered, "I—"

"Pearl's much better," said Beryl. "Could you make her a little toast with butter and jam, please?"

Helen blinked, as if startled by Beryl's civility. Guilt once more ran Beryl through.

"I will," she said quickly.

"Thank you. Bring it upstairs when it's ready, please," said Beryl.

Helen's eyes shone with sudden hope. "Of course."

What are you thinking? Beryl wondered as she climbed the stairs once more. *How do you know you can trust her?* The truth was that she did not know, but the weight of the past year's anger and bitterness had grown far lighter in her chest.

She returned to the guest room to find Pearl sitting up and gazing out of the window at the stable yard below. Despite the early hour, Jack and Finn bustled around the stables. Someone sang a Christmas carol, which drifted through the glass, distorted and distant.

"Your mother is bringing you something to eat," Beryl promised, resuming her seat.

"Thanks." Pearl hesitated. "You mean *our* mother, don't you?"

Beryl looked away.

"I'm not an idiot, you know," said Pearl. "Mama thinks I'm too young to understand these things, but I've worked out by now that you and I don't have the same papa. I don't even know who my papa is, and I know that Mama wasn't married when she had me, not like she always said."

Beryl lifted her head. "She lied to you, too."

"Yes." Pearl shrugged. "I don't like that very much, but I do know that Mama would do absolutely anything in the world for me."

Beryl sighed. "I wish she would have done anything in the world for *me*," she confessed.

Pearl smiled. Her eyes held the wisdom of a child who had had to grow up too fast and know too much. "I think the Mama she was when you were little and the Mama she is now isn't the same person," she said. "I didn't know how she lost you. She told me the same story that she told you, Beryl. But now that I know about it, I think it haunted her all these years. She would talk about you all the time, especially around Christmas, and I often found her crying by herself. I know it was over you."

"She talked about me?" Beryl asked.

Pearl nodded. "She never stopped talking about you. I couldn't wait to meet my big sister. To hear Mama tell it, you were an angel from Heaven." Her eyes filled with tears. "I know you saved my life. Mama was right. You *are* an angel from Heaven."

Beryl struggled with a lump in her throat. "Oh, Pearly, it's not true. An angel would never have turned you away like I did last Christmas. I'm so terribly sorry. You would never have become so ill if it wasn't for me."

"You saved me now," said Pearl. "It's all right."

Beryl wrapped her arms around Pearl and gave the dirty little street girl a tight hug.

"I think you need a new dress for Christmas," she said, releasing her, "and I'll draw you a hot bath as soon as you feel strong enough."

"A new dress!" said Pearl, eyes shining. "Did you hear that, Mama?"

Beryl turned her head. Helen stood in the doorway, holding a tray that contained two plates of toast and two cups of tea. Tears shimmered in her eyes, but she quickly blinked them away.

"I heard that," she said quietly, placing the tray on the bed. "I made tea and toast for you, too, Beryl. You must be exhausted after looking after Pearly all night."

"It was only my pleasure," said Beryl sincerely, taking the teacup. "Oh, thanks so much."

"I didn't know if you took milk or sugar, but I put both in," said Helen nervously.

"I take both." Beryl smiled.

Her mother's eyes met hers, and a nervous smile played over her lips. Then she wrapped her arms around Pearl and hugged her closely, her shoulders trembling with suppressed sobs. Beryl watched and struggled to recognize the frightened young woman who had sold her on that cold Christmas.

Helen had been little older than Beryl was now, she realized, when that happened. She remembered being on the streets without Jack, alone and afraid, and an inkling of empathy curled through her mind. But it was for the girl who had abandoned her. The woman who now hugged Pearl seemed like an entirely different person.

"I'm sorry, Helen," Beryl blurted out.

Helen raised her head. "Oh, Beryl, how can you apologize? You saved Pearl. I'll never forget it."

"But I mistreated you," said Beryl.

Helen's tears threatened to spill over.

"I know you wronged me too," said Beryl quietly, "but I should never have treated you the way I did. I gave you no time to explain... I had no grace with you. I see now that you have changed." She glanced at Pearl, who was gulping down her toast and tea. "I should have given you the chance to say that. You came all the way from London, after all, and you were the one who searched for me.

I should never have chased you off as I did... let alone ignored you for the better part of a year to follow." She raised her head. "Please forgive me, Helen."

"Oh, Beryl." Helen wept, tears rolling down her cheeks. "Oh, Beryl, I'm so sorry that I sold you, that I lied, that I let you down, that I didn't try to come back here... I'm sorry for everything I ever did to you, I truly, truly am."

Pearl watched intently. "So do you two forgive each other?"

Beryl smiled at Helen and felt the shackles falling away from her heart as she said the words. "Yes. I forgive you... Mama."

Helen flung her arms around Beryl's neck. Though she hesitated for a brief moment, Beryl leaned into the embrace, then gently returned it.

Though only a few days had passed since she'd lain nearly lifeless in Finn's arms as he carried her into the cottage, Pearl seemed to glow with an inner light. She sat at the end of the kitchen table, laughing, wearing a silly paper crown on her hair, which tumbled in soft, shining curves over her shoulders now that she was clean. She wore a new green dress.

"All hail Queen Pearl," Beryl teased, prodding Pearl's shoulder.

Jack's attention quickly returned to his wife. His heart swelled with love at the joy and light in her eyes as she tickled her little sister, laughing as though they had never been apart. The crumbs of mince pies lay on the tables before them, and the candlelight reflected on the Christmas tree in the corner, the tinsel leaving fragments of light all throughout the room.

"Time for your cracker, Finn," Pearl announced, handing him one end.

Finn chuckled as he gripped it and pulled. The paper tore, and tiny treasures showered the table—roast chestnuts, small boiled sweets, and a scrap of paper with a blessing written upon it. They couldn't afford the nice crackers sold in London, but Beryl had stayed up making homemade ones late into the night. Now, her face was transfixed with joy as Finn combed through the treasures and chuckled at the blessing.

A church bell rang in the village, and Beryl jumped up. "That's the goose ready!"

"Let me help you, dear," said Helen.

Beryl barely hesitated. "Thank you, Mama."

They went to the stove together, talking and prodding the goose as they decided whether or not it was properly cooked. It was only a simple conversation, and Jack sensed that the road forward would be a long one yet. But those first painful, tottering steps had been taken on the road to true reconciliation. He smiled, knowing that they would get there. Beryl's mother was finally part of her life once more.

As they carried the goose to the table, accompanied by much applause from Pearl and Finn, Jack turned to the window and gazed outside. The snow fell in a thick curtain of white flakes that danced on the wind and sparkled in the candlelight. Laughter filled the room, yet Jack had to swallow the lump in his throat.

He pressed a hand against the cold glass. "I'll find you someday, Mama," he whispered.

Mabel knew by the delicious smell filling the kitchen that the goose was nearly ready. Laughter rolled from the drawing-room along with the crunch of brown paper and the pop of crackers.

She knew that she should return to the drawing-room and sit with her family, yet she stood and gazed through the kitchen window as snow fell thickly upon her white-blanketed fields, and quiet tears rolled down her cheeks.

"I'll find you someday, my Jack-Jack," she whispered.

"Mae!" Percy called. "Is the goose ready yet? Mags wants to open her present!"

Mabel shook herself and turned away from the window, wiping her tears. "It's ready," she said. She pulled on her oven gloves and lifted the golden-roasted goose from the oven, then squared her shoulders, found a smile, and returned to the joyful laughter of her family.

Yet it was not her whole family. They were not all together.

All would not be well in her life until they were.

Part Seven

Chapter Twenty-Two

One Year Later

Beryl lumbered into the kitchen, grunting with effort. The washing basket on her hip brimmed with sheets and towels, bumping on the banister as she manoeuvred down the stairs.

"Beryl!" Helen chided, turning away from the stove. "What are you thinking, carrying that around in your condition?"

She hurried to Beryl's side and gripped the basket. Beryl gave a sheepish laugh and wrapped one arm around her swollen midriff, cradling the broad curve of her belly.

"They're just so dirty, Mama. I have to do something about them," she said.

"You have to sit down and take the weight off your feet," Helen scolded. "I was just about to bring you up a cup of tea."

She pulled out a chair at the kitchen table and gently guided Beryl into it. Her daughter sat with a sigh of relief and lifted her feet onto the stool Helen provided, her ankles puffy with pregnancy.

"I can't wait for the little one to come into the world," Beryl confessed, rubbing her belly. "For more reasons than one."

"You must be so overjoyed to finally have a baby of your own and soon in your arms," said Helen.

"It's about time." Beryl smiled, eyes shining. Although I'll admit that I'm also quite relieved not to be in the family way anymore! It's so uncomfortable! "I know." Helen chuckled. "I remember your father having to help me into my shoes and stockings in the last few weeks when I was expecting you."

Beryl's eyes softened as they always did when Helen discussed Adrian. "Jack does that for me, too."

"Jack is a good man, darling," said Helen, "just as your father was. Adrian would have loved him."

Beryl smiled.

"Now, let your mama do this washing for you," Helen added. "If you really want to keep yourself busy, you can knead the bread."

"Oh, Mama, you must be so tired of laundry," said Beryl.

"Not anymore, darling." Helen laughed. "I'm not saying that I miss it, though, and I enjoy working for Mrs. Fletcher." Jack had talked the old milliner in town into giving Helen a respectable position there as a seamstress.

"Mrs. Fletcher is nice," Beryl agreed. "I love the dress she sent Pearl for Christmas."

"Me too. It was very good of her to let me have two weeks off to look after you. Speaking of Pearl, she should be home from the market any minute." Helen glanced at the clock on the wall. "Do you mind if I go out for a little while when she gets back? Pearl can help you with anything you need."

"Of course not, Mama." Beryl tilted her head, curious. "Where are you going?"

Helen smiled. "To the market myself. I need something that I forgot to ask Pearl to get for me."

Beryl still looked curious, but she didn't ask; instead, her gaze darted to the majestic Christmas tree in a corner of the cottage kitchen. Parcels tied with ribbons and wrapped in brown paper lay at its feet, each bearing a handwritten name in one corner. A gleam of excitement came into Beryl's eye.

"Of course," she said, nodding. "Tomorrow is Christmas Eve, after all. If you need something, you might not have the chance to get it before then."

"Precisely." Helen nodded.

Pearl returned a few minutes later, bringing a brisk, cold breeze with her as she entered, snowflakes shining on her hair.

"My, it's cold out there!" she said, placing paper bags of vegetables and sugar on the table. "Oh, Beryl, you poor thing, you look huge."

Beryl laughed dryly. "Thank you, Pearl."

"Pearly!" Helen chided. She pulled her shawl around her shoulders. "I'll be back in a jiff. Make Beryl some tea, would you?"

"Of course I'll make tea for my favourite big sister," Pearl teased, "even if she's as large as a house."

Beryl threw a wooden spoon at her, laughing.

Helen left the girls giggling together and crossed the livery yard, which, as always, bustled. Customers arrived and left with horses and carriages as Finn and their new stable hand ran about to get them ready. Jack stood at the gate, taking a fistful of coins from an old gentleman who had hired their best hack.

"Thank you very much, sir," he said, doffing his cap.

"You said you were planning to build more stables in the spring?" the old man asked hopefully.

"Yes, sir." Jack smiled. "When you ride to Yorkshire to visit your family next, I'll have horses for your entire family."

The old man went away beaming as Jack tucked the money into his pocket. He turned and nearly collided with Helen.

"Oh, Helen, where are you going?" he asked.

"To the market for some last-minute things," said Helen.

"I could go for you," Jack offered.

"No, you couldn't." Helen laughed. "You're much too busy with this splendid stable yard of yours. I'll be back in a flash, my boy."

She patted his arm and turned away, but glanced back when she reached the end of the drive. Jack stood in place, gazing at the horizon, his eyes scanning the distant line of the sea as though searching for something.

He often had that faraway look of pain in his eyes at this time of year. Helen knew how much he longed to find his mother. Her hands tightened on her shopping basket in determination as she strode to the market.

It had stopped snowing when Helen reached the market, and a few glimmers of sunlight peered through the layers of clouds, illuminating the sparkling white blanket that lay over all the rooftops and the boughs of the Christmas tree that always stood at the centre of the square. The smells of fresh baking and smoked fish filled the air, but Helen didn't turn aside. She walked straight up to the young man on the corner, who held a stack of newspapers in his arms.

"Fresh News!" he called. "Get your papers here!"

But Christmas was no time for news, and most of the people hurrying by didn't spare him a second glance.

Helen fished money from her pocket as she approached the boy.

"Good morning, Jordie!" she called.

The lad looked up and brightened immediately. "Good evenin', Mrs. Nicols!" He held out his hand, expectant.

Helen noticed the desperation in his eyes and didn't hesitate. She placed the coins in his palm and smiled. "Any news?"

Jordie was no ordinary paper-seller. Unlike most, he was literate, thanks to a few years of schooling before hard times struck. His father owned the village printing press, but in a town so small that few people even bothered to read the papers, it was a struggle to feed their large family. Still, Jordie's ability to read set him apart, and Helen often paid him to tell of the latest news, sparing her the time.

"Blimey, Mrs. Nicols, this means the world," Jordie said, tucking the money in his pocket. "All this just for readin' the papers."

"I'm too busy, especially with Beryl's baby on the way," Helen replied. "But tell me, did you find anything?"

Jordie hesitated, glancing down. "I might've done."

Helen gasped. "You have? You've found Mabel Finch?"

Jordie held out an expectant hand.

Helen pressed a penny into it. "Tell me, Jordie!"

"Well, it's not Mabel *Finch*, not exactly," said Jordie, whisking the penny into a pocket before Helen could protest. "But I thought it was something. Here, this is it."

He handed Helen a page torn from the paper with an article circled in pencil near the bottom.

LADY FARMER WINS FIRST PRIZE

Mrs. Mabel Mitchell (42) of the farm Finchley Hollow has won first place in the pig show at the Country Christmas Fair last

Sunday. Mrs. Mitchell's pig, Delilah, was the most correct specimen of her kind on the day. She attributes her success to feeding buttermilk from a pure Jersey cow.

The article was so brief and so mundane that Helen's eyes skimmed over it. She frowned, puzzled.

"I know it ain't Mabel Finch like you told me to look for," said Jordie, "but the lady's name is Mabel, ain't it? And look at the farm's name." He tapped it. "*Finchley Hollow*. This paper is from the next village over, you see. I know the farm. It's maybe an hour's drive from here."

Helen tilted her head, her thoughts racing. The more she considered it, the more it could be true. Jack often spoke of his mother and how she had always told him about a farm outside London, one which her late husband had owned. If Mr. Finch had died and somehow left the farm to Mabel, surely she could have remarried and carried on living there?

"Mabel Mitchell of Finchley Hollow," Helen whispered. "*Mabel Finch*."

"It could be, couldn't it?" said Jordie eagerly.

Helen laughed. Excitement thrilled through her veins as she seized the boy's hands and squeezed them. "It very well could, Jordie. It very well could! Thank you!"

She turned and ran back across the market square, the cold air biting her lungs. The growing dusk made it impossible to journey to Finchley Hollow that evening, she realized, so she slowed to a walk and clutched the clipping in both hands. She would have to leave Pearl and Beryl alone with the morning preparations for Christmas Eve.

Yet, if her suspicion were to prove true, it would all be worthwhile.

Harness bells jingled on the black mare's coat as she trotted along the country lane, the trap rattling along behind her. Although Finn had lifted the top before they set off from Sea Crescent, a chill wind nipped Helen's hands and feet as they drove. The bright midmorning sun did little to allay the cold. All around them, the fields lay wrapped in white, a patchwork between their seam-like walls. Wisps of smoke rose from the odd farmhouse and candlelight shone in all the windows, painting them gold.

"Do you think they believed our little story?" Helen asked.

Finn shook his head. "Beryl looked suspicious, but people are accepting of white lies around Christmas. They must think we're preparing a lovely surprise for them."

Helen gulped. "We might be."

Finn looked over at her. "I can't believe you were paying Jordie to look through the papers for Mabel all this time."

"Not at first," Helen confessed. "I used to buy the papers from him and look through them myself, but with Pearl working with her tutor most of the day and Beryl needing my help at home, I grew too busy."

"All the same, Helen, why were you searching for Mabel?" Finn asked. "I think Jack has all but given up. He hardly looks through the papers for her at all anymore, and he used to do it every night. I asked him why and he said he had to concentrate on his baby being on the way."

"That's precisely why I started searching," said Helen gently. "Jack has been so good to us, Finn—all of us."

Finn nodded. "Including Pearl and me. After all, he pays her tutor."

"He's the one who brought our family back together. I felt..." Helen sighed. "I felt that the only thing I could possibly do to repay him was to bring *his* family back together, too."

Finn nodded. "He spoke of his mother all the time when we were boys. I envied him for it. I never knew mine. But Mabel sounds like she was always lovely."

"I hope this is her," said Helen softly. "Thank you for agreeing to take me to her farm. I know it's a long shot."

"Sometimes, long shots are all we have," said Finn, "and after all, the yard is quiet today. Like I told Jack, I had to take this girl out for exercise in any case." He gently rubbed the mare's toiling haunches with the whip, and she flipped her head as though to acknowledge his voice.

They drove onward, and Helen sat very straight in her seat, heart pounding with hope.

Mabel ran a brush over the goose, spreading a golden mixture of garlic, herbs, and butter over the pink dimples of its skin. She smiled with pride at the goose's sheer size as she worked more butter over it. It had been waddling around the yard that morning, and the meat was delightfully fresh; it would be perfect on their table for their Christmas Eve feast that evening.

"Mama!" Maggie burst into the kitchen, furious. "Eddie says that I look like a cabbage in my new green dress. I can't go to Christmas service looking like a cabbage!"

"Edward!" Mabel bellowed. "Don't tell your sister she looks like a cabbage!"

Eddie flounced past the kitchen with teenage callousness. "All right. Sorry, Mags. You look like an asparagus."

"I'll kill you!" Maggie yelled.

"Children!" Mabel shouted, pushing the goose into the oven. "Stop fighting!"

Her sheepdog barked from the drawing-room as someone knocked on the front door.

"Percy, can you answer the door?" Mabel called, turning the platter carefully into its place.

"Hands a bit full right now, Mae," Percy called.

The sheepdog barked again. Grumbling, Mabel slammed the oven door shut and hurried past. She forgave Percy—who stood on a ladder to hang the Christmas Angel at the top of the Christmas tree—and marched to the door.

Another knock came as she reached it.

"All right, all right!" Mabel called. "I'm coming!"

"Mama," Maggie moaned, "Eddie's taking my ribbons!"

"I am not!" said Eddie, hiding them behind his back.

"Edward Finch, give those back right now," Mabel ordered. Maybe Eddie would have been easier to manage if his older brother had been present...

She fought down a familiar thought of dear Jack, knowing she would never see him again, and pulled the door wide. A weathered woman about Mabel's age stood on the doorstep, clutching a piece of newspaper. Her large, brown eyes were wide with hope and fear.

"Mrs. Mabel Mitchell?" she asked.

Mabel glanced past her at the trap and horse waiting in the lane.

"I'm Mrs. Mitchell," she said crisply. "I'm also terribly busy at the moment. What's this about?"

"My name is Helen Nicols." The woman gave a tiny curtsey. "I saw the piece in the paper about your pig."

Mabel stared at her, shocked. "It's Christmas Eve, Mrs. Nicols, not exactly a good time to do business."

"What? No—oh, I'm not here about the pig," said Helen. "I'm here about your son."

Mabel ran a hand over her face. "He's not a bad boy, Mrs. Nicols, merely a lad trying to find his way in the world. What has dear Eddie done this time?"

"Not him." Helen shook her head. "Your... your other son. Do you have another son?"

Mabel froze. She stared into the woman's dark eyes, and panic grasped her so tightly and with such biting cold that she could barely breathe.

"A son you haven't seen in a very long time," Helen went on quietly. "A boy named—"

"Jack," Mabel croaked.

"Yes," said Helen. "Jack Finch."

Mabel clutched her chest. Her heart felt as though it was about to burst from between her ribs.

"You knew him?" Mabel whispered.

"I *know* him, Mrs. Mitchell," said Helen. "He's married to my daughter."

Mabel's knees felt as though they had turned to water. Every part of her thrilled, no matter how hard she tried to push her excitement down, to tell herself not to hope.

"If you come with me," Helen added, "I can take you to him right now. He runs Sea Crescent Livery; it's not a long drive."

Mabel gasped.

"Mae?" Percy was suddenly by her side. "What is it?"

Mabel gripped his shirt with a trembling hand. "Get the children," she croaked. "Ask the maid to look after the goose in the oven. We've found Jack."

"What?" Percy cried, his face lighting up.

"We've found Jack!" Mabel sobbed the words she had longed for. "*We've found Jack!*"

Jack threw the rug over old Warrior's chestnut haunches with an expert flick of his hands. It settled neatly over the old horse's body, and Warrior contentedly champed his hay as Jack fastened the straps and made sure that he was warm and comfortable.

"There you are, old boy." Jack patted his neck. "Snug and warm."

"Jackie!" Beryl called.

Jack left the stable and hurried to the cottage door, where his wife stood waiting for him, her arms wrapped around her swollen belly.

"Oh, darling, what are you doing outside?" he asked.

"Calling you." Beryl smiled. "Is Helen with you?"

Jack frowned. "No, she isn't. She went with Finn to exercise Crow."

"When?" Beryl asked.

A thump of nervousness ran through Jack's chest. "Hours ago."

Beryl's eyes widened. "Oh, Jack, you don't think—"

"It's all right, darling," said Jack. "Go back inside. I'll take Warrior out and look for them."

"But it's Christmas Eve," said Beryl tearfully. "The goose is nearly ready."

Jack kissed her forehead. "It'll be all right, don't worry."

Pearl suddenly emerged from the doorway behind Beryl. "Look!" she said, pointing. "There they are!"

Jack turned and saw the black mare trotting into the yard. Snowflakes settled like stars on her dark coat and her harness bells jingled as she strode into the yard. Finn and Helen sat behind the reins, smiling.

"See?" Jack grinned. "Everything's all right. Go inside now, darling. I'll help Finn to unharness the mare and we'll all soon be ready for our Christmas supper."

Beryl went inside, smiling, and Jack headed toward the black mare. A moment later he heard the clopping of more hooves, and a chestnut horse with a soft flaxen mane trotted up the drive, pulling a carriage that Jack didn't recognize.

"Hello, Jack!" Finn jumped down from the seat. "Sorry to be gone for so long."

"What happened?" Jack asked. "Did she throw a shoe?"

"Ask Helen," said Finn.

Jack turned to his mother-in-law, perplexed, and gave her a hand down from the carriage. She clutched his arms, breathing hard, and her face was flushed with excitement. She smiled widely, her eyes shining.

"Helen?" said Jack. "What's going on?"

"Oh, Jackie," said Helen, "a Christmas miracle. That's what's going on!"

The chestnut horse halted in the yard and a woman jumped from the carriage at once.

"Who is this?" Jack asked. Suddenly, his mouth was dry, and his heart pounded madly against his ribs. "Helen… who is she?"

The woman turned. Something about her gentle eyes seemed strangely familiar... but Jack couldn't place her.

Helen squeezed his arm. "Jackie, my dear," she said softly, "this is your mother."

Jack's heart leaped. The woman staggered toward him with arms outstretched.

"Is it true?" Jack whispered, slowly approaching her. It felt as though his feet could not quite touch the ground. Hope and awe filled him like a leaping fire. "Are you—"

"It's me," Mabel whispered. "It's me, Mama. It's me, Jack-Jack."

Only one person in the world had ever called him that, and when he truly looked into her eyes, he knew it was her. He knew that he had found his mother at last.

Jack rushed forward. When he ran into his mother's embrace, she clung to him as though she would never, never let him go again.

Chapter Twenty Three

Everyone barely fit into Jack and Beryl's cottage. The small space was filled with laughter and conversation, the remnants of the Christmas feast scattered across the table—cold slices of goose, bread pudding, and mince pies. A Christmas tree, slightly bent to fit into the cosy room, glowed softly in the corner, casting a warm light over the gathering.

Mabel sat with a contented smile, watching Jack and Beryl as they exchanged quiet words and glances. Around the table, the chatter continued: Finn balancing a spoon on his nose, much to Pearl's delight, and Mrs. Whitmore sharing stories with Reverend Samuel and Mrs. Brownstone from London.

Helen sat by the window, cradling a cup of tea. The room was lively and filled with warmth. She closed her eyes for a moment, whispering a silent prayer. *Thank you, Lord*, she thought, her heart swelling. *For this family, for Beryl's forgiveness, for letting me be here today. I don't deserve this grace, but You've given it, and I'm so grateful. I need nothing more.*

She opened her eyes and smiled softly. Everything she could hope for was in this room.

"Mama?" Pearl's soft voice broke through her thoughts. "A penny for them?"

Helen smiled, shaking her head gently. "Nothing I would ever sell, my dear," she said, her voice light and content.

Before Pearl could respond, a knock echoed through the room.

The conversation halted. Every face turned toward the door.

Helen blinked, startled by the sound. Mabel stood up, her brow furrowed. "Who could be knocking in this weather?"

Jack rose beside her, frowning. "We're not expecting anyone."

Another knock, more insistent.

"I'll get it," Mabel said, standing up quickly, and making her way through the room.

Mabel opened the door to find two men standing on the doorstep, snow swirling around them. One of them stepped forward, his face familiar, but his expression filled with confusion and disbelief.

"Mabel?" the man asked, removing his hat slowly, as though he couldn't believe what he was seeing. "It's me, Mr. Goulding."

Mabel's eyes widened. "Mr. Goulding? What are you doing here? You've spent years searching for Jack but—"

Mr. Goulding shook his head, his gaze shifting past Mabel and landing on the man standing inside by the fire. He froze, as his gaze locked onto Jack, the resemblance to Mabel unmistakable. His breath hitched as realization dawned. "Could this be — Jack?"

Jack's brow furrowed, and he stepped forward, sensing the weight of the moment but unsure of who this man was.

"I'm Jack," he said quietly, watching Mr. Goulding carefully. "Do I know you?"

Mr. Goulding blinked, his mouth opening but no words coming out. He took a step closer to Jack, his eyes wide with disbelief. "Jack... I've spent years searching for you." His voice trembled as he spoke. "I was hired to find you... by your family. And now, after all this time..." He shook his head slowly, as if struggling to comprehend. "You're here."

Jack exchanged a look with Mabel, confusion giving way to recognition. "Is this the investigator you told me about, Ma?"

Goulding nodded slowly, still staring at Jack as though he couldn't believe what he was seeing. "I searched everywhere... and never found you. I tried my best, but I failed."

Jack stepped forward, offering a small, humble smile. "Well, now you've found me. And I found my way back to my family."

Goulding let out a breath, shaking his head, the shock still heavy in his voice. "I can't believe it... after all this time. But," he cleared his throat, "I'm actually here tonight for a different reason."

Mr. Goulding nodded toward the man standing in the shadows. "I've come because of him."

The man stepped forward, slowly removing his wide-brimmed hat. The firelight illuminated his face—older, weathered, but unmistakably familiar.

Helen squinted, her heart pounding as she struggled to make sense of the familiar yet weathered face before her. She took a step closer, her voice trembling with uncertainty as she stood. "Adrian...?"

For a moment, the silence hung heavy between them. Then Adrian nodded, his eyes filled with years of longing. "It's me, Helen," he said softly. "I've come back."

Helen's knees weakened, and she gripped the chair for support. "You're alive," she gasped, her breath coming in shallow bursts. "But how? I thought..."

Adrian stepped closer, his voice raw with emotion. "I survived the shipwreck, but I was stranded for years. I tried everything to get back to you, but it took so long. When I finally reached England, I couldn't find you."

He paused, glancing at Mr. Goulding. "That's when I found him. I'd heard of his reputation for finding people. I thought if anyone could help me, it would be him."

Mr. Goulding, still shaken by seeing Jack, nodded. "Adrian came to me looking for you, Helen. When I traced you to your village, we came immediately. Your neighbour directed me here. I didn't expect..." He shook his head again, still processing. "I didn't expect any of this."

Adrian's gaze softened as he looked back at Helen, his voice growing quieter. "I never stopped thinking of you, Helen. Not for a single day."

Helen's body trembled, tears streaming down her face. "I thought you were gone forever," she whispered, her voice breaking. "I thought I'd lost you."

Adrian reached for her, his hands shaking as they touched her arm. "I'm here now, Helen. I'm not going anywhere."

Beryl, who had been standing quietly nearby, finally spoke, her voice thick with emotion. "Papa?"

Adrian turned toward her, his eyes softening as he saw his daughter standing there, tears filling her eyes. "Yes, Beryl. I'm here."

Beryl crossed the room and fell into her father's arms, tears spilling down her cheeks. "I thought you were gone forever," she sobbed, holding him tightly.

Adrian closed his eyes, pulling her close. "I'm home now," he whispered, his voice thick with emotion. "I'm so sorry I wasn't there for you."

Helen watched them, her heart full yet breaking all at once. After so much pain and loss, he was finally here.

Pearl stood to the side, watching the reunion unfold. Her mother's joy, the emotions filling the room—it all felt like a piece of a story she had only heard in fragments. Pearl's heart ached, but she understood.

Adrian's eyes met Pearl's for the first time, soft and questioning, as if searching for something in the face of the daughter he had never known.

There was no need for words.

His gaze lingered for a moment longer before he gave a small nod, acceptance clear in his expression. The unspoken understanding passed between them—the time for explanations would come, but not on this day.

"Mama," Pearl said softly, stepping closer, "he's home."

Helen turned to her daughter, tears still spilling down her cheeks, and gave a small nod. "Yes," she whispered, her voice filled with gratitude. "He's home."

The room stirred again, the family gathering around, the air filled with the joy of watching a miracle unfold. Jack watched as Beryl hugged her father tightly, her emotions raw from the long separation. He placed a hand on her back, quietly supporting her, knowing how much this meant to her.

He exchanged a glance with Mabel, whose eyes were still filled with the weight of their own miracle just a day ago.

Jack's heart felt full—not just for himself, but for the family now finding each other again.

In that quiet moment, Jack understood—some journeys, though long and painful, led the right people to exactly where they belonged.

The soft crackle of the fire filled the room, mingling with the faint sound of heavy snow tapping against the windows. Outside, the world was blanketed in white, but inside, the warmth of family, love, and forgiveness wrapped around them like a familiar embrace. It was Christmas, a time for hope and new beginnings, and tonight, the Finch household had been blessed with both.

Jack gave Mabel a small nod, the kind that spoke more than words ever could. They had all been through so much, but this night—this moment—was one they would carry in their hearts forever.

The End

*I hope you enjoyed
the final book of this series*

Are you ready to Discover a New, Unforgettable Series from Iris Cole?

Step into the world of an evocative journey through the streets of Victorian London. In **The Daughter's Silent Promise,** Molly Turner's fierce loyalty to her Yorkshire roots leads her into the heart of London's shadows, where every step holds the risk of losing what matters most.

Pre Order The Daughter's Silent Promise on Amazon

Click Here

OVER THE PAGE YOU WILL FIND A LINK TO JOIN MY NEWSLETTER AND A LIST OF MY OTHER BOOKS

LIST OF BOOKS

Christmas Books

The Forgotten Match Girl's Christmas Birthday

The Christmas Pauper

The Little One's Christmas Dream

Victorian Romance Saga Series (Three Books)

The Widow's Hope Book One

Little Jack: Book Two

The Lost Mother's Christmas Miracle Book Three **(This Books Title)**

Other Books

The Waif's Lost Family

The Pickpocket Orphans

The Workhouse Girls Despair

The Wretched Needle Worker

The Lost Daughter

Printed in Great Britain
by Amazon